KEEPING Chris

SHANNON DICKINSON

authorHOUSE®

AuthorHouse™
1663 Liberty Drive
Bloomington, IN 47403
www.authorhouse.com
Phone: 1 (800) 839-8640

Published by AuthorHouse   01/11/2016

ISBN: 978-1-5049-6918-5 (sc)
ISBN: 978-1-5049-6919-2 (e)

Print information available on the last page.

FOR MOM …

MY BEST FRIEND FROM THE BEGINNING.

CHAPTER ONE

A MOMENT OF CLARITY

This is how my heart stops beating—not from a heart attack or a body growing old—but from divorce papers I hold within my hands. I just woke up in a lake of sweat.

Oh my God. My husband is dying.

When I fell to the floor two days ago, filling doctors' faces with stunned expressions, I didn't care what anybody thought. With my heart breaking, I can barely believe that I'm breathing right now.

Although it is 7 o'clock in the morning, I stand with my back perfectly straight, amazingly without sobbing. A rainbow is lingering at the edge of the horizon, and I am gazing down at a stack of papers that is covered with print and stamped with a scrawled signature. Reality has finally hit. Tears hover on the edges of my lashes, and my eyes raise, softening against the rain.

I am holding a pen in a hand that is trembling. Memories scatter through my mind as I toss a hand through my hair and lift my eyes to the bed behind me. The dress I had planned on wearing five months ago is sprawled out on the pink bed tapestries with its original tags still attached. I look up for a moment and wonder what could have been.

A diamond ring is sitting on the dresser in my room, and my left ring finger is vacant. The diamond sparkles and shines like stars in a night sky that is still dense with the warmth of day. I run my hand over some old photos, which sit on my dresser in such an order that I feel I could trace my memories into the sand on the edge of my backyard. My life seems to be coming to an end, and the dense fog outside the window seems to mirror my heart at this moment.

Now, staring down at a tray full of pills, I hold up a green capsule as I picture my life without my husband, Chris. I stand here above my dresser, once again recalling my husband's soft fingers combing through my hair and his warm hands upon my face. Although recent events of my marriage have caused my heart to beat more quickly, I can't let go of the only man I've ever loved.

Holding a hand tightly against my heart, I stare and sniff quietly. I run a tissue under my nose and wipe away tears that have been building for five months now. No one sees it behind my smile, but deep within, my heart is breaking.

My marriage seems to be a complicated issue these days. It has been neither blissful nor horrid, but it is an accomplishment that I am proud of. For me, marriage was not a flurry of kisses and amorous hugs. No, it was a friendship that started with a boy and a girl who were so helplessly in love that they couldn't bear to be apart.

After our nuptials, there was no honeymoon. There was no frolicking into the sunset. I didn't mind the mediocrity. I didn't miss the lavish honeymoon that everyone expected us to have. Don't think that we didn't want a romantic getaway. We did. The thing was that we were poor. In spite of my efforts to make that honeymoon possible, I realized that my husband and I had each other. Love was all I wanted, and it was all I needed to stay happy and sane.

Chris is in his hospital bed, blissfully dreaming or wishing he had picked someone else. I have fought for our happiness for ten years. And by giving our love my all, my mission as a wife has been fulfilled. At the end, there was no thank you. Our marriage was nothing fancy. There was no sympathy for my efforts to keep Chris. In the beginning, there was hand holding. There was me clutching Chris's fingers as he struggled to cross a short bridge that led out to his boat. I love him so much. I grabbed his hand and promised never to leave. So here I stand, gazing at my trembling hands and wondering what went wrong. Do not put me up on a pedestal. I am your typical soul—one who believes in helping the man she loves, in spite of the hardships that marriage brings along. My love for Chris will never waver, nor will it perish the moment I die.

Our parting is not a tragedy in his mind. I wish I could reverse his feelings, but changing a person's mind is not something that is easily carried out. However, I refuse to sign my name on the final divorce papers. I see the hospital's phone number on my cordless phone every morning and know that I am doing the right thing by answering.

However, reality is crashing into me more harshly this morning. I know that the end of our marriage looms, as the papers have gone through the lawyer's hands. No request for reconciliation has been sent. Dense emotion fills my being, as I run my hands across the crisp, white paper.

Oh my God. I just can't do this. This can't be happening. This can't be happening. Oh my God, I'm going to die without him.

No effort on my part can stop the clock from ticking or lift me out of my rocking chair at night. It's become somewhat of a meditating place for me.

Perhaps, if I sit there long enough, the pain will fade away. I'm looking down at my hands and tracing the life line on my palms. A palm reader examined it long ago. The line appears longer now than it did years ago. I have always thought I'd live to be ninety. I enjoy the thought.

Today, like every other morning, I stand at my dresser and, sobbing deeply, examine each word on the 'intent to divorce' paperwork. Now, I ask myself why my life has come to this. I try to touch Chris's hand in an attempt to remind him of the time when we were teenagers and divorce was a foreign concept. People who are so much in love should never have to think about that.

I'm not expecting a miracle or a total change of heart. Chris's mind is made up. His heart has changed. In another year, our life together will end, and our marriage will be nothing but an abstract filed away at the social security office. There are a few moments every morning that I want to dial Chris's number and beg for him to change his mind. He's a changed man with a changed heart. But to me, he will always be the boy next door I swore I'd love forever.

However, the love of my life wants nothing to do with reconciliation. Knowing this, I place my head in my hands each morning and allow the tears to flow. Trying to be the perfect wife is never easy.

This morning marks a new day, and I plan on trying to make Chris see me in a totally different light. Some would call it a leap of faith. Chasing a man who no longer has an interest in you really breaks a woman's heart. As I stand here in front of the mirror and sniff, tendrils of my curly brown hair fall around my face. I can barely bring myself to breathe. The love of my life is leaving me, and I simply don't know why.

My bags are packed. I'm ready to go. The taxi outside has been waiting for me for some 30 odd minutes, and I still don't have my things together. At the moment, I'm agonizing over some pill vials, trying to make sure the Ativan is in its proper place. Chris couldn't keep the painkillers down, and the chemo is destroying him. Four more weeks, and I'll be a widow. Well, technically one month. But these days, I seem to be breaking down time into manageable increments of existence. Four weeks–that's 672 hours, just over 40,000 seconds. This morning my heart is aching.

I'm not the perfect wife by any means, but I've done my best to show Chris that he can cross the lake without falling down. The lake behind our backyard radiates a sparkling shade of blue, glistening against a slowly rising sun.

But things got difficult. Chris's condition has made walking hard for him. He trembles. He moans, but he loves the water so much. So many times I held his hand, as he teetered over to the canoe. These days, he finds it harder to walk.

In his prime, Chris was absolutely beautiful. He used to love the racing water, the wind on his face. These are all recollections that encapsulate my time with Chris.

I'm feeling particularly spunky this Tuesday, despite the fact that it's four in the morning and I haven't slept a wink. The warm milk never called my head to the pillow. The coffee is wearing off. So today, it's back to my morning grind. I lay out photos, trace the lines of Chris's face in our pictures, and wonder why I have subtle wrinkles at the corners of my eyes. A marriage of ten years and a separation of five months—I suppose we've had our ups and downs.

Our schnauzer, Molly, is on the floor and stuffing her nose into some smelly slippers Chris wore for years. God knows I tried to get him to throw those things away. I reflect on these memories only because I know that in a few weeks, the present will be the past, and my life will be transformed.

I will sit in the sunroom, wondering how our next boating venture would have been. I will look at a collage of photos of my former husband to frame in a picture box long after he's gone. My life may not sound extraordinary, taking care of my ailing husband. It may make me sound like a saint. It's not a name I've earned. Honestly, I don't deserve the title.

"Molly, get your nose out of the wool," I say, gazing at a dog whose eyes resemble those of a deer caught in headlights. The white fur on Molly's snout ruffles as she takes her snout out of Chris's slippers and sneezes quickly.

"Daddy loves those slippers. Now, be a good girl and grab your bone. I need these today," I say, motioning her in circles and wiping a tear from my eye. "I love you. I love you so much," I cry, briefly patting her head.

I would have loved to have heard those words from Chris a few months ago. I wonder when the insomnia will end. I wonder when I'll be able to be proud of myself for the goals I've accomplished. Nothing says success like dirty laundry, a dishwasher full of scratched plates and potatoes that are stuck to pans. My life is established. I'm here all the time. I am ashamed of my appearance.

What about my heart? Well, that is another story—one that I have far too little time to recite without falling to pieces. Chris, my dear Chris. I don't have time to think of him in a negative light.

At 35, I would have expected I'd have more, perhaps a booming career, frequent trips to the city, a circle of friends perhaps. I would have loved to have joined a professional organization. The dreams I could have accomplished for myself were at one time right under my nose. Pondering what could have been isn't going to do me any favors, let alone lift my husband out of a bed that is dense with sweat-soaked sheets. He barely talks to me anymore.

I look at him every day at noon when the nurse opens the doors and gives me the opportunity to vent about the chemo. I make it sound like I'm the one taking the pills, the one losing my hair. When the doctors look at my green eyes, they must wonder why I'm here. The thing is that I'm a good wife with good intentions. But even the most well-intentioned spouses have their shortcomings.

As for my husband, he's somewhere in dreamland, presumably dreaming of a life that is different from the one I have given him. I'm not your typical suburban housewife, but instead the epitome of commonplace existence. I sit in the house. No, I take that back. Sitting would imply that I twiddle my thumbs all day, that I read magazines until it's time to eat dinner. I have a heavy heart. My eyes trail down to the moss-colored rug in our living room.

I'm becoming more observant these days. I'm beginning to take notice of the little things, of children throwing leaves on our front lawn and the brisk air ushering in the commencement of fall.

The phone rings, and I lift my head. I shake a blanket off my lap, glance at my watch, and walk to the bedroom. It has to be 10:00 o'clock in the morning, and dew is still fogging up the windows. The coffee maker gurgles in the kitchen, and I don't hear the sloshing of cars against the rain sloshed streets. No one is raking leaves outside, but the wind is blowing at a speed so rapid that the trees will soon be bare. I stand in my bell bottoms, which have loosened around my waist and a cotton blouse that is now too large for my shoulders. I close my eyes and hear the coffee maker gurgle once again.

Ralph, the cab driver I hired two months ago, has yet to lay on his horn. His tardiness is a fact to which I've grown accustomed, but it's his angst that bothers me the most. I am soft and tender, but there comes a point when an even-tempered woman hits her breaking point.

My arms are shivering because of the October air, which seems to have come much earlier than usual. I blow out my breath and look out the window. The crimson and gold shade of the leaves outside has caused me to stand by the windows more often than I used to. The chill of the glass windows stings my fingers, yet I can't seem to find another place that brings me such comfort. I smile for a moment, remembering the first kiss I placed on Chris's lips and the soft fingers that caressed my neck in the 90s. In spite of the throbbing ache on the right side of my head, now is a time for remembering and for starting anew. I'm tossing away my old clothes, reminiscing through old memories that still bring me comfort. I'm running my fingers spread wide open through a tray full of green pills. Their texture is smooth, waxy. I've tried to be the best wife. Thankfully, I've found a way to stay sane.

I try to show him my best, I really do. Every day at noon, as the doors slide open, I widen my eyes in excitement and wave to the man who picked me up off my parents' front porch and ran his hands through my hair. I've never been the type to strive for a picture perfect life. All I ever wanted was that smile—that hand that combed through my hair 19 years ago.

Thankfully, Chris still lifts his head to me from time to time. He looks at me for a few moments and looks away. These days I find amusement in getting Molly to dance circles on the kitchen floor. Our son, Ben, just started preschool.

Matilda, our babysitter, drove Ben to school this morning while I attempted to conceal the circles under my eyes. It isn't easy to hold it all together, nor is it my intention to push Chris away. These days, Ben spends most of his time with Matilda.

My eyes linger when I think of the times that I brushed his hand away, as he brought his lips to mine. I had postpartum depression and, for several days, I thought I wanted a divorce. Perhaps it is those memories that trigger the migraines.

The headaches have a way of getting worse. My hand is on my head, and I can't figure out for the life of me what is going on. God knows I'd love for Chris to hold my hand when the pain gets too strong. I'm not sick by any means.

My heart is strong, my legs full of vigor. In spite of my musings, I hear Ralph out front of my house lay on the horn multiple times. I called him 20 minutes ago, and I can't seem to find my composure. I often wonder if they get paid extra for dealing with distracted customers like me. I have my composure, at least for now. A second later, I bring the cab driver's face into focus as my thoughts pull my eyes away from the pounding rain. It makes it hard to see. I look up, hear the rain pound against the roof, and feel for the first time that I am fully alone.

I write stories and post them online. I also design websites. It takes my mind off my mistakes—for not loving him enough, for not showing my affection as often as I should have.

With regard to the stories, the most recent masterpiece I published was a small novel featuring a woman with dementia. My blog has gotten 5,000 hits. Writing stories and designing websites tends to draw my thoughts away from the nights I spend alone.

Chris smiles at me from time to time, but he doesn't talk. To him, I am an annoyance. However, I am a distraction from his illness. I suppose these thoughts come around during my most desperate moments. As my eyes return to the window this morning, like any other morning in Seattle, I squint against the grey streaks of rain that are falling in sheets. Now, I race down the front porch, pull open the door to the cab, and look briefly at Ralph.

"I'm in sad shape," I think to myself, taking a mental picture of the driver's face, which is porous, and strangely familiar. "West 74th Street," I say, raising my eyes to the streetlights, which have illuminated because of the darkness of morning. The sun, slightly visible in the distance, draws my eyes toward the horizon. Even so, the rain pours like a waterfall. It's a typical occurrence, considering the fact that we live in Seattle. As the cab pulls away from the hospital's exterior, I race through the hospital's sliding glass doors. I listen to beeping heart monitors and wonder if my husband's will be the next one to go. Green lights blink behind me as a series of beds and curtains turn into a blur of white behind me. Finally, I have reached the door to Chris's room. And I am greeted by a soft and knowing smile.

"The chemo's been done. He's resting now," says my favorite nurse, Susan. She pats my back. Then, she darts away, her heels clicking in rhythm across the linoleum floors. A woman wearing read high heels hovers over Chris, her hands hovering over needle syringe. She looks up, smiles softly, and returns her eyes to Chris.

"Okay, Mr. Rylan, time for your treatment," says Susan, Chris's nurse for the day. "Time to get that chemo going again, okay? Just a little pinch," she says, wiggling a needle into a vein.

My eyes glide over his skin, radiating pure beauty from his soft, porcelain flesh. His hands tremble, and his chest rises and falls shakily with each breath he takes.

Susan nods as Jackie, another nurse, steps in. I pause and lean forward in my chair. "Should I say something?"

I watch in silence, tugging softly at my eyelashes and sniffling under my hand. He's leaving me. Yet, he is still so beautiful, I realize, seeing his soft hands and beautiful arms. Dancing in the background is the soft sound of music at the nurses' station.

I look at his face and see his eyes open in acknowledgement of the nurses. It's amazing how much a person misses when they don't note the emotion in another person's eyes. His face, still vibrant and fresh, brings me closer. And I touch his hand. His breath, now rising in a steady rhythm, draws me closer. As a matter of routine, I softly place my hands on top of his trembling fingers. Then, I gaze at him with a look of love. Warmth radiates within me as my eyes linger on his face. And right now, I smile, knowing I will love him forever.

"You are so beautiful, Chris," I say, placing my hands on his arms. "I love you."

The doctors say it helps to read to them. I know he's conscious, although talking seems difficult for him these days. I hope that reading might recapture the love we share and make him call off the divorce. Drawing a deep breath, I smile for a moment, seeing those eyes, those beautiful blue eyes. Now, rolling a book over in my palms, I feel its rough exterior against my fingertips.

"Okay, Chris. This is the beginning of our story," I say, pushing a lock of my hair behind my ear. "This is where it began."

Having conquered all my dreams as a child, I believe in the power to move mountains, to make hearts and bodies whole again. So I'm placing my hand on his chest right now, hoping he will lace his fingers into mine and mend the broken pieces of my heart. With a little love and determination, perhaps I have the power to bring his hand back into mine.

God knows I'd move Heaven and Earth for him. With a little love and determination, hopefully I can bring his eyes toward me and make him see me in the light he did long ago. It is human nature to want to be held, to be loved by another person. They say that babies would die without human touch.

Chapter Two

Blissful April

The rushing whir of the wind behind me slows to a hush as I inch my car into the parking lot. Lifting my eyes to a blue, yet cloud blanketed sky, I exhale a deep breath. And for a moment, I lose myself in the breeze. The wind funnels up in a dizzying haze, seemingly being conjured up, like dust suspended in sand.

It is now 6:42 in the evening on a frigid October morning, and the heat turns on in Chris's room. I glance at my watch and see the sun dimming behind the blinds. I look around, and drawing a deep breath, I sit down in my plush hospital room chair. The chair is a grayish blue and sounds like it is exhaling air as I sit down. Knowing Chris's feelings about me, I have to be cautious when I come around him. I shouldn't be here, but I have to be. I can't lose him.

As I look at the tubes encircling his body, I feel as though I am living in a dream. The beeping of the heart machine draws my eyes toward the door. I feel my sleeves fall carelessly on my arms as I stand up and hover over his bed. Now, I close my eyes for a moment, shuffle a hand under my nose, and draw a heavy, prolonged breath. Now, my eyes lift, trembling like green saucers floating on a table of white. I tug my fingers through my hair.

I need to read to him. With my laptop in my hands, I can feel my throat being choked with tears. Perhaps this is where my story begins. Right now, my story's on my laptop, but that's not where it began. Right now, as I fight my quivering lip, I listen to Chris breathing.

Lifting the screen to my laptop, I breathe out, remembering a day I lived so many years ago. Breathing deeply, I look at Chris. "Okay, here it goes."

For me, it was the typical story of boy-meets-girl. I was a girl with a carefree spirit who loved to lose herself in the wonders of nature. All through the warmer months, you could find me gazing up at the junipers, the oaks, and the maple trees. I remember a day in the spring of 1998. As the sun blazed upon us, Chris danced around me, creating a memory that seemed to crystallize in my heart. This story is in my diary, my forever treasured diary. When I was a teenager, Chris used to pick me up and throw me over his shoulder.

As I read my first entry, I see Chris twirling around me and dancing. The memory is fresh. It is now a relic that prompts me to wipe my eye and slump my shoulders. In an attempt to regain composure, I stare against the sun outside the window.

This is the beginning of a love story, the love story that brought my hand into Chris's 19 years ago. I power up my laptop and bring the text into focus. I smile at Chris, shuffle a hand over the touchpad, and begin reading. Clearing my throat, I press my hand against my heart.

Sadness tugs at my throat as I look at him and picture myself letting go of his hand. I blink, and for a moment, I feel like the child within me is one again smiling against his face.

I blow out my breath and touch a finger to my laptop. "Okay, sweetheart. Here it goes."

One day in early spring, Chris and I found ourselves in my parents' front yard, goofing around. Chris was brushing his fingers over my face. Trees and flowers were in full bloom, and I looked up from the front lawn, taking in the sweet smell of the air. The sweet sound of birds surrounded us, creating a song of peace and brilliance.

"I'm so happy to see the warm weather," I said, gazing up at some cherry blooms and throwing my arms around Chris. As Chris's eyes rose softly to mine, I brushed a lock of my hair aside my face. Slowly, I looked at him.

"I'll bet you can't catch me," I squealed, catching Chris's gaze with a sudden smile.

"I'll bet I can," he giggled, throwing his arms around me and spinning me around.

As I ran forward across the lawn, he followed me, put his hands around my waist and picked me up.

"I can't believe you're here with me right now," I grinned, allowing myself to fall back on the ground and smile at Chris. My smile brightened against his face and, for a moment, I felt as though I could see eternity. I stared into his blue eyes, and like a child, I giggled.

"Have you ever done this before?" Chris smiled, as cherry blooms danced, and he breathed into my neck. "Have you ever done this?"

"Done what?" I asked, curling a lock of hair around my index finger and noting a fleeting look of amusement on Chris's face. A smile curved his lips, and my eyes rose to his, beckoning me forward.

"This," he said, grabbing me by the waist and throwing me over his shoulder. "You're the only girl I can do this to."

Slowly, he released me, bringing me back to the ground.

I looked up and smiled, realizing that words eluded him. His smile was soft and adoring, and his body seemed to mirror mine.

"Huh?" I asked, looking up and feeling my eyes float over him.

"You're the only girl who feels like this," he said, tracing my jaw with his hand. "You're just so soft … you're just so beautiful."

I rolled over on my side and felt tall blades of grass trail my chin. "Oh, so tell me more about this beautiful girl," I said as he bounced forward and pinched my nose.

He looked up, turned to look over his shoulder, and returned his eyes to me. "Have you ever thought about being close to someone?"

My eyebrows rose. "Being close to someone is nice." My voice fell to a whisper. "So what are you saying?"

"Have you ever done it?" he said, as his voice trailed away. Chris looked at me, and for several seconds, I found myself drifting toward him, as though another force had beckoned me. "Hold up your hands," Chris said, opening the spaces between his fingers and drawing my fingers in between his. "Feels good, huh?"

I couldn't say a word, but I stared back, taking in his soft breath, feeling his soft hands, and allowing my eyes to drift closed against his shirt. A tear emerges from my right eye as I continue to read the entry. As I reflect on this memory, I sniff, returning my eyes to the screen.

"Here's what happened next, Chris. Here's what happened next."

As Chris lifted me and threw me over his shoulders, I looked up and broke into laughter, enjoying the feel of his fingers upon me. That was a beautiful day. The world was in bloom, and I was about to do something I'd never expected.

As Chris and I held hands and chased each other, he chuckled giddily. I paused to pinch his nose playfully. Unrestrained laughter escaped my lips. Feeling a sudden thrill, I turned to run to the front sidewalk. As I did, Chris stomped, running toward me, and shot me a smile. His thick-lipped grin drew my gaze to the dusty blond wisps of hair that dangled from his head as he came toward me.

"So here we are," Chris said, his eyes trembling upon me. "Yeah," I said, my eyes gliding across his face.

"This is like so awesome," Chris said, ruffling his fingers through my hair." My heart pounding within my chest, I lifted my head and took in the crystalline beauty of his fragile blue eyes.

"Yeah," I smiled, suddenly moving closer.

I felt my green eyes deepen in the sun, as I turned toward him, focusing on the soft skin of his lips. His statement caught me, stirring within me a mixture of feelings I had never felt before.

"You don't seem enthused," he said, a soft smile slowly curving his lips.

I chuckled, looking at him thoughtfully. "I've never had a boyfriend, but someday, it will happen." I paused, feeling a mixture of delight and excitement in the pit of my stomach.

Looking at me intently, Chris's crystal blue eyes lingered on my face, and I detected a flicker of intrigue. Mirroring his body, I combed a hand through my hair.

He paused. "Does it make sense that I don't want to be anywhere else but here right now?"

"It makes total sense," I said, looking at him silently and placing my hand on my cheek.

"Come here," he said, slipping his arms under my armpits and lifting my chin toward his face. "There ya go. This is where you need to be."

No words could convey my feelings at that moment, as I took in the smell of his shirt against my face. It was April of 1998 and what quite possibly classifies as one of the greatest days of my life. Stargazer lilies and tulips were bursting into bloom, and I began to lose myself in the childlike wonder of the world.

That month was wonderful, for it was spring—a time for renewal, rebirth, and in my case, the month I met my soul mate. Looking up at the trees, I sprawled myself lazily over my parents' front lawn and stretched myself out, giggling against the lush grass that rose up to my chin.

"So, this is it? This is what you do with boys?" Chris said suddenly with a soft, yet amused look.

The statement rattled me for a moment, and I looked down, my green eyes trailing the soft blond hairs on Chris's arms.

"I'm not sure," I said.

"Let's go somewhere," Chris said to me, grabbing my hand softly and turning his head in distraction. "Come on," he said, taking my hand softly and leading me to the backyard. I stared back quietly, lacing my fingers through his before spinning around him.

"Let's do something," he said, touching my face.

"Okay," I breathed, feeling my eyes flutter and my mouth curve upward into a smile. Slowly, my eyes trailed his body, from the top of his head to the tips of his tennis shoes.

He stared back, his eyes flexing in surprise. "Wow, you really are clueless," he said, flashing me a fleeting look of joy. "Come on," he said," grabbing my hands. "Come closer."

Slowly, I lifted my eyes to his brilliant gem blue eyes, which trembled as he examined my face. As his gaze floated over me, I grabbed for his hand and pulled him toward me, feeling his velvet soft skin. I drifted toward his chest, and his arms folded possessively around me. I felt a tendril of hair upon my shoulder, and breathed deeply.

"You've never done this to me before," I said, trailing a finger over his nose and leaning down to kiss him. His lips were soft against mine.

"I've done it now," he said, opening his eyes and drifting slowly out of our embrace. "Let's do something else," he said, drifting forward before pulling me back into his arms.

Instinct drew me forward, and my mouth seemed to melt into his, as he breathed deeply. His breath was deep, growing heavier as his hands began to roam.

"Okay, I'm ready. You said you wanted to do something to me?" I asked. Slowly, he drew me closer.

The feeling deepened, bringing me closer toward him. The warmth of his hands wrapped around my shoulders, and he kissed me slowly and deep. Before I knew it, the warmth of his hands grew more intense upon me.

His gaze lifted slowly, his eyes trailing me with a glint of anticipation.

"Do you, huh? I'm not your slave, and you can't just order me around," he said, drawing my hands into his. Then, he lifted me and clasped his arms around my warm and eager mouth. His touch grew more intense and more eager as they descended to my hips. The world seemed to stand frozen in time as his eager hands traveled wantonly between my legs. I breathed as he looked at me and continued in silent concentration.

"You like this. I see it in your eyes," he said.

"Uh huh."

Slowly, his mouth curved upward.

"Do you know what you're doing to me?" I chuckled, feeling a sudden thrill fly through my body, which grew more intense as his fingers traveled over my torso.

I could tell he was playing dumb. "No. I have no idea," he said.

A sudden laugh escaped my lips, and I tilted my head. "I think that's called foreplay, Chris."

"Oh, is that what you call it?" he said, as his fingers halted and traveled upward.

The world seemed to disappear around me as Chris giggled, whispered, and pressed his lips into mine.

"Should I go slower?" he asked.

Minutes passed like seconds in a dream, seemingly bringing him closer—closer to my mouth, closer to my soul, closer to the temple I called my body. Suddenly, I was free. I smile, reflecting on the memory.

It was never my intention to find the love of my life at the age of eighteen, but things just happen. All I know is that on that beautiful April day, birds were chirping, and every moment felt magical. For the first time in my young life, I found total comfort in another person.

After releasing me, Chris threw himself on the ground and propped himself up on his elbows.

I wanted to say something, but words seemed to elude me at that moment. I pause, staring at the Times New Roman text.

"Have you ever felt like you want to be with only one person?"

"Well," Chris paused, looking around. "I've never been like this with a girl."

I couldn't think of a thing to say, so I stared forward, feeling a sudden rush as he looked at me.

"Well, aren't you gonna say something?" he said, chuckling briefly.

My eyes lingered on him until his mouth curved into a grin. Sailing briefly on the wind, Chris's blond hair called out to me, once again awakening a feeling I never knew was there.

Days came and went, and before we knew it, it was Friday, our day to be together. We spent Friday evening together until the sun set, and we had to return to our parents' houses.

Then, along came Saturday. Yes, it was Saturday. And I knew in my heart of hearts that something was about to change. Chris and I spent the day talking and walking through the neighborhood.

Then, I felt a sudden yearning that drew me closer. As we walked, I felt my eyes wander, searching for a place to be alone with him. We found a bench in the neighborhood and sat down. Looking up, I took in the warmth of the sun and felt the sun kissed breeze against my skin, as his eyes trailed me.

Turning to me, Chris raised his eyebrows. "Let's go somewhere."

"Where?" I replied, raising my eyebrows in response to his sudden laughter.

He chuckled, and his blue eyes trailed from my shoulders and farther down. "Anywhere."

I felt a smile curve my lips. Sliding a hand under my soft brown hair, I eyed him briefly and grabbed his hand. Then, as Chris's eyes trailed me, we ran back home. We spent the next hour talking. As we did, I tossed my head back in laughter, knowing that something was different. There was a certain connection between us—the kind that few people have, but so many people yearn for. From my head to my feet, I felt a culmination of emotion and anticipation, and I instinctively moved toward him. Then, as his smile broadened, I locked his gaze and lingered.

Later that evening, we found ourselves in my parents' backyard. "Do something," he said, sitting next to me on the ground. "Do something else to me."

I felt my every inhibition melt away as Chris put his right hand on the back of my neck, suddenly drawing me closer.

A sudden tumble filled my stomach as he brought his mouth to mine. I drifted away slowly for a moment, drew an expectant breath, and glanced at him nervously. Slowly, his eyes returned to mine, and he smoothed a hand over my shoulder.

"I have a feeling someone feels pretty good right now," he chuckled, pulling me into his arms.

"Whatever do you mean?" I asked, quietly laughing. Grabbing my hand and ushering me forward toward the fence in the backyard, he smiled, slowly pulling me toward him. As his hands trailed my arm, a chill of joy fled through me, causing my arms to drift around him.

Moments I spent with Chris took me back to my grandmother's wise words. "I tell ya, Lil, one of these days, you're gonna find the right one. And when you do, you'll know it's forever. It may sound cheesy, but when you meet the right guy, you know."

My grandfather traveled to Europe years ago in search of my great grandmother's emerald necklace. She had died years before, leaving the necklace behind, because she believed it would bring her great grandchildren luck long after she was gone. No one has heard from my grandfather since, even though he had promised to return.

As I lay there with Chris on the ground, I looked at his face and rested my head on my chin.

"Looks like someone's deep in thought," Chris said, rolling onto his right side and pinching a finger over my nose. At first, I wasn't sure whether or not to take his affection seriously, considering the fact that I was 18 and had yet to even think about a committed relationship. Commitment wasn't yet a part of my vocabulary. "You're not the type to be coy," he said, chuckling softly and smoothing a finger over my nose.

I chuckled. "Coy. That's a sex word, isn't it?"

His eyebrows lifted, and he smiled. "You think coy is a sex word? Seriously?" he chuckled, throwing his hand forward. "Get your mind out of the gutter, girl."

"What?" I said, shaking my head in an attempt to hide my smile. "Coy is a sex word."

"It is if you want it to be," he said, ruffling my hair. I loved his warm touch, and it drew me toward him. Slowly, my mouth drifted into his. He held me, running his soft fingers through my hair. Before I knew it, the bright daylight that kept us awake faded into a dark night sky.

I scroll to the next page and smile with a soft giggle.

The night faded, I remembered, as I drifted to sleep in the backyard. Such peace envelops me now, as I place a finger on Chris's warm hand and gaze at him.

"You know," I coo softly, "this is what happened next, if you remember." For a moment, my eyes tremble and fall upon his skin. Now, I scroll to the next page.

"This is what happened next, sweetheart," I whisper before kissing his hand.

Two months later, we found ourselves stretched out in my parents' backyard, horsing around behind a lush azalea bush. Crickets chirped seemingly in unison. As we looked up at the stars, the dense heat of the world departed, and the sun faded into the landscape.

Finding privacy was a daunting task, especially when we were so loud together. But that evening in mid June, I was content to be beside him and looking into his eyes under the moonlight.

"How long have we known one another now?" Chris asked, glancing over at me as I stretched my arms above my head.

"Beats me," I chuckled. "Two months feels like an eternity when you're trying to get laid," I snickered, averting my eyes to the sky and propping myself up on my elbows.

"Wow." His eyes widened with a mixture of amusement and eagerness. "Someone's a little eager there," he said, trailing an index finger to the tip of my nose and bringing his mouth to mine.

"It goes back to the whole foreplay thing," I said. "Come on. You can't tell me you've never thought about getting laid."

"Hmm, getting laid?" he said, grinning. "You wanna get laid? We haven't known each other for two years yet." I rolled over, my eyes widening, and gave him a playful slap. I could feel my eyes tremble as he looked at me in examination.

"Ya know it's called 'sex,' right?" he asked, as his eyes drifted.

"Yeah, I know it's called 'sex,' Chris."

He nodded, seemingly distracted. "Ah, sex is good. So you've thought about this?"

Suddenly, my nerve endings tingled, and my senses heightened. I fumbled the collar of my shirt, feeling my eyes upon him.

Chris's mouth curved into a smile, and he snickered. "Say it again, Lilly. You think about it all the time."

I exhaled an excited breath and looked at him. "Sex."

"Say it again," he said, smoothing a finger across my bottom lip. "Say it again. You know you like it."

"Cut it out," I said, giving him a playful slap.

"Ouch, don't beat me up for making an observation," Chris cracked, flinching. He folded his arms against his chest, grabbed my hands and allowed his head to roll over and meet my eyes. "Besides, have you?"

I shook my head. "Nope." I closed my eyes momentarily and then opened them. His hands, now upon me, drew me closer.

"Interesting," he said, as he looked around and placed a possessive hand on my shoulder.

"Wow," he said, looking around. "I would never have thought. But like I said, I have a timeline of two years. Until then, there will be no hanky panky. Just admit it. You want all this, he said, holding a hand above his body.

I looked at Chris and detected a hint of yearning in his eyes. My head fell into my palms, as I examined his porcelain skin and imagined my soft tongue against his. "Yes, I've thought about it, Chris."

Feeling his eyes upon me, I lifted my head, searched his eyes, and lingered.

"You've done this before?" I asked.

His eyes lingered as though he was looking for an answer that would please me. "No."

"No one's ever touched me," I said, trembling and reaching for him.

A playful smile curved his lips. "Prude. You're a prude," he said, grabbing my hand and tugging me playfully toward him.

I laughed loudly and tugged him to my parents' basement steps. I had left the door unlocked intentionally that morning, knowing that night would be special. My parents never checked it, anyway.

"Come on," I said, tugging him by the hand. "Let's do it."

"You're not serious, are you? Your parents' house?"

"Dead serious," I smiled, tugging him in through the door. "Come on. Don't be coy."

"There's that word again," he snickered, "the sex word."

"It's not a sex word," I insisted.

"Uh huh," Chris said, his deep chuckle calling to my senses.

I struggled to hide my smile as his eyes searched me as he stood, somehow mirroring my body. He had yet to touch me again, but I detected a flicker of yearning in his eyes. He paused briefly and ducked through the door, attempting to avoid the doorframe. He lifted his eyebrows as we walked slowly, somehow mirroring me.

"So here we are," he said, lifting up his palms. "This is a nice place," he said, taking my hand and pulling me forward. He chuckled and grabbed my shoulders as I looked at him, feeling safe. He moved slowly and cautiously behind me before halting and smiling, seemingly unable to draw his eyes away.

Slowly, he tugged me in through the door to the laundry room and spun me into the hallway leading into the giant box-shaped basement. Fully furnished and lavishly decorated, the basement was clearly the product of a house that was built in the 80s. Never in my life had my senses been so heightened, as I tugged unwillingly at the soft fabric on my sleeve.

"So this is it? This is the place?" Chris asked, allowing his eyes to glide over the sheer cardigan sweater I was wearing.

His hands rose, and he tugged the sweater from my arms. "Are you sure you're ready for this?"

"Yes," I said, biting my lip and searching his eyes, as he removed my bra and tugged down my shorts. He tossed them to the floor and looked at me with silent yearning. Pulling down his boxers and taking a step toward me, Chris smiled and tugged my hand toward his torso. Time seemed to move in slow motion as I looked deep into his eyes.

"Wow," he said, his eyes lingering on my body. "We're alone and naked," he breathed, gently pulling my hand toward his torso, which beckoned my mouth toward him.

A gentle stroke of my hand upon him solidified my desire. Slowly, his eyes rose to meet mine. As I examined his face, an unexpected culmination of desire and urgency took hold, and I felt the warmth of his breath upon me, as he moved closer. Desire drew me forward, and my tongue met his. Running his hands over me, Chris lowered me to the plush carpet and paused to examine me. Lifting his hands to my face, his eyes held a sudden fire.

My hair fell over my shoulders as he came closer, lowering down and allowing his tongue to envelop my chest. Placing his hands upon my shoulders, his touch brought me closer, as I examined his face, and his hands roamed. My lips parted briefly, as his fingers rose, softly inching above my legs. It felt exciting, almost forbidden, as he moved forward. My eyes rose, and I felt a sudden thrill as he examined me. His breath was warm against my skin.

"Beautiful," he said, circling a finger around my belly button. "This is it, love. This is me," he breathed, lowering himself to my torso and stretching his arms out and over me. His lips wrapped around mine, and his hands cupped my face as I drifted back, feeling him linger above my hips. I looked at him intensely, and he enveloped me.

Feeling him within, I inhaled, and my hands traveled instinctively to his back. Slowly, my mouth melted into his. His scent was warm and seducing, as I wrapped my legs around him, feeling my every inhibition drift away. Desire deepened within my skin, and slowly I drew him in deeper.

"I wish I could do this to you forever," Chris said, placing his hands upon me, breathing against my skin, and nipping hungrily at my neck. His hands were like soft mitts growing warm against my skin.

The night was like any other time I spent with Chris. We were playful, intent, and passionate. He pressed his nose into my shoulder and trailed a hand down my leg, as we looked at one another in a new light. By his appearance alone, Chris exuded a raw sexuality. His eyes were bright, his form energetic. And his body possessed a magnetism that brought me naturally to him at that moment in time. I could feel him deep within me— with every surge of passion. Slowly, he withdrew.

"Back in we go," he chuckled, releasing his hands from my chest and returning to my hips.

Keeping me locked in his gaze, Chris tugged his fingers through my sweat-soaked hair and brought his open mouth to mine. His hands traveled over me, and shivers of joy swept through my body as he danced circles around my chest with his mouth. "It kind of feels like swimming," he said, easing back into me. "You take the plunge and find a wet spot to stick yourself," he said with a prolonged surge of passion. He stretched his arms around the nape of my neck, moving rhythmically within me.

I ran my hands over his chest and brought his affection to fruition with an upward surge of my hips. Even in a moment of passion, Chris rubbed my shoulders, just as he did when we gazed up at the stars and wrestled each other to the ground.

"Feels good?" he said, as I tugged him into me and threw my head back. I nodded, feeling his eyes upon me. Unable to hold back my pleasure, I exhaled. His hands were warm on my skin, soaking through the sensation within me.

"Come on, don't be a prude," he said, touching my chin and smiling softly. "Get on top of me."

"Okay," I chuckled giddily, straddling over him and bringing my chest to his open mouth. I hovered over him and took his mouth hungrily as my hand traveled toward his torso and lingered briefly at the crevice of his leg. He withdrew for a moment, lifting his eyebrows. And I looked at him, feeling warmth as our hips connected, intertwined like vines wrapping around one another.

A grunt of satisfaction escaped his lips as he moved against me.

Slipping his hands under my armpits and cradling my shoulders, Chris pulled me close to his chest. I squealed playfully and allowed my hands to trail over him, taking in his warmth. My hands slid under his back, and I breathed in, taking in the mysterious musk of his skin.

Closing my eyes for a brief moment, I tugged him in deeper. He surged within, and his pleasure was made manifest in a sudden jolt of his hips.

"Oh my God," I breathed, as sensation pulled at my senses and fled through my body at rapid speed. It was the most intense moment of my life, and I couldn't resist the urge to jolt as his hands traveled over me. His eyes froze haltingly as he exhaled a grunt.

My breath deepened, as sensation climbed through me, pulling me into an aura of sensation. As his eyes trembled haltingly, I closed my eyes, feeling waves of pleasure radiate from my torso to my fingertips.

For a teenager who had never explored the wonders of physical affection, I became instantly aware of the joy that could be derived from another person's body. Chris's body.

"Hey, Lilly," Chris said, breathing deeply and retracting his open mouth from mine. "Well, you had your way with me," he said, chuckling deeply and bringing his moist forehead to mine.

"I did," I said breathlessly, leaning down and allowing my lush hair to fall upon him. Then, I brought my mouth back to his and watched his chest rise and fall. Utter peace floated over me. Looking deeply into his eyes and panting heavily, I lowered my back to the carpet beside him, exhaling a deep breath.

"That was great," I said, regarding him and bringing my eyes to his face. "You liked that."

"Uh huh."

"Now do me a favor," he said, lifting my chin to meet his eyes. "Promise me you'll never forget this." He drew a dense breath and enfolded me in his arms. "Because you're no longer a virgin."

There are only a few things in a woman's life she can say she'll remember forever. One of those moments is her first time. As I rolled over to Chris and reached for him, I once again felt sudden warmth.

"That was fun," he said, rolling over and reaching with possessive hands.

CHAPTER THREE

RECAPTURING YOUTH

"Okay, sweetheart, that was the beginning of our life," I say, gazing at the screen to my laptop and feeling its cold metallic surface against my fingers. "That was the moment you fell in love with me. That was the first time you touched me and felt the connection of our bodies."

I smile before scrolling to the next page.

Chris's blue eyes lift, rising slowly, and linger in the silence, but he does not bring his gaze to me. I look up and hear rain gently falling outside the hospital window. My eyes rise as rain continues to fall, my heart becoming one with the sound of its soft and steady rhythm.

"Do you remember that?" I ask, gazing at him pleadingly and holding a finger above the computer screen. He is clearly in pain. His muscles tense every time the chemo goes into him through the IV, and I hear him moan every so often. "Chris baby, it's okay. I'm here," I say, gazing at him with my soft green eyes and smoothing a hand over his mostly bald head. "That was one of the best moments of my life."

I touch a hand to the silver rail on the side of his hospital bed. "Anyway, back to our life together," I say, as I sit down and return my eyes to the screen. Slowly, the Times New Roman font comes into focus.

"You hear me, don't you?"

Life brings unexpected miracles our way. I touch a hand to my right cheek and sniff deeply. I have my composure once again, at least for the moment. "Okay, I'm scrolling to the next page, Chris." Pressing my lips together, I sniff. Like a blur, the text flies before my eyes, causing my heart to pound.

I look at the next page and exhale a dense sob. Now, after pausing briefly, I continue to read.

It was June two months later, and I had just graduated from high school. You and I were dancing at my graduation party, while my dad was dancing rodeo-style to a country song he adored. My dad's dancing made me cringe with embarrassment. However, I was used to the songs he called "good music." Soft rays of sun illuminated my parents' back yard on that June day, bringing a golden shine to the lush green grass below the porch. It caused my eyes to lift to the clouds. As the sun's rays thinned into a soft shine on the lawn, Chris nestled his head into my shoulder.

My arms wrapped around him, as they did instinctively, and I found my mind drifting back to April of 1998. If I had been dancing with anyone else at that moment, I wouldn't have given him a second glance.

As Chris's hands descended to my waist, I knew in that moment that my world would be shattered if he ever let me go. His presence made me feel connected and safe in a way that nothing had before. He was so close and attuned to my heart as people danced past us. It seemed as though we were the only ones there, as he rubbed his nose against mine.

The soft rain that had been falling outside the hospital window thins into a hush. Now, I look up, taken into silence. Susan is assigned to Chris again this afternoon. She marches in, her characteristic red high heels tapping the linoleum floor. Though she has gotten used to my daily ritual of reading to Chris, I can see the confusion in her eyes. I know she thinks me reading to him is a bit odd. He is divorcing me, after all.

"You love him?"

The question makes me pause, and I look up, caught between sadness and the will to smile. "Yes. He's everything—"

"Oh, hang on just a second," Susan says, holding up a finger. She moves over to the IV drip pouch and restrains its shrill beep. "The chemo's coming along," she nods, wiggling a syringe into the tube.

My eyes lift and tremble and it feels as though this moment is frozen in time.

"You're doing great, Mr. Rylan. I see your lovely wife is here," she says, withdrawing the syringe. "If you need anything, just give me a buzz," she smiles, sliding her hand over the door to the room and tugging it closed behind her.

I stare at the door for several moments and then return my eyes to Chris's face. It is an emotional day, like all the days that came before this Wednesday. They say that divorce rates are high when one spouse has cancer. Usually, one partner can't take the strain of being a caregiver. Yet, here I am, a caregiver who is still head over heels in love with her soon to be ex-husband. I stare at his face, cough and am tugged back into memories.

We had so much fun at my graduation party as the sizzle of grilled burgers buzzed through the warm air. Even at the age of 18, I understood the beauty of being that close to someone, both physically and emotionally. As I linger in the memory, tears choke my throat.

As we danced at the party, Chris's hands wrapped around me like lace.

"Oh, Chris," I squealed as he reached for my hand and twirled me around in a circle. Chris knew me in a way that no one else ever had, not even my parents. As I drifted forward against his chest and his arms clasped around me, I seemed to give off radiance.

"All right. It's time to slow things down," the disk jockey said, speaking into a microphone. Moments passed so quickly with Chris that time became irrelevant. As we swayed, I closed my eyes.

"How about this one?" Chris nodded, releasing me with a smile and giving the disk jockey thumbs up. Our song began playing, and I grinned broadly against Chris's face, as we moved slowly with the music. Then as I moved closer, his hands cupped my cheeks, and he drew me closer.

"You didn't know I had it in me," he said, smiling softly and rubbing his hands against my lower back. Some would say that at the age of 18 you have no idea what love is. At that very moment in time, I knew exactly what love was, because I felt it in my heart. Chris and I danced slowly. His boxy white tennis shoes were untied and flopping against the ground, but it didn't matter; it never did. All I needed to be content was for him to be there.

That was the year Chris took up boating and bought his first canoe. His family owned a beach house, and we were there so often, swimming, sunning ourselves, and dancing on the shoreline. His canoe was dusty brown and fit perfectly against the boat dock. I liked the boat for the most part, though I was a bit skittish about stepping into it too quickly. The boat itself was made of cheap wood and had a tendency to wobble when you lifted a foot into it.

"Take it easy, sweetheart," I said to Chris as I helped him climb into a canoe on a balmy day in late July of 1998. The water was rocky that day, and the tide rushed in, shaking the fragile boat. "Lilly," Chris screamed. Feeling my heart in my stomach, I let go of the boat dock and plunged into the ice cold waters.

"Chris, baby," I said, stretching my arms around him and kicking to keep us afloat. I tossed my water-soaked hair behind my back and jerked my neck. Clasping my hands behind his neck, I pulled him to the shore. My eyes were instantly drawn to beads of water that lingered on his arms and shoulders, and I jerked my head, feeling water drip from strands of my hair.

"See," he said, pointing his fingers toward my face. "You can't take your eyes off me. And by the way," he said, breathing deeply, "thanks for saving my life."

"Anytime," I said, clasping my hands into a locked position behind his neck. "If I'm going to marry you someday, I have to make sure you make it to our wedding."

"So you're talking about marriage? Let's not get too ahead of ourselves," he said, smoothing a hand over my hair. My green eyes froze, and I stared back at him.

"What?"

His eyes grew mellow, and he pulled me close, running his hands across my skin.

I wanted to get married. I wanted to marry him more than I wanted to do anything else. Chris was aware of my affection for him, as he had come across a diary in which I kept all of my thoughts about him. When we were very young, Chris once opened the book and saw his name at the beginning of an entry.

Every day after that, he snuck into my room to look for the diary, which to my elation, resembled many other books that I kept on the bookshelf in my room. So it was often hard for him to find my most current entry. My stories featured him as the main character.

At the time, Chris had no idea of my intentions for keeping my diary. It was my attempt at a self-fulfilling prophecy. I wanted to marry him more than I wanted anything else. If I could make my dream real on paper, chances are I had a good shot at making my dream of marrying him come true.

I keep telling myself that I have four weeks left to be with him. In four weeks, he will pass away and will leave me with nothing but memories. Still, my memories call me back to the diary.

Right now, in Chris's hospital room, I look at him for several moments and note the subtle lines of his face. They've gotten deeper now and more pronounced.

"Do you remember that, baby? Do you remember the diary? You're Chris. I'm Lilly. I love you," I say, leaning down and kissing his head. I press a tissue to my nose and lower a trembling hand to the armrest on his bed. "I don't want a divorce."

I still have more memories to relive, I realize now, as I scroll to the next page. Our happy moments together are fleeting. I remember looking at him and seeing sadness in his eyes when I told him I was going off to college without him.

"Chris, sweetheart," I said. "I've been accepted into a college on the east coast. It's a wonderful opportunity, but I can't leave you. I love you too much."

Chris's eyes trailed away slowly when I told him. "Sweetheart," he said, "I would never keep you from doing something that would make you happy."

"Oh, Chris."

"But," he said, "I can't bear the thought of not seeing you, so I'm applying to the school." He pulled down his baseball cap, shuffled his hands through his hair, and sat up straight. He was accepted four weeks later, and we each boarded a plane and headed to the east coast.

It was September 3, 1998, and I found myself reflecting on our relationship from its start to its current state. As far back as my memory stretched in my high school years, Chris was always a part of my life. He had not been there for the first year of my high school career, but my years with him were the only ones that mattered. The rest could be tossed aside without a second glance.

On my first day of college, I was sitting in a grand lecture hall, gazing up at steel-beamed rafters that overlooked the giant lobby to the science building on the large and sprawling campus. Placing a notebook with fresh white paper on my lap, I held a pen loosely in my hand, and a strand of my hair fell in front of my eyes. I looked at my watch, gazed briefly at the door, and blew out my breath.

As I contemplated the possibilities of what college would bring, my head lifted when a loud male voice ricocheted against the lobby's walls. As I looked up at the glass doors, the sound of that voice met my ears. Excitement rose within me, and I touched a hand to my cheek. Moments passed as my eyes lingered. Returning my eyes to my lap, I scratched down some notes. Then my eyes lifted to see the blond hair, the blue eyes, and the beautiful face I had known for so long.

The sight of Chris's boots made me feel like I was sitting in paradise, as I stared at him, breathed out, and slowly lifted my eyes to his.

He raised a hand to my cheek. "Well, you did it," he said, smirking. "You made it to college without telling me where you were." He grinned, sliding across the plush bench on which I'd been sitting.

"Why are you in this building?" I asked, as my eyes lifted and hovered helplessly upon him.

"Biology 503. I told you I'd meet you here, bonehead," he said, smoothing a hand playfully over my head and reaching for my face.

I looked up, feeling safe as I gazed into his vivid blue eyes.

"I thought you were trying to avoid me," he smiled, tilting his head. "Your seat was vacant, so I had to come get you. No one is in the classroom yet."

I raised an eyebrow. "And my seat is vacant?"

He tilted his head and ruffled a hand through his hair. "You're gonna follow me, right?" he asked, grabbing my hand and tugging me up the escalator. As I gazed up, marble walls came into view, and the sound of feet pounding the linoleum floors met my ears.

These memories bring tears to my eyes. And as my eyes scan the screen to my laptop, I draw a dense breath, knowing in my heart that there's a reason I am doing this. True love lives in the heart, never changing, never wavering. When love is like the air you breathe, you never stop chasing. You always follow the one you love. And that's forever what I plan on doing.

I glance at my watch and run a finger under my nose. Then I stand up, place my right hand over his heart, and breathe deeply. Looking behind me to make sure no one is here, I bring myself to speak.

"Sweetheart, can you hear me?"

I can feel my eyes tremble, and I look down at the stubbly whiskers on his face. He draws a deep breath, and his eyes lift to meet mine. The rising of his eyes is slow, but meaningful.

I sniff for a moment, and the door creaks open. Susan is his nurse again today. Her high heels tap the floor, and I smile at her as she comes into view.

She pauses and looks at me softly. Her face radiates a sense of warmth that I haven't seen from any of the other nurses.

"You love him, don't you?" she asks, eyeing me softly and glancing at the IV pouch.

"I do, more than anything." I sniff and press a tissue to my nose.

She nods. "I can tell. He's been improving ever since you started reading to him, and he sees it."

"Sees what?" I inquire, feeling my eyebrows rise.

"Your love …"

She smiles for a moment and holds up a finger. "Excuse me for a second," she says, moving toward the IV pouch and clicking a button.

"It's time for your chemo again, Mr. Rylan," she says, eyeing a needle briefly. "Just a little pinch here, okay? You're doing great," she says, wiggling the needle into Chris's arm and withdrawing it quickly.

"Thank you so much, Susan."

She pats my arm and looks at me kindly. "I see a big change in him. He brightens up the moment you walk in."

I nod in acknowledgement. Now, as Susan closes the door, I stand up once again, feeling a flip of joy in my stomach. It is an hour later, and here I stand, looking back at regular intervals to see if anyone is watching. Five hours have passed since I got here, and I am still standing above his bed, scanning my laptop, and scrolling through our life.

I have been a hopeless dreamer since Chris and I first met. Those things never change. As I look at his blue eyes, I once again take a leap of faith.

"I love you Chris. You have no idea how much."

I trail a finger across his arm and kiss his cheek softly.

Now his eyes turn to me. He reaches for my hand.

CHAPTER FOUR

EPIPHANIES

My mouth drifts open as Chris lifts his left arm and touches his index finger to my hand.

Neither of us says a word, but his eyes search me as if we had met for the first time. Slowly, my mouth opens, and I murmur a hushed thank you. Now, as I tilt my head, I wipe my eye and look at him.

The epiphany is starting, and it seems almost surreal that he is looking at me. The mere fact that he lifted his finger to touch me almost makes me weep. For the first time in months, I feel that I can breathe again. I exhale softly and smile with my head tilted.

The look on his face is strangely familiar, reminiscent, as his lips part, and he tries to speak.

"Lilly."

His eyes linger. His breath rises with stronger vitality. Memories of his hand laced in mine come instantly back to me, and I smile, cautiously smoothing a finger over his hand. Then his lips part, tremble briefly, and curve into a smile. It has been so long since he has seen me. His eyes search my face, pausing briefly in amusement. Slowly, I bring my hand to his and rub it softly over the top of his hand.

"Chris, it has been so long."

He trembles for a moment, but manages a soft nod before speaking. "Yes."

I feel the emotion in his touch as he rubs my hand and looks at me for several moments. His eyes glide over my face, and a look of regret radiates from his bright blue eyes. He wipes his eye.

"I love you. Don't ever forget that," I say, feeling a soft tug in the pit of my stomach.

Vivid recollections of our moments spent together as teenagers come flooding back to me. And as I touch his hand, I can feel the soft and slender fingers that combed through my hair and the long arms that lifted me off the ground. He is the same man. As I look at the hospital gown covering his body, I realize while looking at his long legs and trembling lips that this man has never changed. He is still the boy next door who loved my whimsical nature and joy for life.

Although his hair is all but gone, he possesses the same beauty I saw in his eyes the first time we kissed. The love and emotion within his heart shines through as I watch his vibrant blue eyes search me. As I exhale elatedly, I brush my hand over his arm.

"You've never changed, sweetheart. You're still the same," I say, gazing at him softly.

"I—I never meant to hurt you," I say, pressing a hand softly against my heart.

"I know," he murmurs, his gaze dimming as his eyes drift away. "The cancer, it's hurting me."

"I know," I say, my voice quivering as I hear a knock at the door. I look and see Susan. This time, rather than bolting in, her pace slows and her gaze lifts. She stands there, her body like a shadow against the floor, silently watching.

I look at Chris warmly and tilt my head.

"It's been a while," he says, inhaling deeply and shifting painfully against the thin white sheets on his hospital bed. Sniffing deeply once again, he nods. "I remember so much— your parents' house, the basement."

"Our life together," I say, touching my right cheek and feeling worried that I have said too much. His gaze is soft, pleading, and I feel a sudden peace fill my stomach as he stretches out his hand. Once again, I see the boy I rescued from the lake, the boy who tugged me up the escalator in college. In my memory, there is only one Chris. And here he is, right before my eyes.

I smooth a hand over my greasy hair and search his face, feeling self-conscious that I haven't showered in a few days.

"Oh, Lilly." I am not sure if I should laugh or cry, considering the fact that this man is divorcing me.

"You see me," I manage, wiping the side of my eye and combing my fingers cautiously through my hair.

His gaze lifts. "Can I ask you something?"

His question is inaudible at first, but now, as I move closer, I feel a sudden peace.

"Can I have some water?" he asks, realizing my good intentions. "He's perfect," I think to myself, looking at him and seeing compassion in his eyes as they linger upon me. I raise a hand to my chin, close my eyes, and smooth a hand over his arm.

"Are you sure that's a good idea?" I ask, gazing at his IV pouch. He looks up, tugs at the top of his shirt and looks at me, his eyes moving fearfully. "How have you been doing?"

"As well as I can," I say, lifting my eyes to a butterfly on a tree outside the window.

I raise my head, feeling at a loss for words. "Is the chemo working?"

"They say so," he says, "but I'm feeling weak these days."

I sniff, picturing the intent to divorce paperwork I'd been scanning for weeks and feel a sudden denseness in my throat.

"Are you still thinking about the paperwork?"

He draws a dense breath and looks at me softly. "I don't know," he says, his eyes freezing and his arm jolting above his head.

"Chris!" I scream, feeling helpless and wondering what is happening to him. He begins to moan, and his arms and legs twitch wildly.

I want to help him, but I have no idea of what I should do. "I'm calling the nurse. It's okay. I'm right here."

A series of beeps chirp in unison in the nurse's station, as I press my finger into the buzzer.

"My husband is having a seizure," I scream frantically.

"I'll be right there, Ms. Rylan," Susan says, her voice coming through the speaker. I can hear her footsteps against the floor, this time with more vigor and persistence than usual. Dashing through the door, Susan throws her brown hair behind her shoulders and looks at Chris.

"It's okay, Mr. Rylan," she says. "You're having a seizure. We're gonna get you right out of this one, okay?" she says, holding a bottle and drawing fluid into a needle syringe. "Hang in there, just a little pinch," she says, struggling to find a place to inject the needle.

As she pulls the needle out of his arm, and Chris drifts out of the convulsion, Susan places a digital thermometer in his ear.

"His temperature's up," she says, withdrawing the thermometer and eyeing it briefly.

"Oh, honey," she says, eyeing me fearfully. "His temperature is 104.6."

CHAPTER FIVE

MENDING HEARTS

I feel my body go rigid as my jaw drops, and my lips tremble, unable to do anything but watch. The instinct to cling to him is strong, overpowering. If anything happens to him, I don't know what I would do. Though Chris is leaving me, there is still a part of me that yearns desperately to take care of him. I want to return to the boy who lifted me off the front yard when I was a teenager.

I know he wants to hear something sentimental from me, but saying something of that nature without him feeling the same way would break my heart. There were moments when I felt like throwing in the towel, realizing that there was no hope for reconciliation with Chris. But right here in this moment, things feel perfect, connected. "Chris," I say, watching Susan from the corner of my eye. Looking at me, he seems to have come to life for the very first time. Now he curls his finger, prompting me to come closer.

"Say something to me," Chris whispers with a gruff rasp to his voice.

"I love you, Chris. I always have, and I always will."

Susan is lathering her hands at a sink in the room. She dries her hands, looks at me briefly, and closes the door. His lips part and his breath brings me closer.

"Lilly," he says, reaching for me. And though it clearly takes all of his energy to lift his arms, Chris lifts his head and pulls my hand toward him.

"Yes, sweetheart?"

"There's a reason," he says, inhaling shakily. "There's a reason I filed for divorce."

"Why?" I whisper, shifting in my seat and wiping the back of my hand over my eyes.

He places a hand over mine. "The pain. I wanted to spare you the pain."

I reach for his arm, feeling connected, yet slightly terrified. "But I love you. I'd do anything for you."

He reaches for my hand. "I know, but that's a lot. That's a lot to put on you."

I dab a tissue to my eye and sniff. Noting the remorse in his eyes, I wonder if that is the only thing that led Chris away from me. I have made mistakes, many of them, I know. After I had Ben, hormones kicked in full tilt, and I thought I wanted a divorce.

"Was it because of the postpartum?" I sniff, pausing briefly and remembering the tears in his eyes.

"No. That had nothing to do with it."

I throw my hair over my shoulders and look at him critically. "So you thought about this?"

"It's not something I'm proud of."

I can't say a word. I should be angry, I really should be. But anger will do nothing to solve the problems between us.

His gaze turns toward me and drifts away fearfully.

"Please don't hate me, Lilly. I wanted to do what was best for you. I didn't want you to long for me after I am gone. I want you to move on. And it is better for you to do that now than to deal with the pain of having your husband die."

An explosion of pain shatters within me, and I reach for him.

"I don't hate you. I could never hate you."

"But I'm—"

I hold a finger to his mouth to silence him. "You're everything to me, everything."

He looks at me remorsefully, runs a hand over his head, and shifts nervously.

"Is there a chance? That was a horrible thing that I did."

"Is there a chance for what?" I ask, picturing my days with Chris, picturing a time when we were young. Before my eyes, I see him lifting my veil at our wedding. I see him chasing me through the reception hall, and I see him scooping me up in his arms.

"Chris, I don't want a divorce," I say lowly while shifting shakily. I look at him pleadingly, remembering his soft hands upon me and picturing him chasing me through the backyard.

He pats my arm. "Neither do I." Then, he trails a trembling finger over my wrist.

"You were nervous about bringing this up," I say.

He nods and trembles. "Yes."

"Oh, Chris."

He tilts my chin toward him, like he always has. "Oh, Lilly, you're my girl."

I reach over and caress his face. "It's not the end, you know?"

"Lilly, I have four weeks to live. I think that's the end."

I get up from my seat and kiss his mouth softly. "I love you, baby."

"I wish there were a way to slow down the pace," he says, holding a hand to his lips, which are quivering.

I begin trembling, as I reach for him again. "Don't divorce me, Chris, please. Please don't divorce me," I cry, feeling warm tears trail down my cheeks. "I want to be with you for an eternity."

His expression softens, and he moves closer. I bury my head in his shoulder, breathe in the medicinal scent of his hospital gown, and look up. It has been so long since I have been this close to him. In an attempt to turn off my tears, I look toward the floor and regard the wheels on his hospital bed. Running my fingers along the cold railings on his bed, I stand up and kiss my precious husband.

"Oh, sweetheart," he says, seeing my pain and brushing a tear from my eye. "Don't cry."

I am afraid to speak, but somehow my mouth opens. "Why?"

"Because I'm not divorcing you."

"Oh, Chris," I squeal, leaping and grabbing to clutch his hand tightly. In this moment, as I hold his hand within mine, I speculate what his thoughts are. He hadn't spoken to me in months. I stare forward, picturing the divorce papers ripping before my eyes.

Slowly his eyes rise to meet mine.

"Bring me the divorce papers. I'll rip them up."

"Chris, I was horrible in the past, with the postpartum depression," I say, realizing by the look on his face that it doesn't matter anymore.

His gaze is soft as he looks at me, awaiting a response.

"I have loved you from the beginning," I say, reaching for him.

"Love has no end. It goes on and on," he says, bouncing his fingers on my arm and looking at me the same way he did 19 years ago. "Things change. We get older."

I pause and stare silently, realizing that he is right. Though I haven't given it much thought, I realize that Chris takes a more realistic view on things. A dreamer at heart, I often don't think about such things. We are getting older. And though time may change our destinations, it will never change my love for Chris.

I grab my pocketbook, smile, and stand up. "Well, sweetheart," I say, leaning in and kissing his mouth softly. "I'll be back shortly. I have something I need to get."

"What is it?"

I smile. "It's a piece of paper."

He grins and gives me a wink. "A love note perhaps?"

I smile at him, turn, and slide a hand under my hair, feeling a sudden thrill. And I stand here staring at the man I love more than life itself. I look away for several seconds, and my eyes are pulled toward a bright light that causes my throat to constrict.

CHAPTER SIX

COMING BACK AGAIN

Chris is still going to die, and I have to make the most of every precious moment that remains.

Now, as I reach the car several minutes later, I sniff, anticipating the outpour of emotion that is about to burst forth from my eyes. I breathe out an excited breath, also knowing that I am not getting a divorce. Combing my fingers through my hair, I bite my lip. Slowly, I look up at the hospital's red brick exterior, noting the subtle wisps of clouds drifting across the vivid blue sky.

The past week has worn me down to the point of exhaustion, and it isn't until now that I fully realize the urgency of my drive home. Looking intently at my car, I smile and allow my head to fall back. The cool air caresses my neck, prompting me to tug my jacket high above my shoulders.

"Oh, Chris," I say, exhaling giddily. Now, as I stand here, tears stream down my cheeks. The fact that we're not getting divorced brings me a sudden thrill, prompting my lips to curve upward.

"He's finally back," I think to myself. I haven't been this happy in a long time. Caught somewhere between joy and amazement, I realize now that Chris still loves me, the same way he loved me the first time he lifted me from the ground and threw me over his shoulders. Looking up, I breathe in. I feel warm tears as they continue rolling down my cheeks, releasing a catharsis of emotion. The crisp fall air is cold against my skin. And as I place my hand on the car door, I don't shiver at all.

Moments slide by blissfully, as I smile against the sun before I click my seatbelt upon me and giggle. The world becomes brighter and more beautiful as I revel silently against a bright fall sun, my heart beating with warmth.

Sliding the key into the ignition, I smile and allow my head to fall back against the headrest to my car seat. "Oh, Chris," I say, exhaling giddily.

The car ride home is beautiful, I realize, as I gaze up at crimson trees that are swaying in unison and fading from green to a light yellow. I know my life is changing in a big way. I feel it in my heart as I remember the softness of Chris's eyes.

The wind is blowing harder now, as I turn over the engine and head home. I decided not to take a cab this morning. Ralph has grown critical of me, and I simply can't deal with him anymore. So I sit here, driving against the wind and pausing intermittently to take in the majestic beauty of the trees fading into the distance.

It is now 30 minutes later, and I am pulling into our driveway. After grabbing the divorce papers, I inhale before jumping back in the car. There is no time to waste. I speed onto the highway, attempting to avoid a traffic jam two miles down the road. The drive back to the hospital is magical, watching the trees disappear behind my car as I pick up speed. Time seems to move in slow motion and, with each passing moment, I feel more alive.

As I stand here looking at the hospital, I run forward, race into Chris's room, smile, and rush to his side.

"Here it is, sweetheart," I say, handing him the divorce papers with a broad-lipped smile and joyfully trembling hands.

"Shall we?" Chris grins, pinching a finger at the top of the paperwork.

I bring my eyes to his.

"We shall." I smile and pinch two fingers next to Chris's thumb and forefinger.

"Let's do it," he says.

The sound of the papers ripping is like music to my ears as I watch paper fibers shave away like mist. As we shred the rough grains of the papers, I look at Chris.

His eyes linger on me, and his right hand cups the side of my face. "You're my girl, Lilly."

His blue eyes seem to sparkle as I climb up onto his bed and squeeze his hand. We exchange warm gazes, and I bury my head in his shoulder. We seem to drift together, and I lift my arms to his shoulders, feeling my lips wrap around his. As his lips press harder against mine, I draw him closer, bringing my hands to his jaw line.

That is his move normally, but I find a certain magic in making the first move on the first boy who captured my heart.

He is all man now. As he looks at me, he takes my hand and bounces it on the white sheets, cuddling me softly.

"I think this is how we're meant to be," I say, looking into his eyes.

"I know, sweetheart. I know this is how we're meant to be."

My heart radiates with warmth and joy, as I put my arm around him, taking in the warmth of his skin.

"Are you ready for some freedom? Wanna get out of here?" I ask. I rise briefly from Chris's bed and look at his IV pouch, with my right hand hovering at my chin. "Susan said you'll be done with this round of chemo by 7 tonight. Seriously, we need to get out of here."

His eyes trail downward. "That would be wonderful, but I don't think that's possible," he says, shuffling a hand over his head.

Though Chris is weak, his eyes still hold a vivacious spunk, an unwavering seduction from which I can never walk away. I have worked hard to keep our marriage together. Now that I know it is fully intact, I plan on enjoying every minute of it.

My eyes lift and linger on him. "Do you think there's a chance that they'd let you out of here for a night, a few days maybe?"

As I look at the tubes above him, reality stops me in my tracks. He still has cancer. But as I gaze at his soft blond hair, desire tugs at my heart. There is so much I want to do with Chris. There are so many things I need to share with him with the time we have left.

A loud thud takes me out of my thoughts as I look up and watch a group of doctors walk in.

"Well, Mr. Rylan, we have good news," says a doctor with thick white hair and a deep, angular jaw. He pushes metal framed glasses up on his nose and looks up with a face full of concentration.

My eyes brighten, and a sudden lift fills my stomach.

"Your cancer appears to be going into remission. We found a mistake in your medical records. You're cancer seems to be going into remission, so you might be able to send you home for the weekend. However, I want to run some scans before I let you go home," he says. As Chris's eyes lift, he smiles and nods suggestively. "Then I guess you can unhook me from this IV and let me go home."

The doctor affixes a pen to the top of his ear and smiles. "Not entirely. You can go home for the weekend, but we want to see you back on Monday, just for a checkup. If all checks out, and the cancer isn't growing, you can go home without coming back," he smiles. "We just want to make sure everything's clear."

"Awesome," Chris says.

The doctor shuffles his hands over his clipboard. "All right," he says. "Enjoy a weekend with your family."

Chris lifts his arms sluggishly, yet with more vitality than he has in ages.

As my eyes linger on Chris's large and husky hands, I feel his eyes upon me. His smile makes me pause and turn toward him. Right now, as I gaze at him, I feel once again like the teenager who surrendered to his soft touch. So much has changed, I realize, yet so much has remained the same.

I look at the clock, like I have for five months. It feels familiar, almost mundane, as I watch the third hand glide around the numbers. Watching the hospital clock has been a matter of routine for many months. But right here, as I listen to the clock tick, it feels as though I am doing it for the final time.

"This is it—the moment of truth, when everything I prayed for finally comes together," I say, pushing my hair behind my ears and feeling worried that I have said this too soon. Tears sting the corners of my eyes as I look at him. What if he still has cancer?

"And there you are, still a writer. You are eloquent," Chris says, "you know, with your words."

I sigh softly and sniff, feeling the warmth in his words and realizing in this moment that he can no longer look away.

Chris smiles deeply and reaches for my hand. With my gaze lingering on his soft skin and crystalline eyes, I close my eyes momentarily. Now, I open them, allowing my hair to glide behind my shoulders. I showered before I came back to the hospital, so I feel rejuvenated in a way that I haven't in five months. It hadn't mattered before.

"You are beautiful," Chris says, "just the way you were before."

Looking up, a soft sigh escapes my lips. "Yeah, when we were teenagers," I giggle, tossing a hand through my curly brown locks.

"You still do that," Chris says, chuckling softly and catching my eyes with a warm and sudden gaze.

I pick up a glass vase from his night stand and examine it. The possibilities for our life are endless, I realize, as Chris winks at me with a sudden and familiar smile.

"No, but seriously," he says, grabbing for my hand. "You've never changed."

"Oh, sweetie. Nor have you, aside from the new hair," I say, chuckling.

"It is pretty sparse these days, isn't it?" he laughs, tossing his head back.

I remember that laugh and that warmth as it rises within his voice. My eyes linger on him and I stare into his eyes, losing myself. Time seems to stop as our eyes rise, rediscovering one another.

"Okay, sweetheart," I say, drawing his hand into mine. "Let's get you home."

He trembles for a moment, clutches my hand, and slowly puts his arms around me.

"Let's get out of here," I say, possessively clutching his hand.

Susan, Jackie, and a few other nurses are helping us pack up for the weekend, giving us instructions for Chris's meds and waving before we go through the hospital's front door. As I push Chris out to the car in a wheelchair, I touch his hand, and his eyes reflect a purity I have so long yearned to see yearned to see. "This is a beautiful reunion," I think to myself, clutching Chris's hand, walking out, and fading into a new and mysterious world.

Outside, beyond the sky, the wind feels cold as it wraps around us, enveloping us together.

"Oh, this feels good," Chris says, stretching his arm around me, as we walk forward toward the car.

I raise my right arm for him to grab, but he simply walks forward, breathing in. Chris hasn't seen the world in five months. And it is clear, as his eyes rise, that he is welcoming the world with a whole new outlook.

I realize, as I look at his soft skin and sparkling eyes, that nothing has changed about Chris. I have known him for 19 years. Yet as I look at the subtle lines at the corners of his eyes, I see the same boy, that same smile.

"I'm gonna race you to that car," he says, tightening his grip on my hand and races forward. I squeal as he pulls me forward, watching the hospital disappear behind us and fading slowly into the distance. The world seems to freeze in time, as he stops at the car, draws my hands into his, and kisses me. As I clutch his hands, it feels as though we have done it for the first time, as we see one another in a new light—older, closer, and connected in a way that few couples are.

"All right, sweetie," I say, spinning him around. "It's time to get you home."

We get in the car and exchange expectant glances, as he ruffles my hair and draws my head forward into his palms. I know that move. I have craved it since the moment we separated.

"Let's get out of here," Chris says, trailing my hand with his fingers. His eyebrows lift with silent expectation, as I rev the engine, and we speed away against the deepening night sky.

Getting home quickly is not the point of it, I have decided, momentarily rolling down my window and feeling the crisp breeze upon my face. I smile against the driver's side window, pull out of the parking lot, and get onto the freeway. I take my time, realizing that this is a turning point in our relationship. As we walk up to the house, my eyes grow intense upon him. Chris breathes in deeply and eyes me with silent yearning, his eyes growing intense.

It took us 30 minutes to get home. Now we stand in front of our house, watching the sun sink into the landscape behind us. Standing in front of the house feels surreal now, as I feel my eyes fall upon him. Slowly we walk up the front steps.

"Well, here we are," Chris says, moving toward me.

He touches my hand and it feels like it had when we first came together as teenagers. In my mind's eye, I see my parents' basement. Expectation and desire now rise within me as I picture his boyish face and look up to regard the subtle bristles on his cheeks. He lifts his hands, and I drift back, anticipating the feel of his hands on my face. He holds my cheeks for a few minutes, but slowly, his hands travel lower below my shoulders. His kiss is full and forceful as he rubs my shoulders before allowing his hands to travel lower and to my shirt.

Chris pulls me closer and draws a dense breath. "I think we better," he breathes as his head turns briefly. He nods and smiles, as he regards me with a look of urgency. "I think we better take this inside."

Expectation rises within me, and I take his hand as he tugs me up the steps.

"I think," I nod, drawing a deep breath. "I think that's a good idea."

His hands are warm, and his mouth brushes mine. Spinning me around, Chris drifts toward me, with a suggestive smile. He is beautiful, I realize, as I lower myself to the floor. Slipping a hand under my back, he shakes briefly and lowers his back to the plush carpet as he breathes out and lowers his hands to my chest. His touch feels the same, yet different as he continues, his face full of silent concentration. His fingers spread wide open over my shirt, and his eyes search me.

"Oh my God, Lilly," Chris says, shakily lowering himself to the floor and shuffling his shirt from his shoulders.

"Are you sure you're okay to do this?"

He doesn't say a word, but instead he nods at me.

"Oh, Chris," I breathe, as he combs his hands through my hair and rubs them possessively over my body. As soft as silk, his hands drift under my shirt, slip under the back of my bra, and unhook it. He is still shaky, but there is a look of urgency on his face as his lips part in anticipation. He pauses for a moment, his blue eyes glistening, as his gaze lingers upon me.

His skin, deep and penetrating, melts into my flesh. I am powerless to his touch, too weak to do anything but surrender beneath him. My hands travel over his body, my slender frame crushing heedfully against him, the warmth of my skin soaking through his tattered white shirt and into his skin. Slowly, he draws me closer.

This is so remarkably warm and familiar.

"Oh wow," I breathe, my fingers deepening into his skin.

"Let's get rid of those panties," he says eagerly. His eyes are intent and seducing as he lowers his hands with purpose. His fingers are warm upon my chest, igniting a fire within.

Tugging down his pants, Chris stands in front of me, naked and graceful in front of me. His hands trail the subtle crevice of my knee and slip under my back. Clasping my arms around him, my eyes drift closed, feeling his warmth, as his body melts into mine. His tongue dances circles around my chest, as we drift into a soft and passionate embrace.

"I would love it if we could do this forever," he smiles, lowering his mouth to envelop me. I exhale a heavy breath, as his hips pull him deeper into me. His gaze is sultry and seductive, I realize as he breathes deeply into my skin.

"You know what we're doing, right?" I ask. He places his hands on my chest, caught in between laughter and his deepening breath. He appears as though he is deciding whether or not he should continue.

He chuckles warmly. "Yeah."

With his arms sliding under my back, I feel his warmth against me. As his hands trail my arms, I am instantly transported back to my parents' basement. I remember the way his tongue danced circles around my chest for so many years.

"Here we go," he says, chuckling and drifting into me. The tips of his fingers twirl around every crevice of my body. His breath slows, and he exhales a heavy breath. As he drifts into me, I breathe in and take in the warmth of his body. He pulls me closer, rubbing his chest against me. As his hand floats over me, I am filled with silent yearning, feeling my body melt into his. My fingers hesitate, but I realize, as his hands trail my legs, that there is nothing delicate about him. As he pushes himself in deeper, something within me yearns to be closer. "Oh … my … God."

"Yeah," he says, as he kisses my neck. "It feels good, huh?"

He moves deeper, taking in my warmth as I kiss his mouth hungrily. "I remember this," I giggle, as he brings his body to mine. I am once again helpless beneath him, and I surrender to his touch, panting more deeply with his every touch. His fingers travel over my thighs, and his eyes shine as his mouth lingers over mine. Now, I begin to tremble. A culmination of rising sensation surges from my toes to my head. Slowly, I close my eyes.

"Oh my God," he says, bringing his forehead to mine.

As I feel myself let go of every inhibition, I try to decide whether to hold him tighter or release him as my sensation subsides. He withdraws for a moment and brings his eyes level with mine.

The poignancy I have so longed to feel again comes with clarity, enveloping my senses as he lingers. His eyes are intense, his breath warm. As I pause in anticipation, his warmth surges, sending waves of joy through my limbs. I hold my breath, feeling sensation build.

"Oh God, Lilly," Chris breathes heavily, tugging his hands through my hair and bringing his mouth to my collarbone. He twitches for a few brief moments, exhaling a heavy moan. As I look at sweat forming on his shoulders, waves of pleasure envelop my senses.

"I love you, Chris."

My hurried breath is warm upon him, as my hips move against him in an unexpected wave of sensation and joy. His hands begin to shake as he falls to his side, crashing upon me. "Oh my God. Are you okay?" I ask, struggling to lift him up.

"Yeah, yeah," he says, wiping his forehead. "I just got really dizzy. I think I need to rest for a minute."

Chris lifts himself shakily, and I cringe, fearing an ache in his pancreas. I see his pain as his skin grows yellow. The pain will give way to itching skin, followed by a residual heat on his face.

I breathe out, feeling exhausted, and my eyes rise. "Time has been kind of like a blur, because so much happened."

"Like a whirlwind," he says, lifting a hand to his cheek, which flushes red. "In more ways than you could imagine, it was just really hard."

I look at him and lift a hand to his face. His eyebrows flex. "You thought it was the end. I can't blame you for being so upset." He brushes my arm, drops his hand, and lingers at my wrist. "I heard you read to me. I listened."

His statement means a lot to me, considering the fact that I thought he wanted to hear nothing of my stories. They are real in every possible sense, as my memories drift back to the beginning of our relationship. In my mind's eye, everything is still so fresh, so vivid.

I bounce his hand within mine. "No regrets, Chris. No regrets."

He manages a smile and tilts his head toward me. "I never want to lose you again. I wish that we could be together forever."

"Chris, I promise I will never leave you. I'll keep you with me forever.

If it weren't welcoming gaze, I swear I would cry. Though I understand his reasons for filing for divorce, what he thinks doesn't matter. Love radiates through his brilliant blue eyes, as he brings his lips to mine.

"This is it. We're together," I say, bouncing by his side and lifting my fingers to his temples.

"Lilly, I'm so sorry." His voice trembles, and he sniffs. I'm so sorry I tried to leave you."

His hands are trembling, and he raises his arms to my shoulders. I wipe a tear from my eye. "It's okay, sweetie. Don't beat yourself up. You're torturing yourself."

His eyes are red as they hover upon me, and his skin is clammy. Breathing shallow breaths, tears slide down his cheeks. He looks at me, and I feel his pain within my stomach. It takes all of my energy to comfort him. Within my body, I feel the emotion as it soaks into his soul. Slowly I release him. He should not feel this way. "I feel no anger, Chris. I never feel anger."

Why are you so forgiving? I was horrible, Lilly."

I shake my head, place my right hand on his shoulder, and exhale softly. "I see your pain. I feel it in my body. I couldn't understand why you filed for divorce, but don't ever feel guilty."

I feel my mouth drift open as I close my eyes and rest my head on his shoulder. His breath is deeper now, and he lifts his eyes to mine. "Lilly."

"I know your pain," I say, placing a hand on his heart. "Do you know that angels are all around us?"

I bury my head in his shoulder, breathe in the medicinal scent of his hospital gown, and look up. It has been so long since I have been this close to him. In an attempt to turn off my tears, I look toward the floor and regard the wheels on his hospital bed. Running my fingers along the cold railings on his bed, I stand up and kiss my precious husband.

CHAPTER SEVEN

REFLECTIONS AND MEMORIES

It is now two days later on the edge of dawn, and Chris and I open our eyes. The day before has become a beautiful memory as I rub my eyes and turn to look at Chris.

There is a banging sound in the living room and I raise my arms sluggishly above my head. The sound is deep, distinctive, and it sounds a lot like what Ben calls 'playing the drums.'

Shielding my eyes to avoid being blinded from the impending sunrise, I smile at my husband in our giant four-post colonial bed.

Chris snorts and rises slowly, releasing himself from our dense down covers.

"Ben, what are you doing?" I yell, smiling at Chris.

Chris groans, shuffling his arms over his head. "He's in the pots and pans again."

I roll my eyes and sniff, and my breath, now quickening, makes me feel alive. This isn't the first time this had happened. It seems that every weekend, Ben gets on top of a chair and retrieves our kitchen pans. Then, he grabs kitchen utensils and pounds them on the pans. Even when Chris was in the hospital, he did it every weekend. Sadly, we lost a baby a few years ago. I was pregnant with a little girl.

I rest my head on Chris's shoulder, rekindling the joy I had shared with him before the separation. Chris stretches his arm around my shoulders. With his head tilted, his eyes linger on me as if he is afraid to speak.

"What did you first think when it happened? Ya know, the separation?" he asks.

I stare silently. "I'm not sure."

"Did you write me off as being a pig?"

I look away for several seconds, my gaze frozen, and feel a lump in my throat. I shake my head and bring my eyes back to his. "No. That would have been too easy."

"What do you mean?"

"Calling you a pig would imply that I was angry. I wasn't angry," I say, my eyes rising in contemplation.

He is silent for a long moment and finally brings himself to speak. "You were hurt, though?"

"I would be lying if I said I wasn't."

Some things just aren't meant to be spoken, I realize, as I gaze over at the dresser on my side of the bed. To avoid breaking his heart, I scan the room. It has been so long since I have felt the warmth of his hand or the sound of his voice. Now that I have them both again, I don't want to blow my chances of being with Chris for a long time.

"You're thinking about it," Chris says, his blue eyes dense with a look of concern.

My eyes lift, and I can tell from the warmth in my face that my cheeks are flushing red. "I thought you hated me."

As soon as I say the words, I cringe. I know that hate is not a part of Chris's vocabulary. He has never been short or unloving. "I thought you didn't love me anymore."

"You don't just fall out of love with someone," he says, lifting his hand and placing it over mine. "You want what's best for your spouse. In a sense, you realize you can't meet all of a person's needs. You're going to break their heart at some point," he says. "It's inevitable."

I withdraw my hand from his, and as I swallow hard, feeling tears tug at my vocal cords. "What do you mean?"

As my eyes linger on Chris, Ben's plush slippers pound the stairs. Running into our room with a wooden spoon in each hand, he screams. "Mommy, Daddy, I'm playing the drums!"

As Ben turns, a baker's hat slides off his head, and there is a bang in the living room.

"Yep, he's at it again," I chuckle, gazing at the door to our bedroom. "Ah, the joys of parenthood," I say, smiling briefly before lifting my eyes to the window.

"I'll go check on him," Chris says, shifting against the covers.

My first instinct is to grab Chris and ask him to stay with me. But instead, I bite my tongue, realizing that the world doesn't stop for me. I would have been perfectly happy staying right here with him in our bed, but Ben's voice crashes like thunder against the walls, strong and echoing.

With his feet pounding like drums on the carpet, there will be no peace until we check on him.

"I'll be right back," Chris smiles, patting my right knee before rising. When he returns, the sun is blazing in full, and I can no longer shield my eyes. Tugging down the blind, I turn to Chris and meet his eyes. His face is solemn and pleading. Clearly he wants to continue the conversation.

"So, what were you saying?"

I know what he wants to say is painful and obviously quite serious, and I have a tendency of blocking out those types of conversations.

Chris sits down and his breath ruffles against the covers as he falls back. Regarding me softly, Chris pats my hand, which is still hovering underneath the dense covers.

"I don't mean to put such heavy stuff on you, but when you think about it, one of us will have a broken heart. We all die. Since I was dying, I wanted to spare you the pain."

I shift and look over at him, removing my eyes from the edges of the blinds, where light is struggling to shine through. I crinkle my nose and look back at him. "I love you no matter what, in life and in death."

"God, you're morbid," Chris says, grinning and giving me a playful punch on the arm.

My eyes linger. He is back. My dear Chris is back. Bringing him back to me is one of the greatest accomplishments of my life. And as I celebrate our reunion in my head, I recall all of our childhood moments and the times that mattered.

Right here before my eyes, I picture us together, as we worked on creating Ben. It was a sweet experience. Chris taught me about lovemaking. He showed me passion that is gentle, yet fervent. He taught me everything I needed to know, including how to take my time on enjoying every moment. He showed me sensitivity and patience. That passion and sensitivity radiates in his eyes, as he sits here, holding me. I really have breath and life. Yet as I rise, rolling over groggily, I run my right hand over the top of my back. My wings have all but disappeared, covered up by silky white skin.

Feeling the corners of my eyes moisten, I turn toward Chris, feeling the pillow beneath my head, soft against my skin.

"I'm not like you, you know?"

He turns, his eyes trembling, and he looks at me quietly. "Huh?"

"I knew your pain in the hospital. I felt everything, even the needles in your arms," I say.

He turns and his eyebrows flex. "I'm confused. What do you mean?"

I place my hand upon his and lift my eyes to meet his gaze.

"I am here, but not for the reason you think."

His gaze falls, and without a word, he looks at me fearfully.

"Is there something you're not telling me?"

"Don't be afraid, sweetie. Don't be afraid," I say, placing a hand on his shoulder.

His eyes tremble, and he hesitates for a moment, examining my face. He draws a shaky breath, pushes the covers aside, and lifts a hand to the side of my face.

Chris is my first and only partner. And though many people prefer variety, I will be forever happy with the first boy who touched me and turned me into a woman.

As I sit here, meditating in Chris's presence, I picture us rough housing in the front yard, bringing into focus the thick-lipped smile Chris wore when we were together and laughing.

"Anyway," I say, "we can talk about this later."

"Lilly, it's me," he says, his voice falling to a whisper. "Talk to me."

I pause, and a soft sigh escapes my lips, as I look at him, and memories bring a tear to my eye.

"Just remembering," I say. "You were my first and only partner."

He tilts his head, mocking me. "Is there something you're not telling me? How many guys have you been shacking up with during the time we were apart?"

I hold up my hand. "I would never do that to you."

"I know you'd never do that. Geez, can't you learn to take a joke, woman?"

Smiling softly and allowing my eyelashes to flutter downward, I sink deep into the mattress on and glance at him. "I liked what you called it before we first did it."

He turns with a quick chuckle. "Did what?"

"Chris?"

"Oh! Oh, you mean hanky panky?"

I feel as though joy just ignited under my skin. "You are so cute."

I am so happy. I haven't felt this way in a long time, so I want to take in every moment of it. Yet, in spite of my happiness, I am incredibly emotional. Lingering at the edge of my eyelids are tears—heavy, impending, joyful tears. Lifting my green eyes and gazing at Chris, I reach out my arm and stretch it over him.

His gaze catches mine, and for a moment, I think he has missed the redness in my eyes. Right here, lingering in my right eye is a warm tear droplet, radiating with fresh emotion and ready to burst forth. I sniff for a moment, run a hand over my bare shoulder, and swallow.

"What's wrong?"

"Nothing," I say, my voice cracking as I tuck a lock of hair behind my ear. "I'm just so happy you're here," I cry, feeling my arm tremble against him. "I almost lost you."

Tilting my chin with his finger, Chris looks at me for several moments and smiles.

"I know," he says, his voice falling to a whisper. "But I'm here now. Wow, I haven't seen you this emotional in a long time." He runs a finger over my cheek.

They say that everything happens for a reason. I believe this is true. I know I am going to cry, but I also know that showing too much emotion all at once will keep us from moving forward and into the future. I wipe my eye and sniff with my hand trembling.

"I'm a mess," I say, sniffling and smoothing my hands over my eyelids. "Once I get started on a good cry, whether I'm happy or sad, it's hard for me to turn off the tears."

Chris smiles. "Oh, sweetheart, it's okay. There's still something you forgot to do," he says, holding up something that is gold and glittering. "You forgot to put your wedding ring back on your finger."

My eyes widen like saucers and I smile brightly, feeling a sudden instinct to stretch out my left hand. Chris's face is full of concentration as he slides the ring on my finger.

"What made you read to me anyway? Did you take notes from our past?"

Before I can answer, Chris touches my hand and stands up.

He grabs my left arm and motions me downstairs. It is 12:05 p.m. I could stay here all day. Together, we walk side by side down the stairs, holding hands and reflecting.

"It's the diary," I say, smiling and regarding Chris with excitement. "It's the diary I've kept since we were teenagers. It's sort of a compilation of stories about our life together."

Chris nods in acknowledgement, but appears to be somewhere else. His eyes are frozen on Ben, who is putting stickers on the carpet. "Stay right there, Mommy. I've got more stickers," he says, placing a hand on my wrist and smiling brightly at me.

Ben smiles. "Be right back, Mommy. I've got another sticker for you."

He bounces on the floor, causing a boom to radiate through the living room. Disappearing momentarily into the kitchen, he screams and returns minutes later. Smiling brightly, he presses a dinosaur sticker to my hand and runs off.

"Okay, Ben, we'll wait right here," Chris says, quietly dismissing my gaze, as he stands silently and looks at Ben.

"We'll get back to our conversation in a little bit," Chris says, patting my shoulder and keeping his eyes on me.

Now, several minutes later, Ben emerges from the hallway with several sheets of stickers. Unpeeling them one by one, he covers our clothes with dinosaurs. I squint at Chris and roll my eyes.

"Just go with it," Chris mouths to me as he pats Ben's head. Now, as Chris returns to a standing position, he winks.

The next thing I know, Ben comes running into our room. "I'm a dinosaur. Roar!" he screams, running up the stairs and bouncing with haphazard motions, before disappearing into the darkness of the hallway. A night light flickers by the wall, as he runs.

"Ah, the joys of parenthood," Chris chuckles, as he lays back on the bed, brushes my hand, and smiles.

"Indeed," I say, shifting toward him. I run a hand through my brown locks and rest my head on Chris's shoulder. He smells good, as he always has. Drifting closer to him, I allow my nose to linger on the fabric of his shirt. I don't want to talk too much about the diary, especially when Ben is around. But now that we are alone, looking into one another's eyes, I am ready to talk.

"Let's go downstairs," I say, motioning Chris through the doorway.

I point to my computer, which is sitting on the end table. "So here's my laptop. I'm getting more up to speed with technology," I say, looking over at my computer. I gaze at Chris with a fleeting smile. "I started the diary when we were teenagers, and still write in it from time to time."

He chuckles. "I know. I remember reading it a few times."

My heart leaps as he smiles back at me. I have so many stories and memories in my diary. Now that many of my stories are on my laptop, accessing entries takes a lot less time.

"Well, it does feel good to be worshipped," Chris chuckles, drumming his hands on his lap and bouncing against me.

I roll my eyes and sigh. "Shut up."

What Chris is thinking doesn't matter at this moment. In my mind all that matters is the fact that he is here, that he is alive. I linger on the thought for several moments, realizing that in spite of my doubts and self questioning, I have been a good wife. I sigh happily at the thought, closing my eyes briefly.

"You know it," Chris says, raising his eyebrows and moving closer to my face. "I am awesome."

"Okay, enough!" I squeal, unable to contain my laughter.

"You know I'm great," he says, lifting his eyebrows. "I'm the star of your diary. I'm all you write about. And that, sweetheart, is the ultimate form of flattery."

"Okay, okay," I exclaim, holding up a hand. "Don't get an ego about it."

I rise from the couch, stare aimlessly, clear my throat, and look up. There is so much about the diary that Chris doesn't know. Memories that have come and gone are all kept within its hundreds of pages. And even as we sit here talking, a new memory is being made in my head. I press my fingers to the touchpad on my laptop, and I realize without a word that I have more to write when Chris is not around.

I smile, stand up, ruffle my hair behind my neck, and once again reach for my computer. My eyes linger on the screen as I press my fingers into the power button. I stare in silence, looking at the keyboard. The computer simply beeps and flashes. Now, as my eyes grow intense, the screen fades to black. "Oh God. My computer crashed," I say, frowning and once again plunging a finger into the power button.

Panic takes hold, as I run my fingers frantically over the keyboard, my eyes freezing intermittently and lingering on Chris.

"Oh, please," he says, placing his hands on my computer and lifting it onto his lap. "I just got on it before we separated, and it did the same thing. I can fix it."

He taps a couple of keys with a flourish, and the Windows screen appears before my eyes. In spite of my appreciation for him fixing my computer, there is still a part of me that is suspicious.

I can't believe it. The laptop is my personal property. And though I love Chris more than words, I am infuriated that he had invaded my privacy.

My eyes are intense, slowly narrowing, I realize, as I watch Chris handle the computer.

"You've been reading my personal thoughts on my computer, haven't you?" I ask, eyeing him critically. I don't want to accuse him, I really don't. But at the same time, I have worked so hard to maintain some privacy, when it comes to the diary. It is one of my most prized possessions.

It is clear from his wide eyes that Chris is perfectly innocent. I have known Chris for nineteen years, and never in that time has he ever been dishonest with me. Yet here I am, accusing him of something he didn't do.

His expression freezes for a second, and I regard him, my emerald eyes pleading with regret.

"I'm sorry, sweetheart," I say, smoothing a hand over the side of his cheek and lingering. "I should have never accused you of that."

He flexes his hand in dismissal of my statement, his blue eyes intense upon my face. He knows me in ways no one else ever has. I pause, struggling to remember a time that I haven't loved him.

"You are beautiful," Chris says, raising his eyes to mine.

"Thank you."

"I knew it from the moment you mentioned the diary that I'm great. Now you're questioning my awesomeness," he chuckles, setting the computer up on the coffee table in front of the sofa. He smirks at me and then strides off to the kitchen. Now, as I struggle to stop laughing, he looks over his shoulder and gives me a wink. In the time I have known Chris, I have constantly changed, not only physically, but also in the way I look at things. I stare for a few moments, reflecting. Molly barks in the background. She is in the sunroom on her back, sunning herself in our large picture window.

"A penny for your thoughts," Chris smiles, returning from the kitchen with a strawberry in his right hand. His statement startles me and brings me straight out of a daydream. In his other hand, there is a bowl full of chocolate syrup.

"Memories, huh?" he grins, sitting down and swirling a strawberry in the chocolate. He pauses in silent reflection, regards me briefly, and lifts the strawberry to my chin.

"Close your eyes," he says, slowly bringing the strawberry closer. Closing my eyes, I wonder what he is thinking. I wonder what his intentions are, and I feel a sudden flurry of joy fly through me as he comes closer.

"What are you doing?" I ask, chuckling and feeling the rough grains of the strawberry against my lips. I smile and draw a dense breath.

"Don't think. Just bite," Chris says. He goes silent for several moments, trailing a hand over my arm. A fleeting chill flies through me as his fingers linger and press more intensely. "Close your eyes," he says, touching a hand to my cheek.

Chris has never done anything this mysterious. Whatever he is doing feels seductive, dangerous. As I chew, taking in the sweetness of the chocolate, I feel his hand on my cheek. He continues the gentle motions of his fingers on my arm, and I feel his arms slide under my back and knees. I feel him carrying me. His voice suddenly falls to a whisper, and his warm breath lingers against my skin.

"Where are we going?" I ask, as his hand slides over my stomach.

I open my eyes and find myself in the darkness next to him, his breath rising and falling against my neck. I rise up slowly, combing my fingers through my hair. A second later, he sits another strawberry on the dresser.

"Welcome back to our honeymoon," he says, nibbling at my ear. "Ben's asleep, so we have some time."

I assume a position for lovemaking, figuring that is what Chris has in mind.

He chuckles while looking at me. "Now let's get back to that honeymoon," he says, slipping a hand under my clothes.

A deep moan escapes my lips, as he disrobes and brings his naked body toward me. Bringing his lips to mine and twisting his hips against me, Chris lifts his eyes and moves his hands to my shoulders. Shivers of joy fly through me, as waves of pleasure rise and fall within me. With each stroke of passion, I arch back, drawing him into my body.

Now there is the sudden pound of feet in the hallway outside our bedroom and a loud thud that repeats furiously. Ben's footsteps halt, much to my elation, and he takes off running once again.

"Cannonball!" he screams. Judging by the sudden boom in the living room and the intensity of its sound, Ben has jumped from the fifth step again.

I have wanted to share the diary with Chris for the longest time. I just want to share it with him when we are alone. And because alone time has become such a hot commodity, I relish the opportunity just to unwind. I sigh, sinking into the bed beside him.

I grab him by the shoulder, and he turns around, ready to walk toward the chair in our bedroom. Softly I tug his hand. "I haven't been entirely honest with you, Chris. I can't do this anymore. I can't hide this from you."

He tilts his head as his gaze grows intense. "What?"

"I have to make a choice," I say, placing my hand upon him. I have to choose between staying here or leaving this world."

His voice cracks with emotion, growing quivery. "You're thinking about leaving me?"

"No, no. It's not that I'm leaving you. I just have to make a choice of whether I stay or go.

His voice cracks as his eyes grow distant. "Why?"

My mouth opens, but I am finding it hard to speak. "Chris, I need to get out of here," I say, raising my eyes to a bright light. "It's happening. I have to—I have to go."

The light quickly fades, but as I bring my eyes to his, tears tug at my vocal cords.

Closing my eyes, I am brought out of the light and look at him.

"Don't worry, sweetie. I'm not going anywhere right now."

Because of Chris, I have written the diary in vivid detail, knowing that he has a terrible memory, and at times, a very short attention span. If I can capture every memorable moment, our love will forever be alive.

"So," I say, running a hand over Chris's head and feeling his soft hair. "I must read the diary to you. His eyes grow dim as I stand up and pace toward our dresser. Dismissing his emotion, I turn, realizing that I need to read to him, sooner rather than later. Examining the dresser drawer and tugging it open, I turn to look at Chris. "Hurry up," he chuckles. "I want to see this thing. I'm getting tired of just looking at your naked bum."

"Oh, that's right. I'm naked, aren't I? Let me fix that," I chuckle, stretching a shirt over my shoulders.

I grab the diary from the top drawer, examine its blue exterior in the palm of my hand, and exhale. "Wow, this thing has been mysterious for a long time," I say, gazing softly at Chris and shaking it between my fingers.

I bounce next to Chris on the bed feeling a silent burst of excitement as I look at the diary and bring my eyes to his. "Well, here you have it," I say, gazing at him, extending my arm for a moment and bringing the book back to my chest. "This is the diary, the story of you and me."

I press a finger to the diary's textured cover. His eyes lift to meet mine, and he leans in, giving me a soft and delicate kiss. His breath hushes as he drifts from my mouth and settles back into the bed. Anticipation builds within me as his eyes turn and he rolls over. He rubs a hand over my arm and regards me softly.

"Wow," I say, pursing my lips and exhaling a dense breath. "You've heard a lot of this already. It's a lot to take in, I know, but here it is."

He smiles mischievously and quickly yanks the book from my hand. I slap his hand playfully, all the while watching his blue eyes light up and hover on the diary's cover.

I grin at him and rest my head on his left shoulder. "What are you doing?"

He pauses and looks at me for a long moment, his lips curling in amusement. "Well, if I'm going to read this baby, I want to enjoy it," he grins, silently flipping the pages and bringing his amused gaze back to my eyes.

"No, sir. This is my creation, and I think I should be the one to revel in the glory of its writing," I say, tossing a hand through my hair and brushing his hand. "You, my dear, can sit back and enjoy."

He looks at me with a wide-eyed gaze. "Well, excuse me, Mrs. Creative, for taking an interest in your fine work," he grins, bouncing against a pillow and shuffling the book back into my hands.

"Thank you."

Finally, the secret stories I have written over the years are about to be unveiled, I think silently, looking over at Chris with a contented smile.

"You've already heard the first few stories," I say, scanning a page and tucking a lock of hair behind my right ear. Whether or not Chris is impressed by my stories remains a mystery. But as his eyes lift, lingering on mine, I feel a sudden comfort and validation for my efforts.

"Come on, you can't tell me I'm the only guy you've ever been crazy about," Chris says, tilting his head and slanting me an expression of doubt.

"No, I can't," I say, my eyes trailing downward. "I kissed a boy in my aunt's garage when I was six. I wasn't crazy about him, but it was fun."

"A garage, seriously? Wow, it doesn't take much to get you going," he chuckles before looking away.

As I sit here and tell Chris more about my life, his eyebrows flex as if he is meeting me for the first time. I tell him more about my childhood and about the years before we met, going into vigorous detail about my various pets, including a white rabbit that had a tendency of ripping its nails out and a Bristlenose fish that ate the rest of the creatures in the fish tank.

I don't have the most exciting stories of childhood, but these are fragments of my existence that Chris has yet to hear about. They are not included in the diary, and I don't consider them relevant to our relationship.

"So you picked the needy creatures?"

"Chris, I'm going to say this in the most loving way possible. Shut up."

As I look at Chris, while running a hand over his arm, I realize instantaneously that we have to go back to the hospital tomorrow morning. It is Sunday, and in just under 24 hours, we are going to learn whether or not Chris's cancer is fully gone. As I ponder the possibilities regarding Chris's health, my thoughts are interrupted, and my attention is instantly drawn to the crackling of crisp leaves outside the window.

"I have to open the window," I say, bouncing up and walking to the window. I wrap my fingers around the giant window frame. Popping the window open with a flourish, I throw its dense panes upward and stand in a whimsical pose. Gazing out, I take in the feel of the crisp wind against my face and breathe in the smell of the rustic air. Leaves once again crackle against the sky. Now the air blows against my face.

Looking back at Chris, I pace back to my side of the bed, realizing that we are spending most of the day in the bedroom, a fact that would normally make me shudder. I love to revel in the sunlight and the trees. But right here in this moment, I feel perfectly content holding my diary and gazing into Chris's expectant eyes.

"So," I say, returning to the bed and clasping the diary between my fingers. "We can skip the first 20 pages. I've already read them to you."

"Okay," he says, his eyes hovering on the pages, which contain blue lines and my often illegible handwriting.

"Have you always dotted every 'i' with a heart?" he asks, glancing over at me and allowing his lips to curve upward.

I tilt my head. "I was young, you dork. What do you expect?"

"Yeah, that's right," he says, jumping as the phone rings. "You never grew up." He holds a finger over a cartoon heart I drew in the diary. Nodding and holding my gaze for a moment, he looks at the diary, and holds a hand to his heart.

"This means a lot, you know?"

The phone rings for the third time, and he releases my gaze, quickly grabbing it.

As always, the conversation between us flows naturally, I think, watching him hold a cordless phone to his ear. "Okay, thank you," he says, nodding and pressing a finger into the off button.

"Who was that?" I ask, looking at him with the same fervency I did nineteen years ago.

"It was the hospital, just a call reminding me to come in tomorrow morning."

I nod in acknowledgement and flip to the next page. "Do you remember the day I broke my arm?" I ask, pointing to a page that is filled with red ink. My handwriting appears visibly larger on that page than it did on the others. It had been a stressful day, I remember, as I begin reading the entry.

It was the beginning of September, and, like any other early September day, I found myself packing away our summer stuff—the boats, life jackets, and fish hooks. As I looked out onto the water, I noticed Chris up on the deck to the beach house. My eyes and ears attuned immediately to him, and I abandoned my good sense as I attempted to lift myself over the rock wall that stood between the beach and the backyard of the beach house.

"Wow, I can't believe school starts tomorrow. I just saw a summer concert last week, and it was as hot as blazes," Chris said, straddling a boat paddle over his left shoulder. "Now it's September. So, I don't want to go back to my parents' house. Gets too comfortable out here, you know?" Chris said to his cousin.

I got so caught up in watching Chris that day that I completely forgot that I was standing on the edge of the dock. As I shifted my feet, I went straight to the sand and broke my arm.

I look at him briefly. "You came running to help me. We wound up in the ER, and you held my hand the whole time."

The memory is just as crisp now as it was the day I lived it. Up until the age of eighteen, my life had seemed empty, like something was missing.

"And you've got this all on the computer now?" he asks, tilting his head and lifting his eyes to mine.

"As I said, I'm just getting up to speed with technology, Chris."

He nods and flexes his jaw in mocking. "I will say one thing, Lilly. This is a huge ego booster."

Keeping Chris's ego from inflating is challenging, and I'm trying to avoid it, leaving out some mushy passages I had written. I lift my eyes from the diary and catch his playful gaze. Bringing his lips to mine, Chris kisses me softly, running his hands through my hair. With our heads swaying together rhythmically, his hands cup my jaw line and bring me into a soft embrace.

He withdraws his mouth slowly, releases his hands from my face, and quickly returns with a kiss that is longer, more lingering. Clearly this is not your typical kiss, I think, losing myself in the motions of his tongue and allowing him to remove my clothes.

I gaze briefly at the alarm clock by my bed and am astounded by the time. It is 6:08, just four hours short of our bedtime. However, I am locked in the moment and continue to press my lips hard upon him, feeling his hands comb through my tousled hair.

"This is so hot, you know?"

"Welcome home," Chris says, slipping his hands under my shirt and wandering upward with his hips. Removing the silk top from my shoulders, Chris pauses, brings his mouth to mine, and tugs my hand toward his torso. His hands drift over me, and I see a sudden longing in his eyes.

Our passion is sweet and effortless, as he melts into me, and we lose ourselves in an intense culmination of sensation. Arching our backs, we moan together, allowing our bodies to crash together. We exhale deeply, our eyes rising together, as we meet in a mutual gaze.

"I love you," I say. "But I can't stay."

CHAPTER EIGHT

BREAKING FREE AGAIN

The night before was clear and restful, as we slept with the window open. The morning came far too quickly. And as I sit here silently, I swirl a spoon in my cup of coffee, and breathe out against the warmth rising from my mug. Anticipating the events that lie ahead of me, I look out the window, noting the subtle wisps of clouds floating across a perfectly blue sky.

"Okay, Chris, I think we've got it all together," I say, stuffing some apple slices in a sandwich bag and brushing a hand over his back.

"I can't believe we're doing this right now," Chris says.

"Neither can I, but it's wonderful, isn't it?"

He nods.

I shuffle my coat over my shoulders and slide my hands into my pockets. Now I look at him with an expression of glee, brushing aside a hair tendril lingering in front of my eyes.

This is a big day, one that could potentially change our lives completely. Chris seems healthy and full of spunk, I realize, watching his legs chug down the stairs. However, I am a bit apprehensive about the office visit. "Whatever will be, will be," I think to myself, smoothing a hand over my coat and tossing it over my shoulders.

"This is a big day," Chris says, smiling at me as he rubs his hands together and slides them into his coat pockets. Bulky, dense and green, his coat is beautifully-made, possessing a luxurious fabric that stretches perfectly around his body. As I pause and look out upon the landscape, I shiver against the breeze. Although I know Chris is strong, it is hard to restrain the worry that tugs at my stomach.

"This is going to be great, sweetie," I say, flashing him a sudden smile and grabbing for his hand.

"Yeah," he says, rubbing his hands together and watching his breath against the crisp air. "Let's hope we get good news."

Anticipation tugs at my being as I throw up the hood to my jacket and shiver against the crisp Seattle air. I love this time of year, but this morning, as I look up, I find myself yearning for a scarf. For the first time in ages, I can look up at the world and know that I have the man I want and that he is mine for keeps.

"Okay," I say, chugging down the porch steps. "Ben's with Matilda. Molly's set." I bounce my hands in completion of the thought and smile broadly, taking in the frosty air.

His lips are pursed tight in concentration as he shuffles into the passenger's side seat and fastens his seatbelt.

Pulling out of the driveway, I eye both sides of the road and smile briefly. Unlike most days in Seattle, the sun is blazing in full, illuminating the crisp grass on our front lawn. Chugging out onto the road, we find ourselves speeding toward the hospital at vibrant speed. He looks at me for a moment with a hint of worry radiating in his now dense blue eyes.

"It's okay, sweetheart," I say, lifting my eyes to his before returning my gaze to the road in front of me. "I'm sure everything is fine."

The reassurance seems to calm him as he breathes in, looks out the window and relaxes against the seat. Our house disappears behind us as we speed onto the freeway. A sudden fog permeates the windshield and soon we are at the hospital. As we go up to the oncology floor, I draw a deep breath, trying to think positive. Surely things are fine. As the escalator doors open, we are greeted by Jackie, who smiles and pats a hand to my back.

"It's nice to see you, Mr. and Mrs. Rylan. Did you enjoy your weekend at home?"

I turn and give her a thankful wink, and she smiles back. The look on her face is brighter than it has been for the past few months. With her dark brown eyes twinkling, she walks slowly beside us, clutching a clipboard between her hands.

"I see home agrees with you, Mr. Rylan," she says, escorting Chris and me into an examination room.

As he slides down into a hospital chair, Chris smiles at me.

"It would be wonderful if the cancer is shrinking or at least going into remission," I say, gazing at Chris softly and smooth a hand over his back.

"Yeah," he says, staring forward and puffing as though he can't catch his breath.

It is now 30 minutes later, and we are still sitting here, awaiting Chris's test results. My eyes are watery, and my chest is tight. My hands, though clammy, are trembling again.

The doctor walks in an hour later and smoothes a hand over his bright white hair before sitting down at his desk. Holding a clipboard full of papers in front of his eyes, the doctor regards Chris for a long moment and brings his eyes to the shuffled papers within his hands. He stands for several moments scanning the documents with wrinkled, yet rugged hands. He sits down slowly in his chair, staring quietly at the paper. "I just looked at the scans we took before you left on Friday, and unfortunately, we still see cancer. Do you see that big mass right there?" the doctor asks, swirling a finger around a dark gray mass on an x-ray. "We need to get you up to your room as soon as possible."

"Oh my God," Chris says, slowly covering his open mouth with his hand. "Oh my God."

I stare forward for several moments and breathe in the medicinal air. Tears moisten in the corners of my eyes, and I grab his hand, tightening my fingers around it. Denseness fills my chest, and I picture the IV and the heart monitors. In the distance I hear Susan's high heels tapping the floors.

As I sit here, examining the light blue walls in the exam room, I now hear wheels rolling across the floor. The sound is painful, yet familiar. Now, as my eyes lift upward, Susan rushes in. Her face is dense with concern, and her pace slows as she walks toward Chris. Her eyes are soft and soothing, just as they have always been.

She places a hand on Chris's shoulder, with her head tilted. "I'm sorry you have to come back here, Mr. Rylan. But we're gonna take good care of you, okay?" Her smile fades as she helps Chris get into a wheelchair.

"I can't do this anymore, Susan," he says, lifting his head slowly and meeting Susan's eyes. "I need to go home and be with my wife."

"Chris—"

He holds up a hand. "Lilly, let me handle this."

"But Chris," I cry, stretching out my quivering hand. "We need to make sure you get well."

He turns, exhales a shaky breath, and drops his head into his hands. "I can't take this anymore."

I move toward Chris and stretch out my arms. "Calm down, sweetheart. You can come home, but if something happens, we're bringing you back here."

He doesn't say a word but lifts his hand for me to grab. "It feels so good to be with you," I say, glancing briefly at his eyes and returning my eyes to the road.

"They're not gonna lock me up in that hospital," he says. "We need to go on and live our lives together."

The prospect of living with Chris is beautiful, considering the fact that I have endured so much pain. Lifting my eyes to a crackling red leaf that is falling from the sky, I blow out an elated breath, and feel a smile curve my lips. When we get back to the house, Chris once again throws his arms around me and draws me into a long and lingering kiss.

"Now let's get on with our life together."

I freeze solid, look at him, and feel a sudden sadness soak through me. If it weren't for the million memories we have together, I feel I would be left with nothing. With his hand within mine, I know I have something to hold onto. But the question remains: Will I ever have to let go?

Three weeks have now passed since I brought Chris back from the hospital, and the trees are nearly bare. The fallen leaves are no longer red, and though their amber shade brings me a sense of comfort, I can't help but wonder if the winter will be just as beautiful. A feeling of comfort fills my stomach as I touch a hand to the ice cold window. A shadow of my hand returns to the glass as a tumultuous wind brings fog to the window once again. Barreling away like thunder in a storm, the wind falls to a hush as I walk over to the chair in our living room. I lift my coffee mug from the table, take in its warmth as the steam hits my face, and stare at my husband's pale complexion. Despite his labored breath, his skin once again looks like porcelain, and his eyes are the same shade of crystal blue. "Compared to a few weeks ago, you look great," I say, strolling over to Chris and carefully touching a hand to his cheek.

"I agree," he says, rolling a hand behind his neck, which is resting on the arm of the couch. "Why mess with perfection?" he says, chuckling. "I'm the real deal."

"Is that so?" I say, strolling over. "And what about me? Don't you have something to say about my perfectly sculpted form?" I ask, throwing my head back.

I sit down on the sofa and look at him. His eyes gloss over me, and he groans softly. "Nope. Come here, and I'll show you," he says, pulling my face toward his and kissing me softly.

"Good answer," I say, slowly withdrawing. As soon as we draw out of the embrace, he bounces his legs against the sofa, quickly rising to his feet.

"Will you dance with me, my lady?" he asks, allowing his fingers to drift between mine. Time seems to move in slow motion, as I lower my head to his shoulder and close my eyes. There is no music. We don't need it. Gazing into his brilliant eyes, I reach for his hand, and am tugged into thought, and I picture the times Chris and I danced like this as teenagers. In my mind's eye, I can see him pick me up and spin me around. And I smile softly as emotion takes hold. Warmth stings my eyes. Struggling to fight my tears, I breathe in and close my eyes.

"You're ready to cry, aren't you?" he chuckles.

"Shut up." I toss my head back in laughter, and after several seconds, my eyes search his face. "I'm just so happy."

"What are you thinking?" he asks, smoothing a hand over my hair and pushing lone strands of hair from my cheeks.

I look up, feeling my green eyes moisten with emotion. "I just love you, sweetheart. That's all."

"I love you, too. A little sentimental, are you?"

Chris lifts his hands from the middle of my back and draws my mouth to his, this time stretching his fingers open and combing them through my hair. As he draws me closer, my head sways around his, and for the first time in ages, I feel like I am home. As we pick up a slow and steady rhythm, the doorbell rings. Chris looks at me and freezes with the sound.

"Hang on a second, sweetheart," he says, drawing his hands back before releasing me.

Drawn to the sound outside, I look at the window. A subtle puffing sound draws my head toward the window. The fog on the glass has faded, drawing my eyes to a bright blue sky, which is punctuated with subtle wisps of white clouds.

Remembering my wings, I place my hands on my shoulders, rolling my fingers to the top of my back and remembering the way the wind felt upon my face. My body has grown weak, but I know there will be time tomorrow to reach out to the angels. I am grateful to have the opportunity to live another day in this body. It's confining, and breaks too easily, and I know that tomorrow I will regret smoothing my hands over my shoulders. It makes me long to go home. But without the help of wings, I can go no place other than earth.

I look over at Molly, who wags her tail and rolls over on her back. "Hi Molly. Look, someone is at the door," I chuckle as I motion her in circles. A man dressed in sweats and a red baseball cap places a flyer for a carnival on the front door, rubs his hands together and chugs back down the steps. Chris takes the flyer into his hands and walks in the house, holding it in front of my eyes. His smile broadens as his gaze lifts. As he looks at me, Ben comes down the stairs and pauses briefly to examine the paper.

"What's that, Daddy? What's that?" he squeaks, clasping his hands on both sides of Chris's face.

"It's a carnival, Ben," Chris says, gazing at our son with bright eyes that instantly grow wider.

"Ooh, Daddy, a carnival. Can we go? Can we go? Please?"

Chris's eyes slide toward me, and I nod, wondering why a carnival would be held in October. "It's the cold weather."

"How can they have a carnival in October?"

"Chris's eyes scan the paper momentarily. "Beats me," he says, shrugging and rubbing his hands together. "All I know is that I want to go."

"Okay, but I need you to be on your best behavior. I can't have you getting hurt," I say, watching Ben throw up his hands and grab his toy dog.

"Awesome!" Ben screams, racing up to the top of the steps and turning to jump. I look up and smile, watching him jog in place. He squeals at the top of his lungs, his blue eyes brimming with an excitement I haven't seen in ages.

"Geronimo!" he squeals before leaping to the floor. Chris holds a hand to his chest, attempting to stifle laughter as Ben leaps to the floor, setting in motion a vibration that makes the entire living room tremble. Chris looks up, catches my eyes, and bursts into laughter.

"Okay, sweetheart," I say, turning quickly to look at Chris. "It will be fun."

I close my eyes briefly and open them, while looking at Chris, feeling that connection, that same spark.

"Great," Chris says as he brings his eyes to mine.

Chris and Ben disappear upstairs screaming, as their feet pound the steps. After hearing several loud thuds and a gleeful squeal, Chris and Ben appear in the hallway upstairs and quickly dash down the steps.

"Are we all set?" Chris asks, pulling the collar to his coat up toward his neck and throwing a hood over his head. He is dressed in a puffy jacket, corduroy pants, and boots. From his feet to the top of his head, Chris looks as warm as a bonfire on top of a snow capped mountain.

As I gaze at him, I become instantly aware of his excitement about the carnival. His eyes dance, and he rubs his hands together. Now, he places his arm over Ben's back and ushers him forward with his cold palms.

I stand up quickly. "I'm going, too."

Thirty minutes later, after a grueling ride through the city, we are at the carnival. I decided not to get on the Ferris wheel, but stand here, happily watching Chris and Ben from the ground. As I do, the wind catches my hair, sending it in multiple directions. The cold wind continues to blow, prompting me to wrap my scarf tighter around my neck.

Chris and Ben love the Ferris wheel. As their feet come pounding over the dense metal base to the ride, I throw open my arms and slide my hand around Ben's back.

"Mommy, that was so awesome!" Ben squeals, clenching his arms around me and closing his eyes in delight.

Chris, now walking with his head facing the ground, falls down onto a bench. With his face as white as a ghost, he holds a hand to his forehead. My heart sinks as he continues to hold his forehead with trembling hands. Now he rocks shakily and looks at me. I can feel my throat tighten as I look at his face.

"Woo, that thing is too high for me," Chris says, shaking his head and turning briefly to regard the Ferris wheel. "Didn't you see?" he huffs, pointing to Ben. "A certain son of yours thought it would be fun to point out other rides while we were dangling 50 feet above the ground. I swear the whole thing shook—"

I feel my face turn to stone, and my throat constricts.

"Take a breath, sweetheart. You look really pale. Sit down for a minute."

Chris's brows slant downward, and he places his elbows on his knees.

"Lilly, I still have cancer. I'm sick, but I'm not going to let it keep me from enjoying life."

I freeze in place and fight to hide my quivering lip. My hands are clammy, and as I look at the rides spinning around me, my emerald eyes are drawn back to Chris's face.

"Never mind," I say, feeling my eyes grow suddenly distant. "Forget I said anything."

His hand lifts slowly into the air, and he chuckles as though he wants to lighten the mood. "Why don't you try riding a ride that has you swinging 50 feet above the ground?" he chuckles, pointing up. He gazes up at the ride seats, draws a deep breath, and slides his eyes toward me.

The glance he shot me slowly fades away, as he continues holding his forehead in the palms of his hands. As he grunts, I grind my teeth together, removing my eyes from the Ferris wheel above.

Realizing there is nothing I can do, I blow out my breath and fall back into a bench. The seat is hard and painful against my back, but at least it is a distraction from the fear that filled me when Chris got off the Ferris wheel.

Now, a few hours later, after my emotional storm has passed, we find ourselves pacing sluggishly toward a carousel. The carousel's round multicolor lights blink wildly and hurt my eyes, as I bring a hand to my forehead. Now, as I gaze fuzzily at the other rides, my head begins to pound.

"Chris!" I scream, feeling my legs go weak beneath me.

"Lilly!" Chris screams, his steps sounding like drums as they pound against the asphalt. With his hips bent toward me, he scoops me up in his arms and lowers me to the ground. Time seems to move in slow motion as I look up, feeling my nostrils constrict.

I have no idea what is wrong with me. It feels as though an eternity has passed. I have no idea where I am, but as I feel my breath rise, I bring Chris's face into focus.

"Where am I?"

"Hey, there she is," Chris coos, placing a hand on mine.

A doctor with blonde hair tucks her hair behind her ears and emerges from my right side. Her pace slows, as she puts down a clipboard and pauses to examine my face.

"I'm Dr. Smyth," she says, lifting a hand to offer a handshake. Now she holds up a finger. Ms. Rylan, can you follow my finger with your eyes?"

Why is she looking at me, and why am I in this place? Maybe it's a dream.

Her voice is soothing, and as I look forward, I smell Chris's cologne. As I bring his face into focus, my heart stops pounding, and I can think again.

"What happened?" I ask, looking up at the white walls and allowing my head to fall back on the pillow beneath my shoulders.

"You passed out, Lilly," Chris says, smoothing a finger over my forehead and attempting to hide his trembling lips with his other hand. "You passed out at the carnival, and an ambulance brought you here."

I allow my head to fall back into the pillow and blow out a shaky breath.

"That would explain this headache," I say, rubbing the right side of my head and looking at a bottle on the doctor's desk. Combing my fingers sluggishly through my hair, I squint and breathe in the cold and medicinal air.

The doctor looks at me, her voice mellowing, as though she wants to say something consoling, but can't find the right thing to say. Her mouth opens briefly, but she looks away, returning her eyes to the computer screen at the side of my bed. Feeling curious, my eyes hover over her shoulder, and she turns to smile at me.

"Relax, Mrs. Rylan. You're okay. We just think you got a little dehydrated." Once again pushing her blonde hair behind her ears, Dr. Smyth's eyes freeze on me for a long moment. Her light brown eyes are scrutinizing upon me, and they tremble as though she is deep in thought.

"There's something I don't know, isn't there?" I ask, looking at her before turning my head toward the other side of the room.

She draws a deep breath and pauses, but I hear her hesitation. "It's probably just an isolated incident, so I think you're okay to go home."

We are now walking out of my hospital room, and I am pausing briefly to scan the lobby. Chris holds my hand, and his voice trembles, as we walk out the door. The doors slam closed behind us. I stand and stare for several moments, attempting to avoid Chris's eyes, which tremble and reflect the deepening terror in the pit of my stomach. As we climb into a cab that is parked outside, I breathe out, clicking the seatbelt upon me.

"Aren't we a pair?"

"Yes, we are," he says, sliding his hand into mine and bouncing our hands together.

"Didn't we have a little tiff at the carnival?" I ask, feeling my eyes search him.

He waves his hand in dismissal. "It doesn't matter now. We've got you to worry about."

"What about Ben?" I ask.

"Matilda's got him. He was squealing like a champ when she picked him up."

I nod and smooth a hand over Chris's cheek. He lifts his hands to cup my face, leaning toward me, but he doesn't bring his mouth to mine. His eyes appear absent, or more appropriately, scared. As sirens wail in the distance, he turns and stares at me, his eyes lingering, apparently in thought.

As my fear begins to subside, I drift back into the seat and feel plush leather caressing my back. As soon as we get home, I fall lazily into a cushy armchair in the living room, feeling my soft sweater caress my shoulders. The days are growing shorter now, and I can feel myself relaxing, feeling the cold sink into my skin. I sit down with Chris and Ben and close my eyes for several moments, listening to the relentless tick of our grandfather clock.

"It feels so good to be home," I say, looking at Chris.

Time passes quickly as we sit together, and I hand Chris and Ben each a mug of hot cocoa. Time is irrelevant, I realize, lifting my eyes to Ben, who is playing with marshmallows that float on top of the cocoa. Feeling grateful to be alive, my eyes rise with relief. I am lifting my head upward, but Chris doesn't see me. "Thank you."

My thoughts draw my head upward, and I feel a sudden peace float over me.

Ben's voice, now shrill against the almost total silence of the room, suddenly causes me to jump. Holding a stuffed animal, Ben squeals quickly and throws the toy on the floor.

"That's a cute dinosaur, Ben," Chris says.

Ben looks up, his blond hair sailing on a breeze coming from a vent, as he moves toward a window.

"Daddy, that's not a dinosaur," he says, growling and grabbing the animal by the neck.

"It's a dog named Toughie. Grrrr," he says, squeezing the giant stuffed dog's neck and making it jump with his hands.

Okay, we get it. It's a dog," Chris chuckles.

"Yeah," Ben squeaks. "Matilda got it for me, remember?"

"Oh, that's right. You love Matilda."

As Ben returns to his dog, squeezing its neck, Chris's brows raise in response to my smile.

"Why was Daddy sick?" Ben asks, as his hands tighten against the toy's neck.

"Daddy's not going to get sick again, is he?"

I lift my head slowly and look at Chris, realizing how inquisitive our son has become.

"Why do you ask, Ben?" I inquire, feeling my heart fall as I search for an answer.

"You cried in your pillow every night, saying Daddy was going to die," Ben says lowly, his vivid blue eyes lingering on my face. Now, he wiggles against the floor and looks at me. "What does die mean?"

Chris's gaze, suddenly empty, turns toward me.

Chris is a scientist, but he hasn't worked in the field since he was diagnosed with cancer. Getting back into the field will take time, but for now, Chris's eyes grow intense upon Ben's face.

Chris knew the moment Ben spoke that he would have a hard time finding an answer Ben could comprehend. He breathed deeply in a chair across the room. He needs to find an answer Ben can understand without scaring him. Is it too much to tell him that we're not going to be here forever? Is it too soon to tell Ben about something Chris

didn't understand? "Dying means that you stop breathing."
"Until the tunnel," I say. Looking up, my eyes freeze as
I watch Chris's eyes transform from placid blue gems to
beaming jewels of intrigue.

"The tunnel?" Chris asks, smiling softly as I shift in
my chair.

Fear descends into my stomach, and instantly I realize
that I have said too much. "Yeah, the tunnel and the sun."

Ben is distracted and he grabs his dog. After looking at
me briefly, he turns, tugging his dog behind him.

Finally, Chris and I are alone and able to talk.

"What are you saying? Are you saying that you died?"
Chris asks, drifting slowly back into his chair. The look
on his face is blank, almost disbelieving, as his gaze turns
toward me.

I can't believe I am about to tell this story. Shifting
nervously, I tell Chris about a day when I was nine years old.

"One day, as I was playing a video game, the screen
began to flash. When it did, I had a seizure."

The look on Chris's face is blank, but I continue on,
looking into his eyes. Slowly, he leans forward and fidgets.
He is curious, I realize, as he stands up and moves toward
me. Staring silently, I run my hand under my nose and sniff.
"Anyway, you know how I told you I am not like you?"

"Yes," he says, his eyes suddenly turning mellow.

"I'm an angel, Chris. I'm an angel."

"Are you trying to tell me something?" he asks, smiling
softly.

I shake my head. "I'm an angel. I'm here for a reason."

His face is mellow, as he smoothes a hand over my back,
appearing relieved. "You're my angel."

"I see things. I see things you can't," I say, gazing over my left shoulder. "I left my body years ago,' " I say, trembling briefly and wiping my eye. "There's a beautiful tunnel and a sun. When you see the sun," I pause, my eyes unblinking. "And when you see the sun, you see everything."

As he looks at me, the sun fades behind the closed blinds. Its golden rays, growing dim in the darkening landscape, fade slowly into the darkness.

Lifting himself up from his chair and bringing his elbows to his knees, Chris's gaze grows mellower, and his head tilts.

"So you had?"

I nod. "Yes," I say softly. "I had a near death experience."

I breathe deeply, my head turning and freezing upon Chris's face. As I look at him, I can see his disbelief through his red and unblinking eyes. I can see his thoughts almost transparently, as he looks at me and touches a hand to his head.

"So you think you saw ..."

I nod quietly. "Yup," I say, looking at his face before moving my eyes toward the TV. "It's a beautiful place. When you get there, you don't want to come back."

For a moment, I cannot speak, wondering whether or not I should tell him the truth about what happened when he was in the hospital. I must tell him. Drawing a dense breath, I turn to him, feeling butterflies in the pit of my stomach.

"You were almost there two months ago." His face turns solemn. "Angels were standing at your bed, waiting."

Chris's eyes brighten briefly.

I chuckle. "Why do you think I was there all the time? I love you so much, and they were standing there, ready to take you."

"What? Who was waiting?" he asks, leaning forward with his eyes lingering upon me.

I wave my right hand and slowly turn my head. "It doesn't matter now. Your grandma said you had time."

His gaze moves slowly over to mine, his eyes radiating a combination of fear and intrigue.

I look at him, and my eyes fall downward. "I have a gift. I can see things that you don't."

"What do you mean?"

I look away for a moment, lick my lips, and breathe deep against his silence. "You. I see you," I say. "There are things that people don't understand anymore."

His eyes freeze for several moments, and he appears to be somewhere else. "Lilly, I'm sick," he says." His voice cracks as he reaches for my hand. "I have cancer. I'm afraid."

As he throws his hands around me, my lips quiver, seeing his eyes freeze. "You have no reason to be afraid, Chris."

His eyes are soft and pleading. "I can't do this, Lilly. I can't keep fighting the pain. "You're the only thing that keeps me living."

He pauses, his voice growing softer.

I place a hand over his. "You're not going to die. We're gonna make it together in the end." Although I have tried to calm his fears, I keep getting this feeling that we are going to part ways at some point. There will come a point when he gets sicker, that I have to say goodbye. The thought of it causes my vocal cords to constrict. I am drawn to his gentle ways, and the way he looks at me warms my heart like nothing else ever has before. Deep inside, my heart is breaking. What if things don't pan out the way I think they will? I know the nature of Chris's heart, and as I look at his eyes, I see his fear and pain. He doesn't say a word, but instead he sniffs.

"What if there's…what if I'm afraid?"

I enfold him in my arms, close my eyes, and rock back and forth. Slowly, I kiss his head and draw his hands into my palms. As I bring him closer, with my eyes steady upon him, a cord of sadness tugs at my throat. I don't know what's going to happen anymore. Perhaps I'm not supposed to. I know Chris in a way that no one ever has. And as I look at him, feeling his pain, I draw a shaky breath. Now that he's in my arms, I cannot look away, at least not right now.

The lines at the corners of his eyes seem to deepen. "So what were you saying about this near death experience thing?"

And there it is. How can I tell him? "Well," I say, tossing my hair behind my shoulders. "I died and saw something incredible."

"What?" he asks, his voice falling to a whisper.

"Eternity."

"Uh huh," he says, drawing a deep breath and touching my hand.

His mouth drifts open, and his blue eyes are intense, as I stretch out my legs on the sofa.

The memory of my near death experience is wonderful and comforting.

As I draw a deep breath, I see the rainbow brightening in the distance. I see the sun growing brighter and brighter as I smile against the wind. In my mind's eye, I see the clouds eclipsing the sun. This is how it happened.

I pause for a moment and stare in amazement. The memory is fresh, and it still feels the same as it did over 25 years ago. My lips part for a moment, and I look forward, realizing that Chris needs the truth.

"I could go at any time, you know?"

Chris's eyes lift quietly, almost fearfully, as I smooth a hand over Molly's head. Now, as my breath heightens, Ben comes bouncing down the steps.

"Mommy, let's play a game."

"Not right now, sweetie. Daddy and I are talking."

"Talking about what?" Ben asks innocently.

"We'll talk about that later," Chris says, attempting to pat Ben's head.

"But I want you to play a video game," Ben wails. "Here, Mommy. Here's the controller."

Ben grins broadly, and I throw my arms forward, taking the controller and bouncing it between my hands. Now, as I stare forward, I plunge my fingers into the big red buttons.

"Lilly, no!" Chris yells urgently, his voice growing louder with a mixture of urgency and fear. "You had a seizure when you played a video game."

I turn silently, and I can feel my eyes narrowing.

"So did you in the hospital." As soon as the words came out of my mouth, I realized I shouldn't have said them. What I saw in that hospital was horrifying. But you can't live your life in fear, I realize, pushing my hands excitedly into the buttons on the controller. Finally, I can lose myself again.

As I sit here playing, I fail to notice that Chris is standing just two feet away from me. As my gaze turns, I see him looking at me, his blue eyes blazing a fear I've never seen before. Knowing this, I turn my head slowly toward him.

Despite Chris's presence, I feel myself yearning to stand in the soft wind once again. "I'm sorry," I manage, placing my hands over my eyes and attempting to stifle my tears. *Oh God, this is so hard.*

"I don't know how much longer I can do this."

I resume playing and lose the game before Chris has a chance to grab a controller. Slowly, he strides over to me, his blue jeans looking more like a haze of blue than dense and flowing fabric. His eyes linger on my arm before I turn and catch him staring at me. "Lilly, are you okay?"

"Come on, Mommy," Ben squeals, staring at the screen. "Play another game."

Ben somehow convinces me to play one more game before bedtime. This game has a longer course. And much like the games I played as a child, this one also causes the screen to flash a lot. As I sit here on the floor, my eyes move in unison with the characters on the screen.

Though it is nearly bedtime, I need an escape. Scooping the controller possessively off the floor, I pound my fingers into its buttons once again. Now, as I stare at the screen, my eyes reflect my amusement.

Ben is starting preschool tomorrow morning, and Chris is upstairs, putting sheets on Ben's bed. I sit there, feeling relieved that the video game hasn't bothered me. Feeling the soft carpet beneath my feet, I am at total comfort. My eyes are intense upon the screen.

This is the perfect moment, I think to myself, staring at the screen, as it blinks 'game over' and flashes several times. I sit with satisfaction until Chris returns and motions Ben to the steps to get ready for bed. As I sit here, I feel the urge to follow them, but instead, I return my eyes to the screen, which blinks two more times. I shut my eyes for several minutes and feel a sudden tingling rise within my body. Closing my eyes for a moment, I stand in silence, struggling to stay upright.

Panic sets in, and for a several seconds, I feel my eyes trembling.

Oh my God, my vision is hazy. Suddenly, I am tugged out of reality. Through my eyes, I see a pink aura, which slowly draws me down to the floor. I can feel it happening slowly. Lights blink in front of my eyes, and my arms begin to twitch.

"Help! I'm having a seizure!"

As my body begins to jerk against the plush carpet, Chris's face comes into view. The softness of the carpet does nothing to soothe me. Chris runs down the stairs to find me on the floor. Looking through blurry eyes, I find it nearly impossible to breathe.

"It's okay, baby. I'm right here," he says, as he sits down by my side. His voice is soft and comforting, just as it has always been. I am unable to speak for several minutes.

Utter peace floats over me, as Chris sits beside me, despite the fact that my body is twitching, and I have no control over it.

As Chris looks at me, his eyes freeze, and I hear him crying. Now, after several terrifying minutes, I drift out of the seizure. As my hurried breath slows, Chris rolls over to me on the floor.

As I look at him, I succumb to my emotions, and tears fill my eyes. The tears are warm as they roll down my cheeks, and Chris lifts me onto his lap. Our eyes rise slowly, seemingly in unison, as he cups my face with his hands.

His voice is quivery, but some he manages a few words. "Are you okay? I'm here, sweetheart."

"I love you," I say.

"I love you, too, but you need to go to the doctor. Maybe we should go see Dr. Smyth."

I know that everything is going to be okay. No matter where I go or what I do, I am safe as long as Chris is there with me. I know that going to the doctor will cause more pain. "I think I have epilepsy," I say, lifting his chin to meet my gaze. "If you have seizures, you take medicine. I haven't had one in 25 years, so I think I'm okay."

He stares back and sniffs deeply with fear radiating in his eyes.

I shrug. "The doctors mentioned it to a doctor when I was nine. I took the medicine for a little while but stopped taking it, because it was such a nuisance."

"Are you serious, Lilly? That's nothing to play around with."

"I didn't think anything of it after it happened."

His breath grows suddenly dense, and I see a tear fall from his eye.

"Why didn't you tell me?"

I hesitate, but he simply smiles. And as he does, he lifts me and carries me to the sofa.

It is clear by the quiver in Chris's voice that he hadn't expected this. However, he doesn't get angry with me. He simply covers us up with a blanket, as we sit side by side on the couch.

"You're beautiful," he says, "so kind and so strong."

As we sit here talking, we suddenly forget all about the seizure. As he puts his arm around me, I feel even more connected to him, and my hand drifts instinctively to his arm. It is a place that brings me warmth and comfort. I should be concerned about the seizure, but my thoughts drift away from it, as Chris draws my hands into his.

Chris and I talk for two hours about the past few weeks and how so much has changed over the course of our relationship. The room gets cooler, and the brilliance of day fades into a peaceful, dark night. The night seems much darker now, and the frost on the window draws my eyes up and causes me to shiver. Chris is still sitting beside me, and I glance over at him, giving him a gentle smile. "Beautiful, huh?" he asks.

I chuckle quietly, grab his hand, and in a moment, realize that I need to write something in the book that inspired our love. Chris appears lost in thought as he rises from his chair and rolls a hand over mine.

He looks at me, as though he is contemplating. "Don't you have something to tell me about that diary of yours?" I shake my head, but know that I can't keep a secret for long.

"I'm not the type to be shy, you know that," I pause, "but there are just some things that a woman doesn't share right away. There is a lot in the diary that I can't share with you right away." For the longest time, I am lost in thought, as Chris's eyelids grow heavy, and he drifts into sleep. The night came and went quickly, as I kept my eyes open, watching Chris. I reveled in the moment, in the togetherness, as I watched his chest rise and fall.

In the quiet of the morning, as Chris continues sleeping blissfully, I open the diary, brushing my fingers across the silky white paper. I scratch my pen on the page and pour out my heart.

Chris, my dearest Chris:

Last night, we created a new memory. We sat in the living room, taking in the beauty of the night. I couldn't imagine a more perfect moment or a better man with whom to share my life. And if you're reading this now, know that you are the answer to my prayers and the love of my dreams. You came back with all of your heart, and I give you all of mine.

Love,

Lilly

It is now two days later, and I sit here thinking about the entry, realizing that if Chris reads it, he will know too much about my future. I am getting too overbearing. I have read the entry several times now.

Now, as I sit here, I hear a chuckle behind me. I can feel Chris's presence behind me as I turn around and meet his eyes.

"You sure are beautiful," he says. "Truly beautiful, unlike any woman I've ever seen before.

I sit here for a moment, but I cannot bring myself to say a word.

"I have to go back," I say.

"What? Go back where?"

I close the cover to the diary and stand up. "Just for a little while."

"Go back where?"

"It doesn't matter. No one will believe me anyway," I manage, looking forward as Chris turns to look away.

"What is it?" he insists, stepping forward and looking back at me with fear in his eyes.

"They know me, and for some reason, they're calling me back."

Chris's eyes are dense and reflect a hint of despair. Feeling his fear, I stand for a moment and lift my head toward a soft light.

"I have to go," I whisper, stepping into a tunnel and fading away.

I know this isn't goodbye, but for the moment, leaving is the only option. Maybe I'll come back. I'm not really sure.

As a soft wind caresses my face, and the sun brightens, I step into a white light, which grows brighter and more vivid as I continue forward. Suddenly, I am standing in the clouds, with purple mountains surrounding me in the distance. What seems like hours to Chris turns into seconds, as I stand quietly. Once again, I am here. I stand quietly and lift my eyes to the dense clouds above me, attempting to keep myself from seeing the tears streaming down Chris's face.

Slowly, I allow my fears to drift away, as I prepare for the future. I look up at the clouds, and everyone moves into formation. I lift my eyes to the beauty above me, and I look up, feeling for a moment that I am back where I belong.

Wow, this is amazing.

I lift my eyes above the grass where I am standing and breathe deeply, feeling the need to stay. Now, as I finally bow my head, I see Chris with tears pouring down his cheeks. I see him holding my body, but I make myself look away, once again lifting my eyes to the mountain. Perhaps I am meant to be with him. Perhaps I need to dry the tears on his face.

I look at my purple mountain, with its full and majestic beauty, and breathe in the fragrant air. Now, in front of my eyes, I see Chris throwing his arms around me and sobbing. Pounding a hand against my heart, he lifts up my body in our bedroom. The purple tee shirt I was wearing is draped against my lifeless body, and my jeans are rolled up. Sobbing deeply and sniffing, Chris moves his trembling hands to my shoulders and shakes me.

And now, as I gaze at him from my mountain, I feel sadness choke my throat. "I can't do this to him. I can't leave when he clearly needs me," I think to myself, as I gaze at the clouds and bring Chris's face back into view.

He is the most wonderful person I have ever met. Looking at the tears on his face, I wipe my eye, knowing what I must do. Drawing a deep breath, I look at the pink sky above me, which is now painted with wisps of lavender.

Chris's usually vibrant eyes are suddenly empty, as his face turns pale, and he falls to his knees, screaming.

Like a blur, paramedics race through the hallway and the door is thrown open with a crash. The redness in Chris's eyes grows suddenly deeper. Terrified, he looks up and removes his hands from my shoulders.

Chris's crystalline blue eyes are suddenly empty, and he listens against the silence, looking forward and knowing that no one can help.

"Oh my God, Lilly."

His eyes glide over my body like flashes of lightning in a thunderstorm. His beautiful blue-eyed gaze stays locked in place, and his face is like a bright light fading into darkness. He cannot hear my vibrant voice, but still, he feels the warmth of my body against his fingers.

"Lilly, please!" he screams, staring forward. "Don't do this. Come back into my arms!"

His hands tremble for several minutes, as this is his nature in a crisis.

The sound of footsteps behind him reaches Chris's ears, and he stands up, feeling his legs go weak beneath him.

Rushing into our bedroom, a paramedic appears like a blur in front of Chris's eyes. And his eyes are drawn out of a stare.

A man with dark brown hair and a mustache stands in the hallway. He pauses for a moment and now moves forward. "Mr. Rylan—"

The man looks at Chris's trembling hands, and his face softens. "Sir, I need to look for a pulse," he says, gently brushing Chris's hands aside and pressing his hands against my chest.

Another paramedic runs through the door. This time, it is a woman. Her brown hair, appearing as soft as silk, falls upon her back, and her hands push instinctively against my chest. It looks as though she has done this a million times. And her deep chocolate brown eyes, frozen in concentration, make Chris's throat constrict.

Chris's eyes suddenly narrow, and he wipes tears from his eyelashes, forcing them up toward his ears. He closes his eyes for a few moments and suddenly falls to his knees.

"Lilly, don't do this to me. Open your eyes. Open your eyes. Lilly, you promised!"

Lifting my head and feeling emotion tug at my chest, I hear the words I had repeated to him time after time.

Promised.

My eyes are frozen against the landscape around me as his voice cries out once again.

"Lilly!"

As Chris's eyes shut tightly, tears trail like raindrops on his face, and his head falls back against his shoulders.

"Lilly. Oh my God. Lilly, don't do this to me!"

He picks up my body, as the paramedics' eyes linger on Chris's face and freeze intermittently on my body and Chris.

"That's my wife!" Chris screams. "That's my wife!"

The man holds a finger to his mustache and looks away, attempting to avoid the emotion on Chris's face. As soon as the man turns away, Chris brings his mouth to mine and forces air into my lungs.

Looking back at the beauty surrounding me, a silent tear emerges from my eye. In a flash of light, I once again see Chris's tear-streaked face, and bow my head.

"I can't stay."

The beauty surrounding me slowly evaporates, and I am transported back to earth. Opening my eyes slowly in my house, I see the two paramedics standing beside the stretcher on which I lay. Silently and without moving, I listen to their hurried voices. My eyes are heavy, and they burn, as I open them slowly.

As Chris clutches my hand, I can feel by the taste on my lips that he had resuscitated me. There is an IV in one of my veins, I realize, as pain rises in the crevice of my right arm.

"What's this, and where am I?"

"You're here in our room," Chris says softly. "We got you some fluids in you. You're okay."

I manage a soft nod and allow my head to drift back slowly onto the pillow under my neck.

"I love you, Chris."

"I love you, too. Just lie there a while," he says, patting a hand on my leg. "You're in no shape to walk after having a seizure."

"I didn't have a seizure," I say, my brows flexing. "There was no pain."

"You stopped breathing for a little while, but before that, you had a seizure. I hate to be the one to tell you this, but you do have epilepsy."

"No. No, this can't be," I say, shaking my head and looking at Chris. "I can't have epilepsy."

As the paramedics leave, Chris lifts me onto our bed and smoothes a hand over my head. I gaze at him warmly as he holds me and kisses me softly. As he enfolds me within his arms, I coo, remembering the innocence of his lips when I kissed them for the first time.

Closing my eyes, I can smell the sweet fragrance of flowers and feel the dense warmth that filled the air when we frolicked in my parents' back yard.

I can still feel the soft arms and the hands that lifted me under my armpits. I remember his soft eyes and his carefree heart. I knew him then. But now, gazing into his brilliant eyes, I know him much more deeply.

"How are ya doing there?" he asks, tilting his head and regarding me softly.

"I feel fine."

I attempt to get up from the bed and fall on my side.

"You better take it easy there," Chris says.

After making me a chicken sandwich, he cuts it in half with a knife and fork, and catches my eyes with a smile. Now he hands me some applesauce.

Chris sits down in a rocking chair in our room, and we begin to talk, as though we are catching up. "How are you doing with your website these days?"

"As well as I can," I say, closing my eyes briefly and lifting a spoon filled with applesauce. "Business has been slow," I say, raising my spoon and pausing in contemplation. "But it's bringing in some money. It's paying a few bills."

As much as I want to say I enjoy designing web pages, the job isn't as fulfilling as I had hoped it would be. I look at him and feel my voice getting shaky. Instead of offering advice, as he always does, he simply smiles.

Chris regards me with a look of nonchalance. Clearly, he is no longer thinking about the seizure. However, my mind is still on something else. I want to tell him about the sun and the rainbow. But he wouldn't understand. No one can.

He removes his eyes from his tea and pauses for a brief moment. "Are you okay?"

Telling him the truth about who I am would absolutely break him. To him, I would be a stranger, if he knew my true reason for living.

"You just died. You stopped breathing."

"I know, Chris. I died, but I came back for you."

His gaze halts, growing fearful, and he looks at me, his eyes like trembling blue saucers. "You were dead, Lilly. You were dead."

"Yes, Chris, I died."

His blue eyes fall, and his voice begins to quiver.

"Remember the near death experience I had when I was nine? It happened again. I saw everything."

Chris shifts in his chair, and his gaze grows distant. "Lilly, don't do this to me."

I shift toward him and turn my head to the sun outside the window. "Heaven. I saw Heaven." For a moment, I can feel the soft wind as I stare forward. I pause, look around the room, and feel like I am somewhere else, somewhere unfamiliar.

"Why are you doing this to me, Lilly? I have a giant tumor in my pancreas. And now you're talking about Heaven. Lilly, don't do this."

"Do what?" I ask, putting my arms around him.

"Don't leave me."

I knew this conversation was coming. I just didn't think it was coming this soon. My eyebrows flex as I stare at him, feeling as though my world is about to collapse.

"I'll tell ya this, sweetheart," I say, placing my hands on his cheeks. "We're gonna go out to Colman Park," I say, rubbing his back. "It's just a few blocks away, and the water is beautiful this time of year."

His eyes are still red, and my words seem to calm him. But this is so hard.

His eyes lift slowly, seemingly terrified. He is still in my arms, and as we rock back and forth, the trembling of his body brings me closer. I close my eyes, struggling to find words. When I open my mouth, all I feel is fear in the pit of my stomach.

I can barely bring myself to speak right now, because I feel his pain. I try to ignore the sadness deepening in my stomach. "Don't be worried, Chris. You know you're my love, and I'm not going anywhere."

Chris's eyes fall and hold a sudden emptiness. His skin has grown yellow now. He had a fever this morning, so I gave him some medicine. Now, as he brings a hand to his stomach, my heart aches for him. "I hurt, Lilly. Don't leave me alone in this world."

Deep down, there is a reason for me reading to Chris. I know him like no one else. I love him. Chris has given me everything I could ask for, and I know that we will make it together.

"Chris, baby," I say, stroking his hair. "We're going to the park tomorrow."

His face brightens for a moment, and peace floats over me as I look into his eyes. As I touch his hand, I feel love within my heart, and I release him slowly. As Chris brings himself to a standing position, he seems to be regaining his strength. Closing my eyes as he sits beside me, I draw a deep breath.

I can't let him see me like this. My voice is choked with tears, and my eyes are watering.

I can feel myself staring at Chris as he stretches his arms over his head. He is growing frail, his arms becoming thinner. I place a finger under his chin and look at him for several moments. I feel like crying now, because I see his blue eyes grow denser as he stares back at me. I have to look away for a moment just to calm myself. "Chris, baby," I say, "I have to get you back to the hospital."

He doesn't say a word, but simply lifts his eyes. "Take me to Colman Park. I need to see something beautiful, other than you, of course," he says." I look up and feel all of Chris's pain within my skin, and my heart pounds within my chest, as I hold a finger to my jaw line. Worry soaks through me, taking over my thoughts. I can think of nothing other than his beautiful blue eyes and his hands warm against my skin.

His eyes have subtle wrinkles at the corners. There's something beautiful about the way we're aging. It's beautiful, because we're doing it together.

"You'll never be without me, Chris. I will always be with you."

Instead of responding, he places a possessive hand on my shoulder, his eyes rising to meet mine. He is a shining beacon of light that brings warmth to my heart. "Don't speak, Chris. Don't say anything," I say, pulling his mouth toward mine. "Just feel," I say, closing my eyes and allowing my lips to melt into his. His skin feels so soft against me, just as it has for 19 years.

I can't let him go. I lick my lips and feel my eyes trembling, as I release him from my arms.

"Lilly, is this it?"

"No, Chris, baby. This is not it," I say, bringing my forehead to his. "You know there's a reason I am here. I love you, and I'll never leave you," I say, shaking my head softly as he looks at me. "I will never leave you. I promise you that."

I kiss his hand and bring my eyes level with his.

I don't know what's going to happen to me. All I know is that this is the beginning of the end in the journey we call our lives. Maybe I am not meant to see him suffer like this. Seeing him suffer is killing me. I have to make Chris stop worrying so much. Nothing is going to happen to him. I'm not going to let anything hurt him while I'm here on earth. I run my fingers over his hands, feeling sadness soak through me.

"Is this what it feels like? Is this what cancer does to you?" he cries, his hands tensing around my fingers. I cover my bottom lip with my top lip and try to hide my arms, which quiver as I bring my eyes to his face, lick my lips, and stare for several moments. I am struggling to calm his fears, but at the same time, warm tears sting my cheeks. I don't want him to see me like this. I have to be strong. "Yes, sweetheart, but you're not going anywhere." My jaw quivers as I look at his face. "I promise that I will be with you forever, I may not be physically with you, but I will always be with you," I say, tightening my hand around his. "I promise you this."

And with that, I kiss his hand.

Chris breathes in, pauses for a moment, and keeps his eyes on me before running a hand under his nose. I will put Chris to bed tonight and will lie down beside him. It is now two hours later, and I am shivering. Right now, I am walking to my dresser to grab my diary. As I open the drawer and pull the book into my hands, I look at Chris. "I wrote this for you, Chris. It's yours forever."

"Lilly, don't do this to me. We need to be together forever."

I lift my eyes to meet his, and for the first time in a long time, words elude me. My breath quivers as I look at Chris and look at the diary's blue cover. "The diary is everything. It's you. It's me. It's everything you'll ever need to know."

"Right now, you need to drink," I say, grabbing a water bottle from the end table and sliding it into his hands.

"I need to get you to the hospital, Chris."

He freezes, wipes his eye, and throws his arms around me.

"I don't care about the cancer anymore," he says, sniffling. "I just can't do this."

I can't believe what I'm hearing. I'm the one who got him out of the hospital. I'm the one who brought him back. Why is this happening to me? I know I look terrible right now. I can feel my hair falling upon my shoulders and my eyes turning red. I am silent, unable to utter anything, but like a child, I move toward him. I turn to look out the window, and a leaf falls slowly from a tree.

"How long has it been now, Lilly?" Chris asks, his eyes darting haphazardly.

"What?"

He stares forward, grabs the water bottle, and takes a drink.

"How long has it been since I got cancer?" he asks, taking another gulp.

I place my head in my palms, sniff, and stare forward. My mouth opens, but I can barely speak. "What?"

"Lilly," he says, smiling weakly. "It's okay. You can say that I have cancer."

He touches my shoulder, looks at me for several moments, wipes his eye, and draws a breath.

"Cancer."

I extend my arm to him, grabbing for his hand. "Don't be scared, baby," I say, stroking his hair. "You're gonna live a long life. I know you think it's ending, but it's not. We're going to watch Ben get through preschool, and we're going to live into our 90s, stronger than ever."

He opens his mouth to kiss me, with his lips trembling against mine. "Lilly?"

I reach out to touch him. All I want is a moment to feel him with me. A moment to bask in the eternity I have forever wanted.

"Lilly, you're gonna be here with me. You're not going to let me go alone, are you?"

I hold a finger to his lips, and he stares. "I can't make promises. I don't know what's going to happen. We're here, aren't we?"

"Yes, but—"

"Listen, Chris. We're going to fight to stay together. We're going to chase rainbows. This isn't the end, sweetheart. Let your heart be at rest."

"But Lilly, it's hard."

"Don't look away when you see the light. Move closer, for in an angel's arms you are whole."

He stares back as though he is reliving a thousand memories. "What?"

I pat his hand and brush his shoulder. "We're going to Colman Park tomorrow. We're going have some fun."

I kiss his hand, take him upstairs, and help him get under the covers. He seems stronger. His yellow skin has now faded, returning to its usual porcelain shade. I offer him a hand to get up the steps, but he politely declines, walking forward.

It is now an hour later, and he has finally fallen asleep. As I lay here beside him, I swear I can hear him praying. But his lips are closed, his body at rest.

Ben is in his bedroom talking. I can hear him babbling. "I'm not sleepy. Maybe Daddy is awake."

"It's time for bed, Ben," I say, walking to his door and watching him play.

"But I'm not sleepy." His loud voice fades into silence as his nightlight flickers, casting light onto the wall. Ben's eyes are finally closed. And though I am finding it difficult to sleep, I slip back into our room and lay down beside Chris.

CHAPTER NINE

REDISCOVERY

Seven hours have come and gone, and I am fully rested. I open my eyes and place a hand on Chris's chest. He sniffs deeply and rustles under the covers. "Wake up, Chris," I say softly, tugging at the comforter. He snorts, opens his eyes, and smiles.

"Okay sweetie," I say, grabbing his hand. "Let's go. Colman Park is only a few miles down the road. But first, Matilda needs to get Ben."

Closing the door thirty minutes later, Matilda's car pulls out of the driveway, and Ben squeals through the open window. Smiling this morning has turned out to be a challenge, but I am forcing my lips upward, praying that the brisk wind will bring me solace, like it always has. Chris is beside me, and I have the heat cranked up, attempting to get my mind on other things. But I can't seem to find any peace. I am hopeful that today things will be better and that Chris and I will enjoy the beauty of the park. It is magical this time of year. But where do I begin? As I drive toward the entrance to the park, taking in the sight of the pristine blue lake, I turn to look at Chris. His eyes are steady, intent upon the landscape in front of us.

I close my door, rushing to the passenger side door. "Come on, sweetheart," I say, taking Chris's hand and helping him out of the car. Going to the park was something we did as teenagers, and I am taking Chris's hand, suddenly reminded of the times we have shared outdoors. The lake is placid. The bright orange leaves draw me forward, and I grab for Chris's hand.

This is where we need to be right now. There could be no better place. We are walking side by side, and I feel the wind, soft against my face. As I look at yellow leaves falling, a tear emerges from my eye.

"All right. Let's take it easy, Chris. We'll take it slow."

He turns, smiles at me, and looks at the ground beneath our feet. "No, Lilly," he says. "Let's have fun."

"Okay."

"Do you remember how we did this as teenagers?"

I nod, take his hand, and draw him forward. Instead of trembling now, he tightens his hand around mine.

"I love you, Chris."

Looking intently at me, Chris tugs me to the ground and kisses my mouth, as we roll around in brilliant orange leaves.

"Oh, sweetheart." I say, grabbing his hands and bringing my mouth to his, once again recalling the way his hands brushed through my hair in the 90s. We rub noses, and I am laughing so hard. I haven't felt this way in a long time, and I am finally at peace, safe within his arms. His hands are soft and warm, despite the autumn chill. I laugh and breathe into his shirt as we slow down and lock eyes. Slowly, I brush my hair behind my shoulders, grab his hand loosely, and gaze at him.

"Well, aren't you going to kiss me?" he asks, wrapping his arm around my back.

Without a word, I draw him close and giggle. "We haven't been like this for a while. It feels wonderful."

He doesn't say anything, but instead kisses my mouth and drifts back against the ground. Instinct draws me toward him, and my mouth crushes his. I close my eyes and feel his skin against mine. His soft hands comb through my hair, causing me to smile, like they always have. Laughter envelops me as we roll in the leaves like children. His touch is like no other, though his is the only touch I've known.

"Chris, you are wonderful."

"As are you," he says, rolling over and tickling me. I scream with joy and bring myself to a standing position.

This is the type of moment I used to look forward to, but right now it feels bittersweet. He is perfect, like I've always remembered him. And in spite of my happiness right now, I feel a gentle tug in my throat, remembering a time when he was well and I wasn't worrying.

Slowly, he rolls over, places his palm on a leaf, and looks at me fearfully with tears in his eyes.

I tilt my head, feeling his pain. I press a finger to his lips. "Be still, my love. Don't ever be afraid."

As I soon as I say these words, I pause, realizing that I too am afraid. Yet these are words I have to say. It is now or never.

He tilts his head as if he is taken back by my words. "What are you talking about, Lilly?"

I touch his hair. "I'm talking about you and me."

"What?"

"Just let me get this out, sweetheart," I say, touching a hand to his face.

He rises from the ground, looks at me, and tilts his head. "Huh?"

These are things I need to say before I can no longer say them. "I will stand in the soft winds, and will never stop waiting for you."

I brush his shoulder with my hand, move toward him, and kiss his cheek. This is one of the most painful moments of my life, yet it is needed to make my heart at peace if anything were to happen. "Lilly, I love you. I know I say it time and again, but it's true; it's always true. If only you knew how much I cherish you."

"Don't think about cancer, Chris. We have the rest of our lives together."

His eyes catch mine and linger.

His thoughts are clearly focused on death. However, I am not talking about dying. I am talking about life. The life Chris and I share is beautiful, and doctors tried to warn me that he would die a few months or a year later. However, I am not convinced. The fact that we ran together and rolled around in the leaves gives me hope for decades to come. Does our love ever end? Will he ever leave me? Does he love me the way he did so many years ago?

If my memory serves me correctly, I have written 987 diary entries that are all devoted to our moments together. I'm perfectly capable of keeping Chris with me for as long as he wants, but I know that cancer comes back, even if it's in remission. Seven is my favorite number. Perhaps that's why

I have 987 entries in my diary. Seven rhymes with Heaven, so there must be some magic in it. I seem to find magic in everything these days, especially the leaves. The walking trail here is filled with bright orange leaves that crunch beneath our feet.

We are walking faster now, hand in hand. I wish it could be like this forever. "You know I love you, if only for a moment we are together," I say, looking at him. "Love transcends everything."

The scenery is beautiful. I feel everything—every emotion that I ever imagined possible is alive in me right now. My destiny waits on tomorrow's horizon, because I know the sun may be setting on my once eternal paradise. Where will this road take me?

"You're feeling better. I see it," I say.

He turns to me with a soft gaze, the kind of gaze I've seen on his face a million times. "This is unbelievable," Chris says. "I feel strong."

"You look better."

"It's because I am, Lilly. See," he says, lifting his arm and squeezing his hand around his upper arm.

I swear I must have written this moment in my diary a million times. It feels like all the dreams I have hoped for our future—walking side by side, never being apart.

I'm trying to collect my thoughts right now as I look at him. "I am—"

He completes my thought with a simple sentence. "As beautiful as a princess."

Now I am taken, taken deep into his eyes and deep into our memories. This has been a beautiful day. If only they could all be like this.

I look at him and squeeze his hand. I wonder what he is thinking, and though I can read his thoughts, I can seem to read nothing right now.

"This is beautiful," I say, taking in the crisp air through my nostrils.

"It is, but before we go. I have to show you something."

I pull his hand and lead him toward the water. There is an apple on a nearby apple tree, which I pluck and roll over in my palm. "Take a bite," I say, bringing the apple to his mouth. "It breathes life into the soul."

He obliges, but for a moment, he is silent. I look into his eyes and see light—I feel my every emotion bubble to the surface as he takes the apple.

"It's sweet, huh?"

He nods. "Yes, like you."

It's moments like this that I fight to hold on, to hold on to this world, so he isn't lost. But I know that nothing lasts forever, and having a moment by his side is to me a lifetime of blessings. Who knows what tomorrow will bring? It used to be so clear, but right now, reality is getting fuzzy. How much longer will I fully be able to see?

Our hearts beat as one as we bask in the nature around us.

"Do you feel that?"

"What?" he asks, turning his head as though he is being called back into a memory.

I look at him, feeling a dull ache under my skull, but I continue on with the thought. "The air—it feels the same as it did when we were on the boat."

He stretches his arm around my lower back. "It does, and we're going to walk like this forever."

I hold a finger to his mouth and feel my vocal cords tighten, because I know that things will change. Life changes, taking us in directions we never expect to go.

"For the first time," he says softly, "I'm not worried about the cancer."

I smile, because there is no fear in his eyes. His eyes don't trail distantly like they did in the hospital. Full of vigor, his eyes hold eternal joy, joy that I will treasure for all of time.

He is silent for several moments, and a lump forms in my throat, strong and overpowering. I feel my heart slow for a few seconds, and then it begins beating stronger. "I'm sorry for putting you through all the pain of my cancer."

I hold a finger to his lips to silence him, as he buries his head into my shoulder.

"No need to be sorry, sweetheart," I say, smoothing my hands over his hair. "I'm yours. I'm always yours. We're gonna make it in this world together. I promise I'll never leave. I promise, sweetheart."

"Oh Lilly," he says, cupping my cheeks with his hands and bringing his mouth to mine. "I love you."

My eyes rise slowly, and I kiss his hand. We walk together toward the car and slip into the night. And before we know it, it is a brand new day. The day has reached full sunlight, and I am looking at him, knowing what soon will come. This is it—the awakening. Though Chris is no longer afraid of the inevitable, he has grown clingy. I look at him, enjoying the beauty of his face, all the while wondering if it will always be this way. And then the pain comes. The dull ache under my skull returns, bringing with it a fear I'd never expected. However, I can't fight it. Chris has taught me what it means to be strong, what it means to be resilient and brave.

My life is not what I expected it to be. On a typical day, I find myself writing stories in an effort to distract myself from the fact that I'm not working a full-time job or making a true living off of something that comes so naturally to me. For my entire life, writing has gotten me through all my traumas and emotions, whether they have been good or bad.

"Lilly," Chris says, his eyes appearing intense as he rubs my shoulder. "Let's go outside and see some stars. It's been so long since we've done that."

I smile, feeling a sudden lift in my stomach. Lifting my arm, I look at his twinkling eyes and look at the shining moon outside. It is beautiful, like the memories we have created. Escorting me through the back door, Chris leads me out to the patio and takes my hand softly. "See that one," he says, lifting his hand and pointing at a bright and beautiful star. "It's almost as beautiful as you."

My eyes lift, and for a second, I lose myself in the crisp air. I should be cold, but the warmth of his tender touch keeps me warm. "This is nice," I say, rubbing his back with my left hand and finding it difficult to pull my eyes away from his face. His touch is like silk, soft against my skin and comforting to my senses. I could never live without his touch or the soft kiss of his mouth.

My headaches are getting stronger by the day, although I am not concerned about the escalation of pain. Migraines are typical for people of a certain age, especially for those who have so much stress to deal with. My hands are trembling, but the darkness seems to calm me, at least for now. For a moment, I bring my eyes back to his and wonder what he is thinking.

Now I bring a hand to my head, wondering when the pain will end or if it will ever go away completely. As I bring my eyes to the bright stars above me, I slip my hand into his, realizing that this is the perfect moment, even in spite of my headache. My eyes lift to the sound of leaves cracking against the wind. I can no longer ignore my headache and bring my hand to the right side of my head.

Oh my God. The pain. It hurts.

Doctors have told me in the past that I should get checked out and have an MRI. I have told them in my least defensive voice that neither they nor anyone else can understand my feelings about the issue. I'm not sick, at least not in my mind. I am simply changing.

Chris and I rise two weeks later, side by side. And as I look over at him, I am comforted by the lush blankets enfolding our bodies up to our necks. For the first time in weeks, I didn't lay awake all night, my eyes blinking against the darkness. Last night was different—different in a way that words cannot describe.

The days are getting shorter now, the sun rising at 7:05 and setting before I finish taking in the beauty of the day. I enjoy it all—the brilliant red leaves falling from the trees, the soft autumn winds, and the rustling of leaves on the sidewalks outside. These are the treasures of this season to me, I realize, as my eyes are drawn to the window.

"Yesterday was beautiful," Chris says, drifting toward me and holding a hand to my face.

"Oh, Chris," I say, looking at him. "Rolling in the leaves was wonderful. It reminds me of when we were teenagers."

"It was great. We're going to keep doing that," he chuckles. "It keeps us young, you know? You fell asleep last night before I had the chance to kiss you."

"What kiss?" I chuckle, smiling in jest. "Oh, that's right. The one that went like this," I grin, drawing his cheeks into my palms and kissing him softly.

He tilts his head and chuckles deeply as I look at him.

"I believe this is how our love began—with an innocent kiss."

"Yes," I say, knowing in my heart that this is where I am meant to be right now. I was never meant to walk alone or be without the power of his touch.

"You're unbelievable, you know," he says, catching my eyes with an innocence that is his alone. I have always known his innocence, because it has made me who I am—a joyful soul who loves her family beyond words. He stares at me for several moments, and he tilts his head. I know he's in pain, but he doesn't want to show it. And then he says it again. "You're going to be with me forever?"

I draw a breath, feel my heart slow down, and look at him. His flannel shirt looks worn now, like it has lived a million lives on earth. For me, a million lives would never be enough to do everything I want with Chris, to experience every precious moment with him by my side.

"Have you ever thought of an eternity with me?"

I touch his face. "We will have eternity together."

I look away, feel my vocal cords tighten, and look back at him. He is beautiful, just as he was on that beautiful April day 19 years ago. I want to marry him again. I want to renew our vows, and once again reaffirm the growing love I have for him.

As I look at him quietly, I feel the peace of his presence. He combs his hands through my brown locks and smiles, as if he's recalling a long forgotten dream. Slowly, he brings his forehead to mine. They say that everything happens for a reason, and there is a reason I am looking at him right now, feeling the warmth of his hands.

"Ya know, I wouldn't mind renewing our vows."

He smiles, and for a moment, I am hopeful. "Why?" he asks.

"Because I love you, and it…" I breathe out. "It just feels like we need to."

We talk throughout the day, and I feel even more connected to him.

Now, as my eyes lift to the window, a bright red leaf drifts down on a soft wind. His eyes, now brilliant, rise again to meet mine. Wiping his forehead and breathing out, he looks at me, and enfolds me in his arms.

"You're magical, Lilly, beautiful like no other. You are everything I've ever wanted. You really are perfect, and I could never live without you again."

"Oh, sweetheart," I coo, allowing my arms to drift around him. I want him near me and with me more than I ever have before.

It is now two days later, and Susan and Jackie are meeting us for dinner to celebrate the fact that Chris and I are together and that we are living our lives together. Chris and I sit here, catching up with the two nurses with whom I'd practically lived for five months. And as I smile, I slip my hand into Chris's open palm.

"It's been a wild ride," I say. "I mean that so much has happened since Chris left the hospital."

Susan looks up, tilts her head, and smiles. "Well, you two deserve it. You deserve to be happy together."

Jackie, who is unusually talkative, looks up and smiles at Chris and me. "We have something to give you," she says, holding up a piece of paper that is covered with my scrawled handwriting.

Jackie looks at me in a way that she never had before and smiles. "It's a story you wrote while Chris was in the hospital. One of the other nurses found it, and we wanted to return it to you."

Jackie's eyes trail away silently as she slides the paper into my hands. Sitting quietly, my eyes dart across the paper, and a pang of fear fills my stomach. I hadn't wanted Chris to see this. I hadn't wanted anyone to read this passage, considering that it is so deep, so personal.

As I hold the paper within my hands, silently staring, I begin to read the passage.

How to die of a broken heart

One of the first steps to dying of a broken heart is to realize that you can't live without someone. In my case, I can't live without my husband, my dearest Chris. He is my one true love and my most treasured friend. If I am left alone in this world without him, what would I do?

This is a given. I would die of a broken heart. This really can happen. As I watch my husband pass away, I realize that I can bring myself to that brilliant place, away from my pain, away from my loneliness. When the pain of living without him becomes too great, I don't take my own life. I simply realize that I am hurting, but not in the physical sense. Maybe it is in a physical sense. I don't know. All I do know is that if Chris drifts away to the heavens above, my heart will break. And if my heart breaks because of his untimely death, then I will surely die of a broken heart.

If Chris lives, my heart will grow stronger and more beautiful with every passing day. But for now, I am ready. If he dies, I'm ready for my heart to elongate in my chest. There is scientific proof that this can happen. I really can die of a broken heart. But for now, I am waiting for Chris to see me again, in the light he did long ago.

If he doesn't make it … well, my heart will break. And I know what that means. Chris, I'm coming to the heavens above. I hope to see you soon.

Love always,
Lilly

Fear rises in my throat, as I read the diary passage silently. I had meant to stick that piece of paper in my diary to read later on. Chris wasn't supposed to see it, nor was anyone else. My eyes are frozen on the diary entry, and I sit here, looking at Chris. My mouth drifts open at the thought. Now, as he looks at me, I avert my eyes from his face.

I look away, hoping to avoid his eyes. As I turn my head to avoid looking at him, a lone strand of hair falls over my face, and I bite my lip, reading the passage over and over again. Realizing that Chris shouldn't read this, I hold it by my side and tuck it under my right leg.

"What is that, Lilly?" Chris asks, his eyes smiling, as he leans over to look at the piece of paper. "What is that under your leg?"

"Oh, it's nothing, just something I need to keep."

"What do you mean?"

"Oh, it's nothing … just a diary entry that I meant to throw away."

He smiles softly. "Oh, it's a passage from your diary. I can't wait to read it," he says, smiling.

"No!" I blurt without thinking. "This one is special. It's meant only for me."

Now, as I begin to lift the paper to the table, a group of people walks by. One person hits the paper, shoving it forward, and sliding it over to Chris. He picks it up immediately, and his eyes widen against the text.

As he reads the passage, fear soaks through my being. As his eyes widen, his gaze rises slowly to meet mine. He doesn't say a word, but simply looks forward, his eyes freezing upon me. My gaze lowers, and my eyes trail away.

This is not going to be good. I need to get out of here. His silence is telling.

"Why did you write this entry?" he asks, sounding calm, too calm.

"It's …"

"You were going to kill yourself if I died?"

I feel my voice beginning to trail away. "No, it's just …"

"It's just what?" he asks pleadingly, his voice quivering as he draws a dense breath.

"I was so grief stricken by the fact that you might die, and I read an article online about how people can die of a broken heart."

He lifts my chin. "Why would you read about something like that?" he cries, his voice cracking so strongly now that sadness sinks into my stomach.

"It was in the news."

He stands up straight and leans toward me. "Were you going to kill yourself? Be honest."

"No, no," I say, twisting a lock of my hair around my finger. "I wanted to find out if grief could really do that. Like I said, it just happened to be in the news."

"Oh, Lilly," he says, drawing me toward him and wrapping his arms around me.

"It's not killing yourself," I say, taking a step back and biting my quivering lip. "When someone you love dies, it is possible to die of a broken heart. The pain gets too strong to bear. As a result, your heart elongates in your chest, and I was just wondering …"

I feel my voice trailing off.

His voice trembles, mirroring mine, and his eyes soften. Softly, he puts his hands on my shoulders. "It's okay, Lilly. Really, it's okay."

"I was just wondering. I was just wondering if something could bring me to you, if anything happened. The thought of being without you was just awful."

I lick my lips and look up.

He looks at me and pauses, his eyes lifting quickly. "I just wish you had told me about this."

He holds me, but doesn't say a word.

"It really can happen. I've read about it a million times over, and I know it's real."

His mouth drifts open, and his expression softens in a way it never has before. Now, as he smoothes a hand over my hair, I feel sadness tug at my throat.

"Well, I can understand how painful losing one another could be. I don't know what I would do," Chris says, his voice halting. "I don't know what I would do if I lost you again."

I tilt my head. "Oh, sweetheart."

"So you weren't going to kill yourself if anything had happened to me? Oh my God, Lilly. I'm so sorry I tried to leave you."

I hold my hand in front of me as if to silence him. "Chris, it's okay."

"No, no. I can't believe I did that to you. You could have …"

"I would never kill myself. They would call me," I whisper, my eyes lifting. "They know when I'm in pain."

"Who?"

I pause for a moment and look at him with a knowing smile. A crisp wind caresses my face, and I look up at the darkening night sky.

Keeping his pain to himself is difficult. I can tell, because I see redness deepening in his eyes. Chris knows my thoughts. He knows how I feel about true love, especially when he is my one and only.

Keeping myself from crying is proving to be a difficult task, so I wipe my eyes and succumb to emotion. I look at him for a long moment and pause, my eyes suddenly lifting. "I'm here. I'm always here with you, regardless of what you do."

He doesn't respond right away, but instead, he looks at me softly.

"It's okay. I'm not sure I understand, but really, it's okay."

Chris kisses my head softly and slides his right arm over my back, as we walk slowly to the car.

Ben is with Matilda, so there are no distractions. For the moment, it is just the two of us. As I continue forward, feeling his hand within mine, I smile. I don't ever want this moment to end.

I have no idea what tomorrow or the next moment holds for me. My life has changed so much in the past few months that I barely recognize myself. I have, without a doubt, cleaned up quite a bit. My once greasy hair has been clean and flowing since Chris came home from the hospital. And my face is fresher, the shadows under my eyes fading to reveal my skin's natural porcelain shade.

Now, in the stillness of morning, a thought comes into my mind. It is comforting and freeing in a way my thoughts have never been before.

I'm old enough now to realize that our lives are constantly changing. Our thoughts are changing. I realize now that the point of life is enjoyment. If I were to leave this world tomorrow, would I have done anything differently?

No. Everything happens for a reason. And tonight, as I close my eyes next to Chris, I think about everything that has happened to us. I think about the little girl who died in my stomach two years ago, and I wonder what she would have been like. I wonder if she would have been like me—a hopeless dreamer, a romantic perhaps. Who knows? Either way, she would have been loved far more than she could have ever imagined.

There is another reason for the diary—a reason that is much different than the reason Chris thinks I have kept it. I try to think of the ending, and my imagination fails me, as I try to picture the perfect conclusion to the chronicle of not only my life, but also of Chris's life. It is a book that not only documents our love, but also tries to determine its direction through every season of our lives together.

Finally, it is morning once again.

Chris snorts, and his eyes slide open, squinting against the pillow.

I don't have the strength to tell him. The doctors told me toward the end of Chris's stay in the hospital that I was all clear. They told me the headaches I've had for months are most likely a manifestation of stress and worry. Worrying takes it out of me, and I have given Chris no reason to think there is anything wrong with me.

The seizures are a temporary annoyance, one that will inevitably go away with time. However, there is something wrong. Someone else has told me this, but I can't tell Chris who that person is. He wouldn't understand, nor could he realize my reason for being his wife or my reasons for making love to him. It's a beautiful act, one that I simply could not live without.

I don't feel as though there is anything harmful in my body. My physical health is still wonderful, still vigorous.

I have felt guilty many times for withholding information that a husband deserves to know about his wife. I have dismissed the headaches in front of him. I have smiled in his face, ignoring the guilt of knowing I have failed Chris on many occasions.

Yet still, he trusts me. Life isn't as simple as I once thought it to be. I love him deeply, so deeply in fact that I would give everything I own for his happiness. I know he would do the same for me. But still, there's a part of me that wonders if I have been too vague in my heart-to-heart discussions with him.

Women are complicated, I know. Chris has told me this many times in jest. I have been tender in my words for the most part, almost too tender at times. There are some things that simply should not be said, especially when you're trying desperately to cherish every moment you have with another person.

But for now, in the stillness of early morning, I am looking into his vivid blue eyes, feeling my eyes remain steady on my one true love. All the while, I am concealing the sadness beneath the surface. It subsides after a few moments of not focusing on the pain. As I stand here looking out the window, I hear him behind me.

"Do you want to go out tonight again, just the two of us?" Chris asks, his eyebrows lifting with expectation. "Matilda has Ben full-time for the whole week, so, we can go out on the town, if you'd like."

"I'd love it."

"Have you been taking your medicine?"

"Every morning like clockwork," he says. "So you wanna do it?"

A sudden lift in my stomach brings my hands toward him. "That sounds wonderful. Let's do it."

We go out on the town that night and two more nights thereafter. Every night these days, we frolic through the world and make out like wild teenagers on the street. This evening, we are together again, and I don't care if anyone sees us. Right now, it is our third night out, and I am dancing on the street, as he laces his fingers into mine and halts. He presses his lips into mine and draws a deep breath.

"This feels so wonderful," I say, as I drift back against a park bench, and he kisses my neck in the darkness.

"We're alone and playing like children. So let's act like children," he says, tugging my hands into his and twirling me around in the pouring rain. Despite the darkness and the fury of the pounding raindrops, Chris draws me closer and throws me over his shoulders. With my head over his back, I squeal with delight. As he brings me back to the ground, my eyes lift and hold his gaze. Now, as he puts his hands around my waist, he lowers me to the ground and kisses me softly.

"Oh my God, Lilly, I love you," he says, bringing his forehead to mine before lowering his hands to the sides of my face.

These moments are like rainbows, brilliant one moment, then silently fading into the slowly brightening stars at night. There was a time that I thought I'd never feel like this again, that I would never twirl playfully in Chris's arms, feeling his closeness, feeling his joy.

Sometimes, I think he feels it—feels that things will change at some point. I have dismissed his concern on many occasions when I have brought my hand to my head. Right now, my head is pounding.

It's just a headache. That is all.

Or is it? At the moment, the answer eludes me as Chris brings his mouth to mine.

He is everything I want. He is everything I need in this world. Yet I can't bring myself to tell him the truth about my headaches. I have realized that my relationship with Chris is very different from the relationships between many married couples. We are still passionate and connected. We still laugh.

Yet, we have had our fair share of tragedy and misfortunes. The loss of a baby before it enters the world is heartbreaking. Though we never got to meet her, the loss of our little girl took its toll, not only on our hearts, but also on our expectations of a family. But there are three of us, and for that, I am grateful.

For the longest time, I was sure there would be distance between Chris and me. I was sure I would continue worrying about Chris leaving me. But as I look at him, I realize that is no longer something I need to worry about.

We stand here for several moments, our eyes reflecting love.

"You never fail to amaze me," he says.

"Nor do you, Chris. I'm glad we're here."

If I am called back to my purple mountain and the brightening sun, there is no doubt that I will long for him. But if Chris left this world before his time, I would have a decision to make. Do I let my heart determine my destiny, or do I stay here and remain simply for the safety of my son? Sometimes we have to make a choice.

But for now, I am here, resting against Chris on a park bench. He looks up for several moments, unaware of my thoughts, as he draws my hands into his.

My time is growing shorter now. I can feel it when I see the flashing lights and feel the pain coming on.

The days are utterly beautiful now, I think to myself, feeling the soft wind against my face and allowing my head to drift onto his shoulder. I will worry about the rest later. Right now, my eyes are growing heavy. We are far from home and sitting on a bench near a shopping center.

"I am so tired. I don't feel like getting up. It sure is beautiful tonight," I say, a soft wind caressing my face and seducing me into sleep.

"Come on, Lilly," he says, hoisting me onto his shoulders. "It's only a mile, and you're light enough to carry."

For a moment, I open my eyes.

"One of these days, I am going to read more of the diary to you."

He nods and rubs my head softly, as he carries me through the neighborhood and back to the house.

"I am so tired," I say, looking at him through blurry eyes.

CHAPTER TEN

THE DIARY AND DREAMS

Night came and went in what seemed to be the blink of an eye. As my eyes slide open this Friday morning, they are drawn to the soft rays of sun playing at the edges of the blinds. With a soft sigh, I turn and look at Chris.

"Hey, sweetie." I shift sleepily and pointing to the dresser that contains the diary. "I want to read more of the diary to you."

Chris looks at me briefly and rubs his eyes, watching me as I get up and adjust the collar to my pajama top. It has been a long time since I have really read the diary. I read parts of it to Chris when he was in the hospital, but it seems like an eternity has passed since I have actually paid attention to every detail. All the pain we have endured since our parting comes rushing back and I realize in an instant that this morning marks a new day, a new moment in our life together.

"It's been a long time," I say. "It's been a long time since I've poured out my innermost thoughts to you."

His expression softens for a moment, and he looks at me.

"Getting a little sentimental these days, huh?"

"Have you ever … have you ever felt guilty about deceiving someone?

He looks at me with a face full of worry.

"Lilly, something's wrong. What is it?"

"It's nothing."

His head turns, and his eyes grow dense with worry. "Talk to me, Lilly. Is there someone else?"

"No, no. It's not that. It's just that—have you ever felt guilty about anything?"

He chuckles. "Food. If I eat too much, I feel bad, because I know it will go immediately to my hips."

I chuckle briefly and look deeply into his eyes. Through his bright blue eyes, I swear I can see his soul.

"There's something I need to show you," I say, nestling my head into his shoulder.

"Are you okay?" he asks, searching my face. "You look like something's bothering you."

"No, not at all. You know the diary I read to you when you were in the hospital?"

"Yeah."

"Well, there's more to it," I say. "There are many more stories and memories that I have yet to read to you."

"You're a total sap, writing all these stories about us."

There have been many times during the course of our lives together that I wondered if the diary would really mean something in the long run. Why do I write in it? Does it even matter?

"Something so intimate and personal," I think, "it should be kept to myself, but Chris is undoubtedly a part of me."

There were many times that my mother told me that keeping a diary about my boyfriend was a bit odd. In the end, she thought it would make him a narcissist and would make him think he is better than other people. But I knew that for one reason or another, I needed to keep writing in *Keeping Chris*, the diary.

It may sound cheesy to some, but its meaning is extraordinary, at least in my mind. I want Chris to hear all of the stories that have gotten us this far and have made us the couple we are.

"Want to know the truth about my question about feeling guilty?"

"Uh huh," Chris says, his eyes growing intense.

My voice quivers. "I ate all your cookies in the cabinet."

"Oh, Lilly. No need to feel guilty. I can't count how many of your chocolates I have downed when you're not around."

I stare in silence, feeling my stomach churn with guilt.

How could I deceive my husband? I am usually so honest. It would destroy our relationship if he knew the secret I am hiding. Then again, telling Chris that I think I'm sick would surely break his heart. Could I possibly be wrong about my destiny?

The headaches have returned, and I am sitting at my desk, with my head in my hands. I can't tell him something is wrong with me. I promised to be with him forever. It is 40 minutes later, and I find myself sitting at my desk, writing in the diary. As I scratch my pen across the paper, I can see our future, our past, and all the moments in between taking shape on the pages of my diary. Chris is not in the room, at least not at the moment. And I need a few more minutes to write my latest entry.

Dear Chris,

If you are reading this entry at this moment in time, chances are that you've learned the truth. I love you, and I want to keep you forever, but it's not always possible for you to understand why I do some of the things I do. Right now, after I finish this entry, I am making a doctor's appointment with a neurologist. I'm not quite sure what is going on, but I think I have epilepsy. I know you told me that already, but now, I know it is my reality. I know, because I just had three seizures in a row. As soon as one was over, another one began. I don't know how to bring this up, but something has really been bothering me. I have been having headaches lately. I know I promised you forever, but I don't know what's going on with my head.

I wish I could promise you that I will be well forever, but my headaches are getting stronger. I did some reading about headaches, and have made an appointment with a neurologist to get checked out. I hope everything is fine, but I need to get checked out.

You are perfect, Chris. Don't ever forget that. Know in your heart of hearts that I am taking care of myself … for you.
Love you forever,
Lilly

As I close the diary and feel a giant lump forming in my throat, I place my pen down on the desk. I feel myself getting dizzy and off balance. Suddenly, I feel the pink haze envelop me, and I fall to the floor. The white light in my near death experience appears again as I succumb to a seizure. This can't be happening to me. I promised Chris that I'd never leave. And now I get this feeling that something is going to happen to me. I've been trying to tell myself, for the longest time, that I am healthy. However, the autumn of my life is drawing near. It's not that I want to say goodbye. I want to stay. I really do. But I realize how strongly I am being called, as I squint against the whiteness of the walls around me. Their typical muted color has turned brilliant and bright. And now I turn my eyes away, just as I have done for the past month and a half.

Chris recently got a job as a research scientist at a local university, so he isn't here to catch me when I fall to the floor in a seizure.

For the next five hours, he is conducting experiments, publishing scholarly papers, and returning to the life he used to know. I am so proud of him. And I wish so much that I could tell him about his destiny. I wish I could tell him about where he's going to be if we ever say goodbye. Or will there even be a goodbye?

It is now 8:02 at night, and I feel pain pulsate on the right side of my head. I can't move. I can't speak. I can't …

"Chris, help!"

As the door flies open, I drift deeper into a seizure, unable to see anything but the flashing of lights. I see Chris rushing in, and he runs to me. He is my hero.

Now, as I drift out of the seizure, I look up at him. I am safe as he holds me, and I feel the softness of his sweater upon my skin.

Yet as I sit here looking at Chris, I struggle to appear strong, despite the subtle wheezing I feel rising in my chest.

Several days ago, I came to the realization that being a stay-at-home mom may be what I need to do right now. I have the freedom to get to know myself without being stressed out by the pressures of the traditional work world. Sometimes sacrifices are made for a reason. The seizures keep coming. So in the end, the question remains: Is it really safe for me to work outside the house?

As I gaze down at my trembling hands, I get my answer. Perhaps my dream job will come along at a later time. What my future holds at this point is an open question in my mind.

As I continue pondering the possibilities for my future, my eyes trail away, and Chris looks at me silently.

"What are you thinking about?" he asks, clicking off a table lamp, striding over to me, and smoothing a hand over my soft brown locks.

I shake my head in dismissal, though I feel transparent as his eyes linger upon me.

"Something's wrong, isn't it?"

His gaze grabs mine, though I try to look away. I stand in silence with my eyes watering, unable to bring myself to speak.

"I know the seizures are hurting you. You need to do something about it."

I freeze and stare, finding once again that words elude me. "I know."

"Your left hand is shaking. Your hands shake after you have a seizure. I've noticed. It's most likely an aftereffect of your body moving without you being able to control it."

"It's happening," I murmur, taking a step and stumbling toward an end table.

"I think you need to get a scan—an MRI or something," he says, his head turning slowly to meet my eyes.

"I don't do MRIs or brain scans. They cause cancer if you have them too often."

"Geez, Lilly," he says, curling his fingers in disbelief. "You're having seizures, and you don't want to see a doctor!"

I take a few steps back and look at him softly. "I just don't like MRIs or brain scans."

"They're painless, Lilly. You go in a tube, and they take a picture."

I turn, suddenly unable to bring my eyes to his. Frozen and paralyzed with fear, I feel my gaze trail away. "I don't want to go to the doctor."

"Lilly, I love you," he says, raising his arms slowly. "But I can't bear to lose you again. If you're not going to get the scans for me, get them for your son."

My heart sinks, and I feel a twinge of sadness as hot tears begin to sting my cheeks. His eyes turn mellow. He reaches for my hand, and I turn away, feeling sadness sink in more deeply.

"I'm so sorry," he says, looking at the tears in my eyes and walking slowly toward me.

My eyes rise, slowly at first, but they bounce quickly as he enfolds me in his arms. "I can't bear to live without you. You know that, right?"

I nod quickly, feeling the warmth of tears trailing to my neck. Emotion rises in my throat as I allow my arms to wrap around him. My trembling hands, I quickly realize, are a dead giveaway that I am upset.

I nod. "Yes, I know."

As I stand here, burying my face in his shirt, I sniff quickly and allow myself to drift back, retracting my head from his chest. Though I want to tell him everything, I can't say a word. As my jaw trembles, my eyes lower, and I feel for the first time in our relationship that I am at a total loss for words.

His gaze drops, and he draws my hands into his, only this time, he doesn't reach for my face.

"I know this scares you," Chris says, looking into my eyes. "I know the seizures really scare you, but you have to do something about it."

"What do you want me to do?"

Chris leads me to the kitchen table as though I've never been there before. As he sits down, he holds my right hand possessively and exhales a soft moan.

"Listen, Lilly. I was dying," he says, his voice cracking. "I was on death's door. I didn't know if I would live to see the next day. I don't know what's going to happen to me either, but you need to do this."

"I know. I know," I cry. "I was there. I saw them waiting for you."

I lay my head on the table, my hands trembling as though I am having a nervous breakdown. All I can do is reach for him. I want him for the rest of my life. I want him for the rest of time.

"I already died. I came back didn't I?"

"And that's what I'm afraid of," he says. "They took you from me before, and I don't want him to take you again, at least right now. You deserve—"

My voice cracks. "Uh huh?

"You deserve to be here," he says, slowly drawing my hand into his. "You deserve to be here with me."

I can feel soft beads of sweat forming in the palms of my hands, as my green eyes linger upon him. "And I am here. I'm yours forever, always yours," I say, tightening my arms around him. As I bury my head into his chest, he doesn't see my jaw trembling. "There are some things you just aren't meant to understand."

To get my mind off the seizures, I plan on spending the rest of the afternoon writing a book that I know will inevitably fail to succeed. Today has been a better day than yesterday, though I know that all the days hereafter will be filled with tumbles to the floor and headaches that send me into silence.

Chris hears me as I write my book. He hears me plunging my fingers into my computer's keyboard, lifting my eyes, and lowering my hand to a tissue on my desk. The tissue is now crumpled. My eyes are red, I realize, as I look into a mirror on my desk. Now, I lift a trembling hand to the tissue, bringing it up to my face.

I look into the mirror on my desk, seeing the redness in my eyes and feeling a tingling in my left arm. I bring a hand to my face, struggling to catch my breath. Now, I draw a shallow breath. That's all I can manage right now. I look into the mirror once again, seeing the worry lines on my face and allow a hearty sob to escape my lips.

I am feeling better now, at least for the time being. What the next moment will bring, judging by the frog in my throat, is a mystery to me. A sudden pang of guilt lingers within my throat and goes away for a second. As my eyes linger absently on the mirror, my guilt returns, and is made manifest in a deep and throaty sniffle.

My heart suddenly quickens, and I feel pins and needles once again pulsating through my skin. I'm being taken away from Chris once again, only this time I am not given a choice. The end is coming soon.

"No", I murmur to myself, lifting my eyes toward the clouds. Is it time for me to leave? No. I have to save Chris from the pain of losing a spouse. I simply cannot go. I am here. I am right here in my body, feeling fear envelop me in a way it never has before. Not even when I lost my mother did I feel this much pain. I thought that losing her had been the greatest tragedy of my life. At the age of nineteen, losing a parent is the worst pain you can experience.

Now that I've gotten older, I realize that things that once seemed huge are actually stepping stones to the next stage of life.

This is it, the ending, I think to myself, allowing myself to type a few words on my laptop before losing my composure yet again. Biting my lip and typing a few words, I realize that this is it. Everyone up above the clouds is lining up into formation. The walls brighten, and now I am torn. Should I stay, or should I move on? The thought brings tears to my eyes. My head drifts back against my shoulders, and tears once again begin to flow, trailing like raindrops on flower petals.

Finally, I am alone, alone in my thoughts, alone in my guilt. And yet, in spite of it all, I am still filled with hope for my future with Chris. I still smile at the prospect of him taking me into his arms every night. I smile at the thought of him slipping his arms under my shoulders and spinning me around the city. In my mind's eye, I picture him taking Ben and me to the carnival. I hear his laughter. I feel his kiss.

The next week slides by and fades into the following Monday. For Chris's sake, I am waiting in a neurologist's office. As I sit here, my jaw trembles with fear. My time in the waiting room is spent reading magazines about current events, celebrities, anything to take my mind off the prospect of having brain scans done.

As I sit there lifting my eyes above the pages, I see a nurse with a mask over her nose and mouth. And now I feel myself spinning. For a long moment, my senses heighten, and my eyes are drawn not only to the nurse's face, but also to the many patients walking in and out of the office. Some of them are struggling to walk, and others find it hard to breathe.

Other patients are connected to tubes and have bandages wrapped around their heads. Time will inevitably decide whether or not I too will become one of those people with nerve damage or circulation problems. The waiting and uncertainty are the hardest things for me to deal with these days. But for now, as I release a magazine from my trembling fingers, Chris slides his hand into mine.

And that's the worst part about it all. I don't want to break his heart, I really don't. Despite my worrying, I know that Chris is right here by my side, taking care of me.

"You're nervous. I can tell," he says, squeezing my hand and looking at me warmly. "I'm sure everything is fine. It's just a checkup."

My eyebrows flex as I take in the medicinal smell of the office and lift my eyes to the ornate crown molding up above.

"This is it. This is the moment of truth," I think to myself, watching patients walk through the doors, one by one, side by side. Some are part of a couple. Other patients, I realize, judging by their nervous stares, are obviously here alone. At least Chris is with me.

Ben is at school right now, presumably playing happily. At the moment, I cannot focus on thoughts of anything other than the nurse in the cubicle in front of me. For as far back as my memory stretches, Matilda has only taken care of Ben. She has never accompanied me anywhere. Now, as I hear the door open, and I look up, I find her standing there. She pauses and looks at me silently, as though she is at a loss for words.

As I pause and examine the pained look on her face, I wonder why she is walking over to Chris and me. This is her day off. She should be doing something for herself, something other than taking care of our family, as she always has.

"Good morning," she says in her thick Columbian accent, which I have come to adore over the years.

"Hi Matilda. How are you this morning?"

She pauses for a moment before responding. "I am here for you, just checking in. Mr. Rylan is taking care of you. He is a good man."

She ducks out of the office quickly, so quickly in fact that my brows lift, and I begin to fumble the collar of my shirt.

Chris looks at me with a soft smile, and I realize instantaneously that there is a reason she had come.

Time seems to move in slow motion as I become lost in my thoughts, watching a seemingly endless stream of patients come out of the doctor's office. I sit with Chris in the waiting room, anticipating what the next moment will bring. And then I hear the words I've been dreading. I cringe as the nurse with the mask walks over to me.

"Mrs. Rylan? You can come with me." She turns and smiles at me, ushering us forward toward a boxy white room. The walls surrounding me give me the chills.

I walk in and smile, figuring I should be polite and exchange pleasantries before I find out for certain that I am okay. Or am I sick? I don't know anymore.

Time will tell, I think to myself, sitting down in a dark blue chair. It is hard and cold against my skin. And though I can see fear in Chris's bright blue eyes, I know there is nothing to fear, at least not now. Minutes pass like hours in my mind as I watch Chris's eyes dart in silence. The topaz blue eyes that usually bring me comfort at this moment are a source of doubt and fear.

Am I disappointing him? Am I about to break his heart? I can't be sure. All I know is that my head hurts. Something abnormal is there in my body, but there is no way I am going to succumb to medical treatment.

"The doctor's coming in soon," Chris says, shifting nervously in his chair and grabbing my hand before giving me a soft and reassuring look. He is more clingy than usual. Still, despite his apparent nervousness, he exudes an unusual calm. He must have a lot on his mind.

However, he has been brushing up on his science stuff. Maybe he knows something I don't.

What could he possibly know? And how? Chris knows me like no one else, so it only makes sense that he has researched the subject. Seizures. Headaches. What does it all mean? Or does it mean anything at all? I can feel the questions tug at me all at once, creating a sudden drop in the pit of my stomach. I swallow hard. My chest tightens, and for a moment, I think that I have stopped breathing.

The quiet is maddening, and these thoughts slip through me, intensifying my nervousness, as my breath rises quickly.

As I listen to doors slide open and closed through the hallway, I feel my body shiver each time someone walks by the door. "The doctor's coming, isn't he?"

Chris's eyes rise slowly and reluctantly meet mine. "Yeah, it shouldn't be long."

"But it's been a long time," I blurt, realizing by my suddenly trembling hands that I am not ready to embrace reality. Chris needs me here. I need him to stay with me.

The stillness and quiet of the room cause my heart to quicken, and my eyes rise to see a blood pressure cuff on the other side of the room.

"Do you see that?" I ask, my eyes rising slowly from the floor to the machine, and then back to the door.

"See what?"

"The blood pressure cuff."

"Relax, Lilly. Sit back for a second. You're really tense."

I drift back in my chair and close my eyes slowly. Now, I open them.

Ten minutes later, there is a sudden knocking. And the door slides open with a creak.

The doctor raises his hand and offers a handshake. I oblige, but realize the moment I clutch his hand that more people are standing behind the doctor. They walk away quickly, and their white coats heighten my fear. As I watch, feeling alone, my pulse quickens. Now the doctor sits down.

"I'm Doctor Nelson. Can you tell me a little bit about what's been bothering you?"

Chris is sitting beside me in his hard blue chair, silently watching.

"There's nothing wrong with me," I say, struggling to convince myself. "I just had a few seizures and some headaches."

The doctor, whose brown eyes lower, appears frozen, as he pauses before speaking. "How long have you been having the seizures?"

"A little while now," I say. "They come from time to time."

Dr. Nelson tilts his head. "I see," he says, scratching his pen across some lined paper, seeming disconnected. "How frequent are the headaches?"

I hesitate and bring a hand to my cheek. "I get them about every four days."

The doctor's voice halts for a moment and he pauses as if he is reflecting.

The usual exam routine ensues, and he listens to my heart before slipping the blood pressure cuff around my arm. This is not a routine physical by any means, I think to myself, as my eyes freeze against the bright white walls. He asks me to follow his finger, and fear descends into the pit of my stomach. This is it. This is the moment that I learn my world is crashing down.

I look at Chris, searching for a memory to hold onto. I adjust the collar to my shirt and struggle to smile. Pausing briefly and holding a light up to my eyes, the doctor draws a dense breath, and his voice trembles as he speaks. Oh no, this can't be good.

His brown eyes are persistent and intense, as they linger upon me. He strides over to the exam table and holds a blue sheet in his hands.

He lifts his hands, slowly at first and now more quickly, as he presses his fingers into my temples.

"Ever had surgery?" he asks quickly, almost too quickly. Suddenly, I feel as though the air has been knocked out of my chest. Running my fingers along my jaw line, my eyes freeze.

"No."

The doctor looks at me, his eyes intense, seemingly scrutinizing. "You need a CAT scan to look at your brain. If we detect any alignment of synapses or unnecessary blood vessels, we may need to do some investigating."

"I've seen her hold a hand to her head," Chris blurts, averting his eyes as I attempt to avoid eye contact with him. There is nothing wrong with me.

"I'm fine, Chris," I say, staring at him for a long moment before allowing my eyes to drift slowly away. "Just let me deal with it."

"Hmm," Dr. Nelson says, sniffing and holding a stethoscope to my chest. The next thing I know, doctors are pushing me down the hallway in a wheelchair to the x-ray room. Time at this moment is irrelevant. The moments between my meeting with the doctor and my journey to the x-ray room seem to blur together as my heart plunges through my stomach.

Now, a man dressed in blue scrubs comes into view. His face is fuzzy at first. My eyes descend to his black boots, which bounce against the floor. I feel like I am living in a dream.

"I'm Tom," he says, lifting his arms and looking at me warmly. He is a kind man, I realize, as his eyes soften and reflect an air of concern.

"I'm the assistant for the day. I'll be wheeling you down to the scan room."

"I don't need this thing. I can walk," I insist, twisting my head around and moving my feet as he pushes me down the hall in my wheelchair. My hands are drawn instinctively to my eyes, and I rub the corners of my eyes, attempting to conceal the emotion building within them.

"I understand that, ma'am, but according to Dr. Nelson, you need this." His voice is insistent, and he speeds forward, wheeling me quickly through the doors.

Chris is beside me the whole time. As my fear intensifies, he speaks. "You took care of me. Now it's my turn," Chris smiles, speeding up his pace and following Tom and me down the hall. I attempt to grab for his hand as I go through the doors. The white walls, the medicinal smell—these are all reminiscent of my time in the hospital with Chris.

And I can tell he feels it, too, as his gaze rises and he breathes deeply. "I'm right here, sweetheart," he says.

"This is utterly grueling," I think to myself, as I lay in a plastic tube, listening to the buzz and whir of a machine I have never seen before. At the moment, as my pulse slows and quickens, I lack the ability to formulate words. This is usually the case when I am in a medical setting. My heart is like a bongo drum, pounding deep within my chest.

Gazing up at the bright lights, the atmosphere transports me back to Chris's bed railing, the beeping heart monitors, and the endless chatter of nurses in a cube. It was there that

I spent every day, praying desperately that Chris would come back to me.

These days, Chris is more worried about my welfare than he is about his own appearance. His face has grown scruffy, and his hair is barely combed today. He is, however, becoming more attuned to me—more attuned to my body, constantly watching my every move.

The scan results will come in a few minutes, and I feel deprived of oxygen, because of my mounting fear. I am not worried about me, however. I am worried about Chris.

We are now in another waiting room two hours later, and Chris and I find ourselves sinking into a deep brown sofa in an area that is sectioned off from the x-ray and exam rooms. By now, the midday sun of fall has illuminated the room through tinted windows. The light is muted, yet it still reminds me of the many moments Chris and I have spent together. The sunlight suddenly takes me back to the many nights we lay together in silence, enjoying the intimacy of our bodies coming together.

It is now after midnight, and I find myself drifting back slowly into the plush fabric of the sofa, just as I have done for so many weeks with Chris. With my teeth chattering, I clench my right hand into a fist for several moments, contemplating the future and feeling an anger I never imagined could envelop my being. I hold my head in my hands, blinking against tears that cloud my eyes.

Now, as I comb my fingers nervously through my hair, I come to the realization that there is no delaying my fate. The brain scans will ultimately reveal the future of my health.

I bite my lip, as is my nature, and I allow my head to back into the plush fabric, my eyes opening and closing at regular intervals.

This worry is exhausting. Exhausting to my body. Exhausting to my brain. And as I feel my breath quicken, my hand falls lazily to my side. Now I feel safe.

Chris's voice halts my thoughts, and he leans over as though he has a secret to tell. "You are beautiful. You know that, right?"

I nod. I have heard this before. Chris says this whenever he is emotional or worried about how I feel about him. Of course, I love him. Why would he question that?

"I know. I love you too, baby," I say quietly, shuffling my hands toward the arm rest to the sofa and allowing myself to once again drift into the sofa's plush, cloud-like fabric.

"The doctor's almost here, isn't he?" I ask, resting my head momentarily before closing my eyes. The pain has become a regular occurrence, I think silently, as I feel the right side of my head pulsate.

Two hours and 15 minutes later, I am still here, because of the pain. And I shuffle briefly, hoping that I will be suddenly released from this body, away from the confines of the pain I experience on this earth.

There is a sound and a knock on the door, and I feel my arms limp at my sides. *This is it. The moment of truth.*

As the door slides open with a creak, I can't tell whether I am about to receive good or bad news. Dr. Nelson's expression is blank as he shuffles a hand through his hair and sits down beside me.

"Well," he says, as a demure look overtakes his face. "It looks like we have good news. The brain scan is completely normal. If you look right here," he says, circling his finger around a dark spot, "there's just a little cloudiness."

"Is that unusual?" Chris asks, as he looks at me fearfully.

"No, no," Dr. Nelson says dismissively. "We see that a lot, actually. Often, the camera picks up some scar tissue."

Chris drifts forward, suddenly rising after hearing the doctor's words. "So she's okay?"

Dr. Nelson smiles. "She's okay. You're good to go."

It is now Thursday two weeks later, and I am back to my old routine—writing my book, taking care of Ben, and tending to the house while Chris is at work. My life has become habitual, unexciting. I now find a certain comfort in being away from the hospital, away from medicine, away from worrying.

Yes, I'm back to my old life, taking care of everyone else. Being home takes on a certain comfort, a certain peace. Even so, the journalist within me still thinks routinely about bylines, lead sentences, and cutlines. These are the technicalities of journalism, my chosen field of work. And now, as my eyes linger on the computer screen, I pause in contemplation.

Staying at home isn't the ideal situation, given today's economy and the push for job growth, but this is where I am meant to be, at least for now. Since the local elections took place, I have found that I don't care for either of the political parties.

This morning, as I sit here, sipping some tea, I realize that I no longer desire to earn tons of money from a booming corporate job or an organization that places me in the limelight. No, I am the guardian, the guardian of the ones I love. I am the rock that keeps my family together.

Whether I will be here tomorrow remains a mystery to me. There was something in that CAT scan that I can't quite put my finger on. There are times that my memory fails me, despite my young age. At times, I have a hard time remembering the stuff I learned about the brain in college. However, there is one thing I remember quite clearly. Brain scans aren't always correct, given that brain structure can change. Perhaps there is more serotonin or more epinephrine.

I should remember what those terms mean, given the fact that I started college as a psychology major. But at the moment, the meanings of such terms escape me. My mind is focused on more important things.

As I sit here reflecting, watching the sun rising up upon the impending horizon, I exhale softly. Right now, I feel a certain peace. It is odd and unfamiliar, considering how much I've been worrying recently. But here, as I sit enjoying the beginning of the day, I smile.

I have found that Chris is more relaxed now, much more than he had been before I had the CAT scan. He is once again clean shaven, and his eyes again possess the same spunk they did before I got sick.

It's amazing, I muse, as I hear Ben squeal in the background.

"It's morning, Mommy. I want breakfast!"

After appeasing an excited 5-year-old with a bowl of sugar-laden cereal, I kiss Chris goodbye and smile. Now, as I draw a nervous breath, I open the drawer to my desk and pull out *Keeping Chris*. "Chris," I murmur, raising my eyes. Next to Chris, the diary is my most treasured possession. From the two of us, our family was created.

I know Chris is excited to see me this evening, because we plan to celebrate a future that is once again filled with hope.

The day came and went quickly, and it is evening once again.

The sun sinks into the land, and I stand here, waiting. He is almost home. My heart is quickening, bringing back the fear I thought had gone away. Drawing short and shallow breaths, I bring my hand to my chest and draw a dense breath. *Oh my God. I can barely breathe.*

However, I am fine.

Hours later, Chris walks through the door and slips his arms under my shoulders. Spinning me around, he kisses me deeply, all the while combing his hands through my hair. It is a long and lingering kiss—one that I don't want to let go, because of its pure beauty. Its feeling is reminiscent of the kisses we shared when we were teenagers.

Ben isn't home yet, and our eyes rise in a mutual gaze, recognizing that we are alone. Finally alone. No doctors. No CAT scans. Just us.

"Are you feeling okay?" Chris asks, as he sits down next to me.

"Yes, I feel wonderful," I say, closing my eyes briefly and then reopening them. His mouth drifts into mine, as he lowers me to the floor and looks at me with a twinkle in his eyes.

He places his hand in mine, and we drift back onto the carpet, which is cool and soft against my skin. The carpet is comforting and reminiscent, as his eyes drift over me in a mixture of elation and joy.

"Chris," I say, as he turns his head to look at me. "They're calling me back again."

"What?"

"I can see the sun in my dreams. I open my eyes and lie awake, as the rainbow tunnel fades in front of my eyes."

Chris rises to his feet and looks at me pleadingly.

"Lilly, don't do this, not again."

His arms drift slowly to his sides, and I know it is best to stay silent, for saying a word would encourage a discussion about Heaven.

I turn to him slowly. "The light. You have no idea how beautiful it is."

His eyes rise, and he smiles for a long moment. "I'm sure it's beautiful, but you can't leave again."

"I might have to. Next time they call me, I'm going."

"What?"

"I may not have the chance again, at least not until I'm old."

"You know so much," he says, looking at me, this time lovingly and with an admiration I have never before seen in his eyes. "But you are scaring me to death."

"There are some things you will never understand."

His eyes grow intense, slowly falling downward.

As I lift eyes, I can see the bright purple mountain. I can see everyone lining up into formation, as a soft wind caresses my face. For the moment, I am here with Chris.

"Lilly, don't do this to me again."

I look at him briefly, and my eyes turn slowly to the light against the wall in the living room. It is hard to stay there. It is harder now than it was several weeks ago.

The temptation to leave goes away for several minutes, so I sniff deeply, avert my eyes from the wall in the living room, and force myself to walk away. My cheeks are tear-streaked now, and my fingers are moist from trying to brush them away. My hands are trembling, but I have not yet succumbed to the mounting pain of a seizure.

Another one will overcome me, I'm sure. I can't continue to fight nature forever, although I am sure Chris will urge me to do so. He isn't with me right now. Instead, his hand scratches notes across some lined paper upstairs. Every day, for two hours straight, Chris works on writing intricate in-depth research reports about advancements in science, medicine, and genomics.

Despite all of our years together, my personality has remained the same. I still wake up at the crack of dawn every morning, 6:30 am on the dot. The fact that I get up so early annoys him, given the fact that he could sleep all day.

I constantly distract myself from the urge to return to the purple mountain and the rainbow tunnel by getting on the computer and writing small portions of my book. Typing a few words on the computer brings me a certain thrill, as I gaze back at text that is of my own creation.

As I focus intently on the computer screen, my green eyes rise, and I realize that it is raining. Now, as I scan the room, I jump briefly, as a hollow sound meets my ears. I hear footsteps. As I look up, I find Chris standing in the doorway. Strolling in, he smoothes a hand over a lock of his blond hair, pushing the strand away from his face.

"You're writing your book, I see," he says, bouncing onto the bed. How's it coming along?"

"It's coming," I say, staring at the screen but not typing anything.

I am so utterly distracted. I know my situation. Now that I know I am wanted in Heaven, I am barely living on earth. However, I have a pulse, and there is a reason my heart is still beating. I am drawn to my diary every night to document a new moment and to keep our memories fresh in Chris's mind, for when his days grow long and it is only him facing the world.

Tonight, I start my entry with a very heavy heart.

To my dear Chris,

I know life is hard for you, especially with me seemingly caught between two different worlds. The world I have known with you is filled with nothing but joy and endless happiness. In our later days, I pray that we are together, enjoying the rest of our time on earth, side by side.

But … I know in my heart of hearts life doesn't always work out as we have planned. Every night, as I close my eyes, I am taken back to our first kiss and our first touch. I see your smiling face in my memory, and I realize beyond any doubt that you are forever the one for me.

You are writing your papers now, rediscovering your life and living it anew. And tonight, as I close my diary, I see you beside me. You have given me your gracious love through passionate kisses and hand holding. If am ever taken away from you, don't ever forget that I will always think of you. I will always love you.

As you scratch your final notes on your papers this night, I am smiling at you and loving you with all my heart.

Love always,
Lilly

I know Chris saw me writing that entry, because he lingered by the doorway before nodding and leaving with a chuckle.

Now, as fatigue finally takes hold, calling me to the pillow just minutes before 11 p.m., I stretch out my arms and slip into bed beside him. Now, I roll over to see him in peaceful slumber. His closed eyes seem to tremble in the darkness.

Some would call my writing an obsession, but I have never been one to leave things unsaid. Everything I want to say to my true love is kept in *Keeping Chris*, the diary that has kept me breathing.

It is now three days later, and Chris and I find ourselves at an electronics store. He has the day off, and, now that Ben is in school, we have some time to ourselves. The early November air makes me shiver, and as I look out the store window, I slip my hands into my pockets.

I have a job interview in an hour at a publication house in Everett, Washington. It is a last ditch effort on my part to get back into the journalism field. The company for which I am interviewing is a biweekly publication. It is part-time position, so the job would fit perfectly into my schedule of taking care of Ben.

It is now two hours later, and I am reflecting on the job interview. As I had expected, I failed the interview miserably and received a rejection email two hours later. Obviously, they wanted to dismiss me from consideration as soon as possible.

Either way, it doesn't matter.

I try to make the most of every moment. I am thinking more than usual this morning, realizing that it is my favorite time of year. The months have gone by far too quickly, I realize, as I sit back on our plush sofa, enjoying the evening with Chris by my side.

Chris brought me a cup of hot cocoa a few minutes ago. And now, as we sit together, taking in the scenery, I pat his leg. I love the fall. There's a warm feeling in my heart as I watch the leaves floating gently to the ground.

"What are you thinking, love?" Chris asks, holding up his mug and bringing it to mine.

"A toast," I say, "a toast to beauty and to being together."

He nods in agreement, sipping his cocoa and pulling a blanket over our legs. We are sitting close together, and I realize by his fleece pajamas that we are heading into the end of the year. Soon it will be Thanksgiving.

Feeling warmth within my heart at the sight of the crackling fire in front of us, I turn to Chris and chuckle. "I can't believe we're here right now. The world is," I pause, "a much more beautiful place right at this moment."

"Yeah, because you have me," he cracks, sitting his mug down on the coffee table.

"Oh, shut up," I say, smirking. "You think you're so clever."

"There's a reason for that," he says, lifting his mug and taking a sip before stretching his arm around me. "I am clever."

"Yeah, sure," I say, nestling my head into the crevice between his arm and shoulder. The fleece fabric is comforting against my skin, and I breathe in, reveling in the togetherness.

"Running around the town the other night," I say, looking briefly into my eyes, "that was a lot of fun."

"Yeah," he says, his eyes returning to my mug. "It was nice."

"We should do it again sometime."

Now that we've finished our cocoa, I find the courage to stand up. I stare at my palms after sitting the mug on the kitchen table. They are cracked from washing them too much. The cracks are jagged and defined. Caring for a five year-old tends to do that.

As I turn, smiling, I take a few steps back into the living room. I reach for my face and realize that I cannot move my hands. Perhaps it is a panic attack. I have to keep on walking and wait for the panic to pass, but at this moment, pain rises within me.

I cannot speak, but I need to stay conscious. I need to keep standing. The fear will pass, I'm sure. These thoughts fly through my mind at rapid speed. The red aura envelops me, and I am paralyzed by fear. And now, as my vision turns blurry, I fall slowly to the floor.

It takes me just a few seconds to come to terms with the realization that I am having a seizure. I want Chris to hear me, but the TV is blaring now, and I am in no shape to scream for help. I am now a shining light, and epilepsy is the fire that extinguishes me. Moments later, Chris finds me in the kitchen, flailing against the floor. Seeing him in front of me, I am no longer afraid, as he kneels by my side.

"Lilly, I'm here. I'm by your side."

Slowly, as I drift out of the seizure, my blurry vision now returns to crystal clear focus. I look up without a word. I am shaken. "Oh, Chris."

"Lilly, I can't do this anymore. I can't watch you have seizures and do nothing about it."

I can barely make my voice audible. It is still shaky.

"This epilepsy—it's not going to hurt me. I have a seizure, and that's it. Then, it's over."

His eyes suddenly grow distant, and I find myself at a loss for words. "You say that now, but with all these seizures," he says, licking his lips, "it's gonna catch up with you someday."

"What are you saying, Chris?"

His voice quivers. "What I'm saying is that you need medicine. You need it now."

"Oh my God," I say, reaching fearfully for my face. "I think I feel another one coming on."

He pauses for a minute, and his tone grows softer. He was intentionally harsh only one time before. Now I realize that he was harsh for a reason. I look up at him, torn between the desire to reach for him or look away.

"It's okay. I'm here," he says. "I love you. I just want you to live a healthy life."

His gaze, though still loving, looks somehow different. His eyes grow dense, and his expression is empty. "Why are you doing this to me?"

I gasp, allowing myself to drift slowly to the floor. "I don't know anymore. I just … don't … know."

"You don't feel the same these days," he says, gazing at me softly. "You're not exactly here, you know, in the emotional sense."

Anger instantly slices through me. "What?"

"Lilly, you can't go on this way."

"I know I've been in denial, but you're right," I say softly, as my voice quivers. "There is something wrong with me."

He stares at me for a long moment, and as expected, he begins to weep. I don't actually see his tears yet, but I hear the pain cracking his voice. He looks at me, and a lone tear rolls down his cheek.

"You know I don't like brain scans or tests."

"Lilly, I know you're bullheaded. You've been that way for years. But beneath that, you are the kindest, most gentle person I have ever met."

Emotion tugs at my voice, and I am touched.

"Lilly, I'm calling Dr. Nelson. You know how I feel about science and medicine. It can do a lot, it can save lives even."

I look up fearfully. "But …"

"But I can't let you go on like this. You're killing yourself and … you're breaking my heart."

He picks up the phone, dials a number, and asks for the doctor. I don't know what to do. I stare at Chris and see the phone propped up on his shoulder. Despite the chaos, I am gazing down at my left ring finger, and I look once again at my beautiful wedding ring. It still sparkles and shines, and it reminds me of the promise I made to my husband many years ago.

I look down at my hands and suddenly remember the flood that happened in our house five years ago. Even now, I still feel the rushing tide, the drenched room, and my ruined clothes, wet upon my hands. Yet I still feel no need to get anything for myself. As Chris continues holding, with the phone pressed tight to his ear, I stand up and walk out of the room. I walk at a rapid pace, but still feel like I am next to him, frozen in time.

The heater beside me turns on, its harsh whir making my ears hurt and sending my senses into autopilot. I am no longer used to sudden movements or sounds. I listen as Chris speaks to the doctor, his voice steady and strong. His voice has always been a sense of comfort, but right now, as his eyes dart, his words are a source of fear.

Today, I know there is no way to calm my senses. I fear that I'll soon be on medicine and facing life as an epileptic. I don't want the title, but there's no escaping reality. So I continue standing, knowing that I will be in the doctor's office soon. I linger here, clasping my hands loosely together and feeling pins and needles throughout my limbs. Standing requires all my strength as my legs are weak and possess the ability to easily crumble beneath me.

I continue standing, and the dull ache on the side of my head pulsates and hurts so much that it makes me choke. Right now, there is no escaping. The sound of Chris's voice tugs me back to reality. I can no longer hide from the raging fire in my brain, the pain that cuts through me like a knife. I am powerless to escape Chris's gaze.

I will do the only thing I can right now. And that is to listen. I hear Chris hesitate, but he doesn't say a word. Right now, he is powerless to speak, and there are no words to console me. After an hour of waiting, Chris finally says something.

"Ah, yes, I need to schedule an appointment for my wife. She just had another seizure."

I am now trapped. Allowing a soft sigh to escape my lips, I close my eyes for a brief moment and contemplate the possibilities.

Chris looks up and nods. "Okay, I will bring her in tomorrow at 8:30 a.m."

I cringe for a moment and walk out of the room, realizing that I need to lay out an outfit for tomorrow.

"Okay, we're all set," he says, turning to me. "I'm taking you to the doctor at 8:30 a.m. tomorrow."

I tug my fingers through my hair, realizing now that I need to write in the diary. "Excuse me for a moment," I say, walking across the hall and into the study. Now, as I open the diary, I hold my head in my hands.

"Oh my God," I sob before bringing my pen to the paper.

Dear Chris,

It is Monday night, and I am sitting here at my diary. Time is of the essence now. I love you, and I thank you for taking care of me. As I write this, I know for certain that I have epilepsy, and I want you to know that you are the most wonderful husband I could ever have asked for.

Your heart is in the right place by taking me to the doctor. I know that someday you will read this and know that you took care of me, that you did everything in your power to keep me well. At the moment, I need to be strong. I need to confide in you about my epilepsy. I need you to know my feelings. I am grateful for your love. And I know that tomorrow, I will be on my way to getting well. I do this for you and for Ben. And I do it for me, for I know that you need me here. I am always grateful for your love. And taking me to the doctor is the greatest expression of your love for me.

Love,
Lilly

It is now midday on Tuesday, and here I stand, holding three pills in my hand. Three pills twice a day will do the trick, or, at least, that's what the doctor says. First, there is Lamictal. As I sit here, examining the flat white tablet, I draw a deep breath.

Then, there's the Valproic Acid. This prescription should also do the trick. Then, there's the Keppra. These three little pills are supposed to take away the convulsions. I will have no more numbness. The pins and needles will go away. The red aura will fade away, becoming a distant memory.

My green eyes are now like emerald crystals, locked intensely on the tablets. As I look at the glass of water beside me, my heart pounds at a pace so rapid that I can barely breathe. I wrap my left hand around the glass. I have to take these pills. I really must take them.

I finally put the first pill in my mouth, and it lingers on my tongue. In my reluctance, I forget to swallow it, and it begins to melt in my mouth. The taste stings my tongue, reminding me that I didn't want to do this in the first place.

My heart is pounding, as I quickly take a sip from the glass, feeling bitterness linger and slide down my throat slowly. I have placed the other two pills on a tray beside me on the floor, and I am slumped over the cup, watching white particles float on the top of the water.

Perhaps I swallowed too slowly. Maybe the medicine won't work. I don't know what to expect at this point. Five minutes pass, and after staring at the tray, I bring myself to pick up another pill and place it in my mouth.

This time, I swallow quickly, and the sensation of the water going down my throat takes me back to visions of my seizures. I gulp deeply. As I gaze at the third pill, I know that my existence on earth is being prolonged. My time on earth is extended because of these pills.

Technically, they are not drugs, according to the drug manufacturers who want to put a tender label on something that's strong enough to alter your brain chemistry. They're prescription medications, but they still interact with the brain. I treasure my brain. It allows me to continue with my writing.

The room is quiet and I am staring aimlessly against the silence of the room. These pills have become my fate, my dependency. And I don't want that. I want freedom from chemicals, freedom from prolonging this misery.

I don't wish to be here in this condition. There is nothing to do here other than to keep Chris and to hold him in my arms. I love him. I love him so much. But there comes a point at which you can no longer hold on. And now, as I hear footsteps, I see Chris's shadow come into view.

And now, I swallow the third pill. I smile, because I know that is the only expression that can disguise my displeasure at the moment. I swallow deeply one last time before I bring myself to speak. As I ponder what I am about to say, he sits down next to me.

"I took the pills, sweetheart. Hopefully these will stop the seizures."

I say this only because I know he will be suspicious if I don't react positively to the pills that could save my life and keep me from falling to the floor in the throes of a violent seizure. I know he wants to comfort me, so I drift back against his chest, as he sits down.

Worry courses through my veins, and I turn, lifting my eyes to meet his gaze. It is soft and loving, and I feel the kindness and warmth that emanates from his face during my most desperate moments. I have seen that look for almost two decades now.

As I look up, his eyes remain steady upon me. He smoothes a hand over my hair and enfolds me in his arms, which, as always, bring me a feeling of safety.

The fading light of this early November evening now creates a sense of comfort within me as I look through the window, taking in the fading sun in the distance and the leaves that crackle against the wind. I can feel his eyes behind me, as I stare forward, unfazed by anything at this moment. I look up at the wall and see a still painting. It is the only constant in the room at this moment. The view outside is a fortress of strength as I stare at it, trying to keep myself from succumbing to the medications that now hold me captive. My walls are crumbling beneath my feet.

Still, the landscape seems to stare back at me, colorful and full, exuding a certain comfort within me. For the moment, it is my companion, even though Chris is sitting beside me. I look at Chris and relive a million memories. And despite the fact that I shouldn't touch the pill bottles until my next dosage, I roll the bottles across the floor, as Chris walks out of the room. I put them in a small box under my side of the bed. I pray that Chris doesn't come back to check on them.

And there they go.

Now, as I climb up on the bed, I dip my finger in the water of my glass as gentle as a bubbling spring. I place a hand softly on my stomach and feel a sudden pang of sadness. I moan softly and close my eyes for a moment, feeling guilty that I put the pills under our bed. I know that when I open my eyes, tears will moisten in my eyes, and I will want to throw the pills away.

My guilt drifts away as I rise to my feet and exit the room, feeling the need to go to Chris. My head is in the palm of my hands as I sniff. I hear him in the kitchen as the sudden clinking of pots and pans meets my ears. Ben is at school, so it is not him making noise, but I do remember Chris saying something about making dinner for the two of us.

Several minutes later, I allow my head to lift out of the palms of my hands and I look up, realizing that it is now fully dark. It has taken several hours for me to get over the shock of being on medicine, but not just any medicine—epilepsy medicine.

Dinner with Chris is amazing, I think to myself, bringing a spoon of tomato soup to my mouth. My eyes linger on him as he digs his fork into a dense piece of chicken. He knows me. He knows my habits and flaws. As these thoughts go through my mind, he looks over at me.

"So you took your medicine?" he asks.

"Yes," I say. "We'll see how it goes."

"Anything has to be better than the way you've been living," Chris says. "The seizures will stop. I did my research on the medications, and they interact with the brain in such a way that—"

I raise my arms before he can finish his sentence.

"I know you're just trying to help me, but I don't care how the chemicals interact with my brain."

"But Lilly! The seizures are painful!"

I can feel my eyes narrowing as I stare back at him. "I know you're trying to help me, but I am not going to keep taking them."

Slowly, he rises to his feet. "Lilly, you have got to stop this."

"I can handle this, Chris. I just can't do this anymore," I cry between tears. "Oh God, this hurts," I cry, cupping my cheeks with my hands.

He turns, seeming at a loss for words.

"I told you," I say, feeling content that I am about to put his worries at ease. "I'm going to be with you forever. I'll keep you forever."

His expression turns soft, and he lowers his left hand slowly to the table.

I can feel another harsh word coming my way, so I brace myself and hold the edge of the table with my trembling hands, hoping and praying it will somehow tame my emotions.

"Lilly, you need to stay here. And the only way that can happen is if you keep taking those pills. If you keep this up," he says, licking his lips. "If you keep this up, you're going to die. You're going to hit your head during a seizure and die from it."

He stares for a moment, and I sit silently, trying to find words that will not send him into a panic. Right now, I find myself unable to formulate words that will soothe him, so I simply reply the best way I can.

"Yeah, I almost died during childbirth."

Slowly, he rises from his seat. "See, that's what I'm talking about," he says, his voice suddenly growing soft.

"You have been on death's door more times than I can count."

"Correction," I say, noting the emotion cracking the lines of his face. "I died a few times."

Now I realize that I have taken it too far. Without a word, he sniffs and wipes a finger across the corner of his right eye. Remorse soaks through me and I tilt my head, hoping he can bring himself to talk to me. I have put him through this many times, yet I keep forgetting how much it hurts him.

Since his eyes are fully dense with tears, I lean forward for a moment in an effort to satisfy my need to comfort him. However, I find that I am changing.

"I have been loved by you and have loved you ever since we were teenagers. I want desperately to keep you with all of my heart," I say. "But Chris, please realize there are some things we simply cannot fight."

He looks up for a long moment, and he breathes slowly, as though he is searching for an answer that will satisfy me. He swallows hard and looks at me softly. "It's okay. I understand."

One week later, I find myself standing at the kitchen sink with soap smothered hands. As I lather a plate with a washcloth, I realize that something feels off. I took my pills last night and felt well for the most part. Though the pins and needles have subsided, I suddenly feel as though something is off. I pause for a moment and look out the kitchen window above the sink.

Suddenly, fear slices through me as my eyes lift to the cabinets above me. I am not the same anymore. Though I am on several prescriptions, the pain on the right side of my head pounds and pulsates to the point that I nearly throw up. However, there is nothing wrong with my brain. There is nothing in there that will keep me from functioning properly. Knowing this, I continue to lather the plate, swallow deeply once again, and wipe sweat from my forehead, all the while gulping against the pain. However, it is just another headache that is most likely caused by stress.

I have had cases of the flu that felt worse than this headache, and still, I pushed through them. This one is no different. I can feel the pain get stronger and stronger as I stand here for a moment. The pain will surely pass. Swallowing hard, I look at the cabinets once again and feel like I am in a state of nothingness.

I am no longer the strong woman I once was, but I continue to press on, living my life as though there is nothing wrong with me. I am lingering in the moment, taking in the soft breeze through the window that I have now opened. I am breathing in the rustic air and enjoying the beauty of my favorite season of all.

I have become a person I never thought I'd be. I am weak and no longer able to do a lot of things I was once able to do. I can't have a sip of wine at night. Alcohol will dilute the seizure medications, making them less effective. And though my seizures are under control, I still feel my muscles tense up from time to time. It's a feeling I can't explain, yet it is always there. It's a feeling that courses through my body, reminding me that a seizure is about to come on.

As soon as the feeling overcomes me, I panic, because I know it is only a matter of minutes before something happens to me.

"Oh my God," I think to myself, suddenly holding a hand to my face. *I forgot to take my pills.*

Now, as the fear begins to subside, my eyes raise. I realize, as I hear the faint sound of music that there is nothing to fear. My feet go numb beneath me. Pins and needles overtake my body.

"Help me, I'm having a seizure!" I scream, feeling a fear so strong that it is nearly killing me. I want to die. I cannot speak. I can barely breathe, and there is no one around me. Chris is at work. Ben is at school, and the only soul around is Molly.

As I fall to the floor, panic sets in, soaking through my being. It continues for several minutes as my body thrashes, and I am utterly helpless. As I drift out of the seizure, I am no longer moaning as I normally do during one of my convulsions. It is over, and I am well again, although my voice is quivery.

Tightness rises within my chest, and reality once again sets in. For the first time in weeks, I forgot to take my medicine. And as I lie here fighting my paralyzing weakness, my eyes trace every line on the ceiling. This is my fault. I hope Chris understands that I didn't do this intentionally. Surely he'll understand. He worries only about my well-being and accepts me for who I am, including my flaws. This thought flies through my mind, as I pull the covers to our bed over me and shiver with fear.

I cannot live my life in fear, I know. That is the worst thing you can do. A life lived in fear is a life wasted. Despite my fatigue, I am still awake, and suddenly a thought rocks me to the core.

Oh my God. I tug the drawer to my night stand open and hurriedly slap the pills on my tongue. Chris would kill me if he hears what happened.

Now, as I sit here writing an entry, I shiver. I told Chris what happened, and though he was upset, he was not angry. He knows I am connected to something that's much different than the world we know on earth.

This morning, we are having a conversation—a very serious one. He sits down next to me at the kitchen table and smoothes his hands over mine.

"Listen, Chris, sweetheart, I love you very much. I know you're worried that I'm going to die and leave you. However, there's something I need to show you. I titled my diary, *Keeping Chris*, and there's a reason I did that."

"What do you mean?"

"Sweetheart," I say, standing up and smoothing a hand over his back. "I love you more than words, and I never want to lose you. I want to keep you forever."

His voice cracks with sadness, and his eyes are suddenly empty, unblinking. "What are you trying to say?"

"I don't want you to think that I am trying to leave you. I don't want you to think that I want to go away."

His whole body is quivering. "Then, what are you saying?"

I kiss his cheek softly and wipe a tear from my eye. "You are my one true love, and we will always be together in some shape or form," I tell him, my voice cracking. "I guess what I'm trying to say is that I don't want to scare you with this death stuff."

His expression softens, and he looks at me in a way he never has before.

I pause for a moment, feeling my eyes struggling to stay open. I am closing them for a moment, struggling to collect my thoughts. "We will always be together. Don't forget that, okay?"

Now, Chris is practically bawling, tears rolling down his face, but he understands what I am trying to tell him. If he weren't standing in front of me right now, I swear I would be crying, too. Staying strong for my husband is not easy, especially when tears hover in the corners of my eyes.

Oh my God. This hurts.

The hard part is that my vision is blurry, making me realize that I could have another seizure at any moment. The blurriness comes at the beginning before the aura.

"Chris," I say. "I have something to tell you, and I'm so sorry I didn't bring it up earlier."

His voice is quivering now. "What's wrong?"

"I had a seizure yesterday, but I'm fine now."

He slides his hands down the sides of his face. "Oh my God, Lilly. Why didn't you tell me?"

I open my mouth, but words seem to elude me at this moment.

"Please don't tell me you took yourself off the meds."

I shake my head, seeing fear crack the lines of his face. "No, I didn't take myself off the medicine. I just forgot to take a dose."

My tear choked voice cracks, as I look at Chris, seeing his blue eyes grow empty. He sees my pain, because I sniff deeply and look at him with my lip quivering. I am powerless before him. He can see straight through me.

This is the hardest conversation I have ever had with Chris. However, it is necessary to talk about such things as being together in life and death. Or is being together even possible?

In life, we are here on earth. In death, we are in a different place. I know that place like the back of my hand. The question is: Does Chris know his place on earth?

That night and several nights thereafter were filled with solace. November is nearly over, and as I sit here at the kitchen table, I am no longer worried that Chris is angry or worried about me. Those thoughts are gone now, but I am not about to let go of my yearning for the purple mountain or the sun brightening in the distance.

Days now pass at rapid speed, but I am not concerned about the future any longer. Right now, my heart is beating strongly, and I find comfort in writing. I find joy in pounding my fingers into the keyboard. I now revel in my own emotions, feeling free, no longer feeling guilty.

Chris is now open to talking about my past experiences, and he leans forward in his chair, intently listening as we talk about my epilepsy and the fact that the medications are working. The seizures are gone, though I am not completely happy about being medicated. Synthetic chemicals hurt the body and the brain. I have thought this for many years, and Ben most likely has a predisposition to cancer. Oh my God. This can't be real. Chris still has cancer. What if he dies? What if I am left in this world without him? People die of cancer every day, and losing Chris would absolutely break Ben's heart. It would break me. Pancreatic cancer grows quickly, and it's in Chris's pancreas. Oh my God. My dear God, why is this happening to me?

But today is a day for making new memories, a day for rediscovering joy and forgetting about the things that have held me back. My heart is once again filled with joy and hope. Hope for the future. Hope for the moment. Hope for all the days ahead. My new outlook on life is exhilarating and exciting, and I find a certain comfort in not knowing what the future holds.

"Time means nothing," I think, looking up at a brilliant blue sky in mid November. As I gaze at Chris, I feel at peace. Today is a new day with new possibilities, new dreams and aspirations.

Chris asked me to dress up in the pink dress I have been moving in and out of my closet for many months now. I have been looking at it with a combination of sadness and joy. Now that our emotional storms are over, I finally see the dress as a symbol of the future. Right now, I am standing on the patio, gazing up at the sky.

Wisps of clouds drift above, and I exhale an elated breath, looking at Chris's long legs and blue shirt. As he stands next to me on the front lawn, his hand drifts into mine. And for the first time in a long time, I feel whole again.

It won't be long before we are speeding down the road on our way to a charming Italian restaurant I have been admiring for a month. The food is good, I hear, and Chris is no longer worried about money now that he is working again.

"You're looking forward to this," he says, standing in the front yard, placing his hands around my hips, and gazing into my eyes with a look of adoration. "God, you're beautiful."

I feel so good that I can barely speak, as a smile curves my mouth. Looking into his eyes, I am lost for several moments, feeling the closeness between us, feeling the warmth of his hands as they slip round me.

I know this may not be the right time to show affection, since our neighbor is raking up leaves. But right here, as Chris's hands drift up to my face, it feels so right. And so, I let go of my reservations, allowing my arms to drift around his flannel shirt. A shiver of desire rises within me, as he slides his arms suggestively around my back.

I gaze at him for several moments, and his eyes remain steady on mine. Licking his lips briefly, he moves toward me ever so slowly and allows his hands to slowly lift to my cheeks. The feel of his lips upon mine takes me back to the last time we made love. His hands seem to move in rhythm with my body as I stand here, enjoying the softness of his touch as his fingers softly trail my jaw line. There is a look of silent longing in his eyes.

"Oh, no," he chuckles, keeping his hands on his face and twisting his head to the left. "I think our neighbor may have caught us in a make-out session."

I chuckle and throw my hair behind my neck.

"Who cares?" I grin, slowly bringing his head back to my lips.

"I've missed this," he says, "I've missed the innocence of our relationship."

I nod, my voice falling nearly to a whisper. "Me too."

At this moment, where we are doesn't matter. His embrace, though innocent, makes me want more. More of his kiss. More of his touch.

"I love you," he says.

"I love you, too."

He ruffles his hands through my hair, stands up straight, and pulls a tendril of my hair toward my cheek.

"It feels good like this," he says, pulling me closer. This time, the kiss is deeper and more meaningful, as his hands hover on my shoulders. I relish his warmth and his touch, as he rubs my head and kisses my mouth in a hungering embrace.

I know it won't be long before we are sitting across from each other at a table in that little Italian restaurant. Time seems to linger as he presses his nose against mine. I need to remain in this place, enjoying his joy and feeling his hands upon me. I look up at him and smile. Our bodies are like mirrors, reflecting one another in a radiant glow of love.

"Now let's get out of here," he says, shuffling my hair forward toward my face and escorting me into the car.

"Sounds good. I was beginning to enjoy myself a little too much."

He chuckles, draws me close, and kisses my mouth once again.

Thirty minutes pass and we now find ourselves seated at a square-shaped table that is covered with a red and white plaid tablecloth. Resting back in my seat against the rising sound of people talking, I struggle to see out the windows. The horizon, reflecting a golden hue against the windows of the restaurant, draws my eyes to the window. I find myself listening to conversations taking place around me.

Because it is National Epilepsy Month, a group of activists is shouting outside of the restaurant. They stand in the street, marching like soldiers.

"It's the worst thing you can experience," I hear a female voice say.

Another woman, whose voice grows louder, screams. "I have epilepsy, and we need to find a cure!"

Another woman is talking about complex partial seizures—a subject that brings forth a lump in my throat and makes my fingers tingle with fear.

Our date was not supposed to feel like this, I realize, and I dismiss the conversation by averting my eyes to a waiter, who strolls quietly by our table.

With a sudden smile curving my lips, I look at Chris and tell him about a local carnival that is coming up in our neighborhood next spring. Anything to change the subject. Anything to draw my thoughts away from the negative. Anything to distract myself from the reality that I have a preexisting condition for which there is no cure.

As we leave the restaurant, I feel as though a sudden weight is lifted from my shoulders. Chris places his hand on my back and holds a finger to my chin, drawing my eyes level with his face.

"You're tense. I see it. Try to relax and have fun."

The only sensation I can experience now is the forceful brisk rush of the late fall air hitting my skin. The wind is cold and whipping, but it brings a sudden comfort to my senses. I breathe deeply and look at Chris.

His black boots crush against the ground, and he looks at me. "This is fun."

I pause for a second and look up at the sky. His hands slide under my shoulders, and I giggle.

The feeling of the season is warm and welcoming, though I have forgotten to bring a coat. I am more worried about being together with Chris than I am about keeping myself shielded from the elements.

"Have you ever made out in the snow?" Chris chuckles and grabs my hand tightly before loosening his grip.

"What?" I laugh briefly, turning to him and watching his lips curve upward.

"Look up," he says, lifting his eyes to the deepening night sky. It has gotten dark quickly, too quickly. And as I lift my eyes, reflecting the soft glow of a street light, I breathe in the chill of the falling snow.

His eyes are suddenly brilliant.

"Oh my God, Chris," I squeal with delight, charging forward down the stairs outside before I pause briefly to examine his face. "It's snowing."

"That it is," he says, once again touching a finger to my chin and lifting my head upward.

We kiss in the moonlight, drifting back and forth against buildings in the city and pause only briefly to let a few locals pass.

"This is fun," I say, drifting away from his mouth and pausing briefly to see the expression in his eyes.

He pushes me forward, and we run through the city, pausing to kiss at regular intervals.

"Do you feel this?" he smiles, tugging my hand forward and kissing it.

"Oh, Chris, this is so much fun."

"How about this? Do you feel this?" he smiles, as he drifts quickly toward me. Suddenly, his hands descend to my chest and then lower. He touches my hands, gripping them suggestively, before lacing his fingers with mine. He leans forward, with his arms around me before backing away quickly, and bringing his body back to mine. As his hands travel over me, we drift back against a stone wall.

Chris's hands are like mysterious mitts, stretching over my clothes and sending a sudden thrill through my skin. His hands are the warmth that shelters me from the cold, as our mouths connect, and snow melts into our clothes.

Now, pausing and locking one another in a gaze that is both sultry and soothing, we drift back into an alcove in the western corner of the city. Holding one another by the shoulders, we stare at each other until Chris yanks his hands away. As he lets go of my hands, he drifts back into the dark corner and leads me to a bench that is illuminated only by a streetlight. I look up and see that we are alone in the pale moonlight.

As he touches a hand to my upper leg, I feel a sudden thrill. "We shouldn't do this in public."

"Let it go, baby. Let it go."

As his hands roam over me at a faster speed and he kisses my neck, he holds me on the bench, reaching for the delicate lace collar at the top of my shirt. He pauses for a moment, still standing, and his eyes radiate a sensuality that slowly beckons me toward him. It feels as though we are kissing for the first time, as he drifts forward and trails his fingers over the waistband to my skirt.

I shouldn't be doing this. I shouldn't be doing this, but it feels so … good.

He looks back and scans the area, gazing at streetlights and people revving engines in the distance. The noise of the world seems to have disappeared, and we are left only with one another. As the snow continues to fall, Chris smiles and looks at me, confirming my suspicions that no one is around. Feeling the eagerness in his warm and roaming hands, I drift back in silent surrender.

"We've never done this before, not in public," he says, his fingers descending, as he lowers to my leg, and I feel the warmth of his arousal under my skirt. Inching upward against the moist warmth awaiting him, his hands hold my hips, steady and strong.

No longer restrained by his boxers and covered by nearly full darkness, Chris lifts forward under the crease between my leg and the lace panties beneath. The panties are a temporary obstruction, I realize, as his fingers peel away the layered fabric, exposing a delicate space that yearns to hold him within. He keeps his shirt on and stretches forward onto my body.

Oh my God. The words that come so natural to me at home are barely audible as he shields my now exposed bra, which he quickly peels away with warm and eager hands. Releasing himself from his boxers, Chris draws nearer and allows his body to take over mine. His mouth envelops the delicate mounds of my chest, and his teeth nip reluctantly at my chest.

I can feel every sensation rising as his hands remain upon me. The night is growing darker now, and we cannot be seen by anyone. The streetlight that illuminated us is now dimmed, covered only by thick mounds of snow that continue to crystallize around it.

Every touch and every stroke is magnified a thousand times in the silence of the city. His touch is almost poetic, as his hands travel over me. He softly and effortlessly takes me into a place where nothing else matters. His hands toy with my senses. And as my eyes rise, realizing that no one is around, I draw him closer. The motions of his hands grow stronger, and I feel a forbidden thrill within my body, as he grabs eagerly for my supple breasts and allows his fingers to trail every corner of my flesh.

He tugs my body into him in the darkness, and I feel the warmth of his shirt, which he promptly unbuttons, bringing his chest to mine. As he draws my naked body toward him, my eyes rise, and I suddenly let go of my every worry. My body once again loses control against him, and our bodies melt together as smooth as silk. His touch is soft at first but grows more intense with every stroke of the masculinity of his thighs. He is moist within me, and he brings his lips to mine. An intense culmination of sensation takes over my body, and I feel his moisture within me. Together, we collapse upon one another.

Now exhausted, I allow my head to drift to his chest, as I kiss him deeply. His eyes rise to meet mine, and he wipes his moist forehead. The snow continues to fall in the wake of our passion. And as I look up, taking in the crispness of the snow, I smile.

"Oh, Lilly, I want to do this to you forever."

I look at him but can't find the words to speak. "I know, sweetheart. I want to do it to you forever, too, but I don't know if that's possible."

After slipping back into our clothes, we walk away with an air of nonchalance. All that is left behind us is the falling snow that promptly covers up our sweat on the bench. Despite the cold air, our bodies are warm with the afterglow of passion. Slowly, we disappear behind a nearby building and slip into the car.

"Do you believe we just did that, Lilly?" he says, rolling the keys over in his hands before drawing my head into the palms of his hands.

"No," I grin and giggle, "but I wouldn't mind doing it again."

"It's funny how things change," he cracks. "I once called you a prude. Now you're doing it on park benches."

I chuckle and throw my head back, knowing in my heart of hearts that this is the love I have forever craved. This is the love I have wanted all my life. And here Chris is, holding my hand and making me realize once again that I love him more than I could ever explain.

Chapter Eleven

Remembering

Now, several days later, I find myself breathing deeply, just as I had for the past eight hours.

It's now 8 a.m. on Saturday morning, and I can no longer keep my eyes open. The night before had been a nothing short of a nightmare, as I lay awake listening to the sounds of the night. I was sleepy, really sleepy, and I swear I felt my eyes dip several times. But instead of allowing my eyelids to flutter closed and rest in silent slumber, I kept them open. That was when the seizure happened. It went quickly, and I was fine seconds later.

The image of Chris and me making passionate love in public kept running through my mind that night, and I wished for a moment that I could be there again. The feeling of him upon me was exhilarating and magical, and I wanted to revel in every memory of it, remembering his lips upon me and feeling his touch.

Despite my desire to close my eyes for just a few hours, I am promptly rocked awake by the sound of the heater turning on in the living room. I want to savor the warmth of the moment with my eyes closed, but keeping my eyes closed means that I would miss out on another few hours of life. And those hours are growing far too precious now.

As I prop myself up on my elbows, examining the end table beside me, I pause for a moment.

Where is Chris? And why isn't he lying next to me? It is Saturday morning, I think to myself before grunting and rolling back over. The comforter is dense, as I breathe against it and attempt to lose myself in another hour of blissful sleep.

Despite my best efforts to sleep for at least a little while, my thoughts about Chris cause my eyes to slide open.

Oh my God. Where is he?

Rising slowly and struggling to figure out where he has gone, I walk to the top of the steps and look down at the living room.

It isn't a holiday, and it isn't a weekday, so where is Chris? Is Ben still in bed? These thoughts envelop me, as I walk down the steps in my pajamas and some mint green slippers.

Though the living room is brightly lit, it feels as though I am calling for someone in the dark.

"Chris?" I yell, scanning the living room below. "Where are you, sweetheart?"

When he doesn't reply, fear rises in my chest, and my eyes dart against the soft light of morning. Though our bedroom is still dark, the morning is bright and alive.

"Chris?" I repeat, this time walking into the living room and then into the kitchen. Chris is sitting at the kitchen table, dead asleep. Next to him there is a bowl of pancake batter with a spoon floating in the bowl.

I chuckle for a moment and tilt my head, realizing that he had fallen asleep while attempting to make breakfast. He is snoring loudly, with his hair in some pancake batter on the table. Restraint eludes me at the moment, and I burst out laughing, as his eyes slide open. His eyes rise slowly, and he looks up.

"Hi there, sweetie," he says, lifting groggily and struggling to greet me with a kiss.

"Wow," I say, chuckling with a soft smile. "Breakfast really agrees with you, huh?"

"I guess so," he says groggily before lowering his head back to the table.

The sun is lower in the sky this morning. My eyes flutter, and a strange feeling of sadness seems to overtake me as I gaze at Chris. I don't know whether it is the lack of sleep or the headaches that is making me emotional. But here, as I look at Chris, I see him holding my hand when we were teenagers, and I see him grabbing my arms before throwing me into the pool.

These memories are so vivid and so reminiscent as I look at him. Something is going to change. I can feel it in my heart as I look at Chris. These thoughts draw my eyes back to the window, and I stare out. I want to say something, but I cannot bring myself to tell Chris what I am feeling right now. Something is going to change. Something is about to be taken away. A life is going to change. What's going to happen remains a mystery at this moment. But as I stare up, looking at the bright sun, I know that this is it.

Chris looks at me with a confused look. He tilts his head as he looked at me. "Are you okay?"

"Yeah, just thinking."

The truth is that emotion is about to burst forth from my eyes, as tear droplets hover at the corners of my eyes. I close my eyes momentarily, walk off, and go upstairs. So here I am, standing in our bedroom above the desk in the darkness. Sadness tugs at my throat, but as my eyes lift, the moment feels magical.

I pick up my diary and look at the cover for several minutes, taking in its beauty, taking in the memories. And I realize, while sitting at the desk, that another diary entry is needed. Writing diary entries seems to be my way of living now. I feel a sudden warmth and magic in my soul as I pick up my pen, breathe deeply, and begin to write.

Dear Chris,

I'm not sure if you remember this, but here is a story that you need to hear. It was late September of 2000, and we found ourselves standing on top of a mountain in the Blue Ridge Mountains. We looked out from a mountain top that was surrounded by bright orange, red, and yellow leaves that soared on the beautiful southwestern winds. After making our way across the country and finally landing in Virginia, we climbed to the top of that mountain. It was one I had longed to see since I was a kid.

As we climbed slowly and, cautiously, your arms were steady around my hips, and you made sure that I didn't fall. Your mitten cloaked hands were soft upon me, as we chased the sky and weaved between the trees.

Our clothes sailed on a steady wind, and you put me on your shoulders. It was one of the most terrifying days of my life, given the fact that I could have gone straight down the mountain. But you turned that day into something beautiful by showing me something that I will remember for the rest of my days. As we gazed out, the trees were beautiful. Standing side by side in rows, the trees reflected our stance together. We stood there, side by side, taking in the brisk autumn air.

Finally, as you brought your mouth to mine, I was no longer afraid of heights. Honestly, I could have fallen without a care. With you by my side, I am whole. I am everything I am meant to be with you.

I often think back on that day. We slept on the mountain that night, and I still dream about that day. All the days in between have been just as special. The only difference now is that our love grows deeper and more beautiful with every passing day.

Remember this as you close your eyes tonight. And now that I am resting quietly beside you, I close my eyes in the peaceful space I call my home. In the morning, I will look for you, as your eyes open in my presence.

Love you always,
Lilly

As I finish the entry, I close the diary, just as I do every night I remember to write in it.

I can't believe I almost lost Chris several times. I look at his eyes shut tightly, and I feel myself shiver. I'm not sick. The CAT scan is proof that there is nothing wrong with me.

I feel a terrible headache coming on. I hold my hand to my head for several seconds and close my eyes, cringing against the pain. It is my habit to hold my head as it pounds and open my eyes several seconds later. That's when the pain begins to subside. Time seems to move in slow motion as I lower my hand from my head and attempt to drift into sleep.

Eight hours later, I find myself sitting in the living room after the doorbell rings. I rise sluggishly from my seat and rub my eyes. "Who on God's green earth would be at my door at 8 in the morning?"

The figure of the person standing outside the door comes into view, and I realize that the figure is that of a man I recognize well. The expression on his face is cool and calculating, disconnected.

Ben comes bouncing down the stairs and pauses to look out the window briefly. Even he seems rattled by him. I sit here thinking, examining the lines of the man's face. And suddenly, it dawns on me. It is the cab driver who used to drive me to the hospital.

I struggle to recall his name, but he speaks before I am able to remember. He knocks on the window, and his head twists around the window. "Ma'am?

Was his name Walter? Joe perhaps? I can't remember his name. All I know is that he is standing at my door, and I can't bring myself to face him. He rings the bell once again, and I feel my jaw clench, knowing that I must face him again. I tug open the door and stare in silence, feeling my gaze as though it's crackling into ice.

"Hi ma'am. It's me again. I'm here to take you to your doctor. I hear it's nothing to worry about. That's what the guy who called me said."

"What? You can't be serious. It's 8 in the morning. Who set up a doctor's appointment for me?"

He scratches his head and stares for a moment before speaking. "Some guy—said he was a scientist. I don't know. I'm short on time," he says, looking at his watch. "Get in the car."

And there he is. Ralph, the cab driver. The angry, judgmental, cynical cab driver I tried to get away from. I feel my throat closing as I look at him.

There is a sudden distance in his eyes as he looks at me. "Besides, you're sick now, right?" he asks.

I can't bring myself to speak, so I manage a slow nod. "Um, what did the scientist tell you exactly?"

"Like I said, ma'am, the clock's a ticking. Let's go."

I slink into the cab and pull the door closed. A slow burn rages through me, and I look out the window. The ride reminds me of the mornings when I took the cab to see Chris in the hospital.

I'm gonna kill him, I think, as my eyes rise once again against the streetlights. *Why would he do this to me without consulting me first?*

The thought soaks through me, choking my throat with tears. I pick up my cell phone, infuriated. Chris picks up almost immediately. His voice is bouncy and positive, as it usually is.

I draw a deep breath and close my eyes before speaking. "What ... did ... you ... do?"

There is a long pause, and I worry for a moment that he will not speak. His voice is inaudible. "Uh, I don't know."

"I'm sitting here in a taxi with a cab driver I literally can't stand. You scheduled an appointment with Nelson?"

He sounds confused and his voice quivers. I have no idea what is going on at the other end of the line, but he is calm, too calm.

"You need to go see Dr. Nelson. I saw you holding your head again last night."

I am not in the mood to argue, so I sink back against the seat and close my eyes. Of course, there is no point in fighting. Chris has seen me. I can no longer deny the fact that I have to go back to the hospital.

I suddenly speak slowly and close my eyes. "Oh—okay."

There is no point in arguing, especially when the evidence is there. *But,* I think, closing my eyes. *But when did he see me?*

His voice grows tenser, and I realize that I should stop talking. As I click off the phone, I shove it down on my lap and look up slowly.

The next thing I know, I am standing in Dr. Nelson's office, waiting for Chris to arrive. The hospital is out of the way and situated in between two other medical buildings. I know the place all too well. I know the directions, and I know the pain I feel every time I enter the lobby.

Fifteen minutes later, I am called back into an exam room. I wonder how Chris could be so deceptive. As I stand in the office and look at a bright blue gown, I sit up straight in my chair. My eyes glide over every surface, every diagram on the wall, and the stethoscope sitting on the doctor's desk.

The door creaks open slowly, and I look up. It is Chris. His eyes dart, and he fidgets with his sleeve, obviously attempting to avoid my eyes. His eyes radiate a fear I have never seen in him before. He avoids my face by averting his eyes and sits down slowly in a chair directly across from me.

The smell of the room is medicinal, and I once again close my eyes for several moments, feeling betrayed. For several minutes, Chris just looks at me. I understand why he called the doctor, but it infuriates me that he didn't tell me about it.

Exhaling a heavy breath, Chris shakes his head, as though he is trying to distract himself. His eyes rise slowly, and he suddenly seems distracted.

"I'm worried, Lilly. I'm worried about your health."

I can barely bring myself to speak, so I look up, torn somewhere between anger and sadness. "No," I say. "You're worried about yourself. You're worried about keeping me here."

He simply stares. "Lilly—"

I hold up a hand to silence him. "Why didn't you tell me you saw me the other night? And more importantly, why did you get that cab driver to drive me to this place?"

"I knew you'd get upset with me and refuse to go."

His blue eyes grow suddenly mellow, and I realize that I shouldn't get defensive. "Boy, you really do know me, don't you?"

"Yeah," he says, staring forward.

"But that doesn't mean I'm not mad at you," I say.

This time, I don't look away. Instead, my eyes remain locked on him. Perhaps I have been too hard on him. Realizing this, I smile, seeing the compassion in his eyes. He has my best interest at heart.

"Baby, I love you."

His head tilts, and his arms rise, beckoning me forward.

My good sense seems to elude me, so I do what I do so instinctively. I leap from my chair, get on Chris's lap, and kiss him hungrily. Our heads sway, and for a moment, I forget that I am in a doctor's office. As I drift away from his mouth, I let go of my anger and look deeply into his eyes.

"I'm not mad at you anymore," I say, putting my hands on his cheeks.

As soon as I return to my chair, there is a knock on the door. Now, a voice comes through the wall. The voice is distinctly female. I look up, feeling a sudden comfort.

A tall woman with blonde hair and light brown eyes strides in and sits down in Dr. Nelson's chair. At first, her form is blurry. As I look up, I see the soft smile, the warm gaze, and the gentle hands that brought me comfort a few weeks ago. It is Dr. Smyth. She looks the same, but her eyes appear more intense than they did the last time I saw her.

She sits down and pauses for a moment, examining my face. "I hear you had another seizure."

I nod, and the sides of my lips begin to quiver. I don't want her to see me this way. I'm supposed to be strong.

"I don't mean to scare you at all, Mrs. Rylan, but I think we need to take a more thorough look at your condition."

A heater above my head turns on, and I look up, hoping desperately that it will take away my fear. I tense up and wrap a lock of hair around my finger. However, I should not be scared.

"You passed out a few weeks ago," she says before looking away and typing something on her computer.

Like all the other neurologists, she holds a finger in front of my eyes and asks me to follow it. The next thing she asks me to do seems a bit strange. "Touch a finger to my nose," she says, her eyes growing intense, more focused.

Though I feel self conscious, I oblige and bring my finger to her nose.

"You're nervous," she says, her hair falling upon her shoulders and slowly sliding behind her back. "There's no need to be afraid."

No need to be afraid? What is she talking about? Here I am sitting in a doctor's office and being asked to follow her finger with my eyes.

"Where is … where is Dr. Nelson?" I ask. I stare for several moments and once again realize from the soft look on her face that she is a compassionate soul. They're a rare find these days.

"I'm not sick, am I?" I ask, looking at her and feeling a sudden comfort in her presence.

"I see a lot of patients," she says, "some with bad problems and some with just minor issues. You're in good hands with us, trust me."

I manage a smile, but feel fear soak through me. "Okay."

"Dr. Nelson will be with you in a few minutes."

She pats my shoulder and walks away as I lift my eyes, suddenly terrified. I look at the entire room, feeling as though I am frozen in time. And though I should be nervous, I return to Chris and kiss him.

Dr. Nelson walks in the room 10 minutes later and looks at me kindly.

A week has passed since I had my scans, and the results are still fresh in my mind. No abnormal arteries. No malformations. I am good, as fit as a fiddle. I am in once again for a follow up. Like all the other times I have come to Dr. Nelson's office, my eyes glide over every picture, diagram, and doctor's instrument.

My eyes are suddenly drawn to the door, and I fidget the collar to my shirt. I think I hear a doctor in the hallway talking about brain aneurysms, and my head jerks quickly to look through the door. I catch a glimpse of several doctors, as they stride slowly through the hallway. I take everything in, including the clunk of an MRI two rooms away.

I feel sorry for the poor soul in that contraption at the moment.

"So Mrs. Rylan," Dr. Nelson smiles, as he strides in. "I see that you're in for a follow-up. Let's have a look."

I breathe in. "Okay."

"You're not passing out anymore, are you?" he asks, while swirling a light in front of my eyes.

"No."

It is now an hour later, and I am being pulled out of my second MRI. I hope it will be my last. I don't like the sound of the machine, and I hate being confined inside a metal tube.

Being here in the hospital makes me feel like I am going to die. Now, as we walk through the lobby, I pause and draw a deep breath.

"I don't like that thing, you know?" I say as Chris and I continue forward to the car. As we stand by the car, I linger in this moment, feeling cold air against my skin. "That's all I can take of these tests."

Chris's mouth twists in confusion, and he shuffles restlessly into the car. "Why do you look so happy?"

"I'm happy because I'm not sick."

"Lilly," he says, his face radiating a fear I have never seen before. "We won't get the results back for a month and a half!"

I look at him but don't say a word. "This is too much for me to deal with. I can't take this whole back and forth drama. You say I'm sick, but I am well. The first scan told the truth."

He doesn't say a word. Instead, he just stands there, staring silently. Chris has read about seizures in his office and wrote a few scholarly papers on the subject.

I spin around, and a chilled wind slips under the collar to my coat. In my haste, I look up at the hospital and draw a deep breath. My clothes are now loose against my body, and I pull my jacket tight against my chest. I failed to eat breakfast this morning and the morning before that. The urge to eat eludes me these days.

The rage that has been bubbling within me in recent weeks dissipates, and his silence makes me wonder if I should speak. "Can we stop and get something to eat on the way home? I didn't eat breakfast this morning."

He turns. "What? You didn't eat breakfast?"

"No," I say haltingly and bring a hand to my stomach. "A certain cab driver pulled up before I had the chance."

"I'm sorry," he says as his eyes drift away.

I shake my head, realizing for the first time that I am not the victim.

"No, I'm the one who should be sorry. You're trying to help me, and I'm acting like a baby about these tests."

I look at his softening expression and realize that no words are needed to convey our emotions. The car is still parked and I am quiet.

He unfastens his seat belt and reaches for the sides of my face. His lips meet mine, but I don't give him an open mouth kiss as I normally do. Instead, I let my lips drift into his softly. Now I drift back into my seat, my eyes trembling as he fidgets in his seat.

"You've never seen doctors like this before," he says.

I slowly bring my eyes to meet his.

I am stupid, I think to myself. I should have gone to see doctors long before life came to this. Now I spend my days fighting headaches and trying to avoid seizures.

Chris sits for several moments and stares at me, as though he is awaiting forgiveness. I have spent so much time caring for other people, taking their temperatures, making sure they live, and making sure they have food in their stomachs.

Little did I realize that my family needs me far more than I could have ever imagined. I am a crazy woman. I am crazy in love. I am crazy about my destiny. However, my fascination is not entirely with the physical state of my body.

This is why, 14 hours later, I find myself standing above the diary. My entry for the night is long overdue.

My dearest Chris,

I have forever appreciated the beauty of life and the precious value of our time together. As I sit here writing tonight, I reflect upon a day filled with drama, but a day that was also filled with love—love that will endure long after our existence in this world.

Today, as we sat in Dr. Nelson's office, I felt the need to hold you and be part of you. We will always be a part of one another. So many nights, I lay awake, watching you and wondering where the next morning will take us. I am not so much a realist, but instead a romantic, as you well know. I live my life for you and Ben alone. Today, as you sat across from me in Dr. Nelson's office, I was not angry at you. What you did today was simply a reflection of your unending love for me.

I'm sorry I got so mad at you for scheduling an appointment with Dr. Nelson. I should have appreciated your gesture. I have grown much older since the moment we met. I have learned more about myself, including the fact that I love you beyond words. I'm stubborn at times, and I know I drive you crazy.

I want to thank you for sitting on the side of our bed and for watching me, as I hold my head in my hands. There is no greater love than the love of a husband like you. I honestly don't know how I could live without you.

I know that there are many times that I overreact, and I feel guilty about it. Just please understand that there are other forces at work in my life. There are things you will never understand and things that can only be seen through my eyes. Someday, when the time is right, I'll tell you what they are. Until then, remember that I love you.

As always with love,
Lilly

I close the diary reluctantly and stare at its cover. Perhaps Chris will read it to himself someday. For now, it is my memory, my diary, and the second greatest possession I could ever own. Chris doesn't know it, but I have been his eternal companion from the beginning. And some things never end.

I document our little conversations and our physical encounters in my diary. I am a passionate soul with passionate thoughts. I have a desire to experience everything in life to the fullest extent. I want to hold Chris's hand forever.

Suddenly, pain envelops my head, and I choke, struggling to keep my breath. Everything becomes a blur in front of my eyes. And right now, it feels like it is time for me to go once again.

I try to close my eyes tight and drift away for a moment, just a few minutes to take away the pain. I want to drift away to that purple mountain and see how it feels once more before I return to Chris for the rest of my life. We have chased many rainbows together over the years. They were wonderful. The days are getting shorter. Is the autumn of my life only a breath away?

I look up and realize that not only Chris is looking at me. Someone else reaches out to me from a distance. Her hair as blond like silk, and she holds out her hand to welcome me. Her image is beautiful and pure, unlike anything you see here on earth. My eyes connect with hers. When she sees that I don't reach out, she simply smiles and waves warmly. I know I am here, and it is currently late November. The question is—where will the seasons of my life end, and where exactly did they begin?

As these thoughts slip in and out of my mind, I open my eyes wider. Everything is fuzzy, and my eyes are quickly drawn toward the sound of Chris's voice.

"Where am I?" I ask, looking up at the walls in our bedroom and once again feeling our soft, dense comforter against my skin.

"You're at home, sweetheart," Chris says, grabbing my hand. "Lilly, you passed out again for a few hours."

I lift my head and throw it back down onto the pillow. "Does seeing eternity classify as passing out?"

He tilts his head, seeming confused.

"What's today's date, sweetie?" he asks, stroking my hair.

I know I was born in April, but today's date eludes me at the moment. As I look up, taking in the smell of the room, I feel a sudden tug at my nose. I have been breathing. But I am weak. I don't think I will ever be the same as I once was. The strength and vitality of my youth are still here, but the will to carry out my mission to keep fighting is getting harder. However, I will try to be strong and to be the wife I promised to be long ago.

I stare for a moment and feel a sudden throbbing on my head. I look up and shudder. Now, as I look away, the pain promptly subsides.

"What's this?" I ask, grabbing for a tube that is stuffed up my nose.

Silence suddenly pervades the room, and my eyes lift to find a husky man holding a bag filled with fluid.

"You're getting fluids, Lilly. I have to take care of you. You took care of me, remember?"

"I'm not the woman I used to be," I say.

"What do you mean?" Chris asks, while smoothing a thumb over the top of my hand.

"I'm tired."

Several days later, as darkness descends upon the world, I wake up, feeling fully revived. The streets outside are quiet now, and Molly is curled up in a ball beside me. She blinks her eyes a few times and licks her teeth.

"You're a good girl," I coo, smoothing a hand over her head and smiling. She promptly jumps to the side of the bed and wags her tail. They say that dogs have intuition, and I wonder if Molly can see the future. Her eyes are slightly distant as she gazes at me, and she appears worried. Her brown eyes are locked upon me and trembling slightly.

"You know, don't you, Molly? You know something's wrong," I say as soon as Chris leaves the room.

Now, as I hold a hand to my head, Chris comes back and looks at me with a face full of concern. I do not say a word, however. I will not let Chris see what I see.

"You're not hiding something from me, are you?"

"No. I told you the truth. I saw the purple mountain."

"Lilly, you remember what caused you to see the purple mountain last time?"

My eyes lift. "Yes. It was amazing."

His face grows pale, and the redness in his eyes reminds me that I should not speak. So I stand here, staring. His fingers tremble, as he brings his hands to my face. "You're not feeling well," he says, turning away slowly.

I shake my head slowly. "Chris, you have no idea how hard this is for me. But somehow we're gonna make it in this world."

"What?"

He turns, his eyes drifting away slowly. He doesn't know what to say. I can see it. He is trusting, too trusting. But he needs reassurance, and I need to show him how wonderful it is to be together before I find it hard to speak.

"It's okay to be afraid, Chris. I'm scared, too. But for now, we need to dance and fight through this together."

"Something's going on. You're shaking," he says, pointing toward my trembling hands.

I look at him for a moment, but I don't try to console him. Instead, my eyes drift away, landing on a delicate lace doily on the end table. "We will always be together somehow."

He draws closer, wrapping his arms around me tightly. "I can't lose you. You keep me happy," he says. "I will do whatever it takes to make you happy and keep you by my side."

I look at him softly. "Everything happens for a reason. I am by your side. I have been by your side for 19 years."

"And you're going to die with me," he says lowly with his eyes locked upon me.

I close my eyes for a long moment, and he does not say a word. His worry appears to have subsided, and I feel relieved. Never in my life have I seen Chris this calm about something so significant, something so life changing.

"Lilly, I am a scientist, and never in my life did I imagine that medical science would not be able to cure you. I know that you feel like you're going away, but there's a reason that you're here with me." He sniffs, and his eyes linger on me, pleading. He runs a tissue under his nose, and his eyes rise slowly. And they tremble against the silence, as though he's awaiting an answer.

"I don't know exactly how to say this, but there have been many people in my life who have given me strength," I say, feeling suddenly drawn to him, yet somehow disconnected. "I think I need to talk to one of those people. I'm sure she's still around, but I don't know if she'd have time for me."

"Who?"

"Susan."

"Really, you think she can help you help with your epilepsy?"

My urge to drift away is replaced with a desire to hold him. "Well," I say, feeling sadness tug at my throat. "I am taking my meds, and they seem to be working. I have been seizure free for several days now, so I think all is well."

My heart swells with adoration, and I find it hard to continue speaking. "So Chris, I need you to hold tight while I make some calls. You can't give up on me, and I can't give up on you either. We're going to make it in this world. We're going to make it together."

"Really?"

I kiss his hand and wipe a tear from my eye. "Yes. I promise."

He drifts forward and presses his mouth to mine.

Now, while looking at him sadly and running my fingers over the top of the phone, I bring myself to speak once again. "I'm going to call Susan now. I can't expect a miracle to happen, but you never know."

I grab for the phone, rub Chris's shoulder, and am instinctively filled with emotion. I blink my eyes slowly. Now, I turn the phone over in my hand and watch the buttons light up with green. As my eyes linger there, I realize that I have to keep my promise. Tears choke my windpipe.

"You're beautiful, Lilly, in more ways than you can imagine."

I press my fingers into the buttons on the phone and recall Susan's nurse's station phone number by memory. It has been a while since I last dialed her in a lucid frame of mind. My fingers tremble against the phone, and for the first time in a long time, I am filled with hope.

I breathe in as though I have breathed for the first time. Her phone rings, and a female voice promptly answers. My eyes dart at a speed so rapid that it feels unnatural, as time is of the essence. My heart pounds within my chest, its haphazard rhythm causing my breath to quicken. I pause as a nurse picks up and hesitates against my silence.

"Can I speak to Susan?" I ask.

The voice doesn't answer immediately, but instead pauses, and I hear the reminiscent beep of heart machines in the background. This woman's voice sounds vaguely familiar, although I don't think I ever met her directly.

"She's with a patient right now. Can I have her call you back?"

Panic rises within me, and I respond simply. "Sure."

This is not the first time I've been put off by nurses. But Susan? Susan is different. Not once has she ever failed me. She is my friend in many ways. I don't know if she can help me with my condition. I am trusting. I am faithful. She is the nurse who gave me hope, a friend whose voice brought me comfort in my darkest moments. I will get hold of her somehow.

But this moment has me frozen in time. I feel my spirit weakening as I hang up the phone, but I am not about to give up. This can't wait. I can't sit here and wait for help when a call back is not promised. Right now, time is wasting away, and I can't wait for a miracle to take place. I must take matters into my own hands.

Chris looks at me, and I lick my lips. My heart descends into the pit of my stomach.

"She's not there?"

I shake my head and stare, my eyes unblinking. "No."

His eyes trail away silently, but I can't offer him hope, as hope is not tangible at this moment. I will not die on someone else's watch. I will determine my own destiny. I always have, and I always will. I am a determined soul, a stallion pounding its hooves into dense sand, never sinking lower, never slowing down.

I continue to hold the phone in my hand, and, despite my best efforts to maintain composure, I place it down on the floor. As I ponder my destiny, the soft light of midday shines on the carpet in our room. I have been standing here for far too long.

I look at Chris, but he is silent. I watch him sink down in a cushioned chair on the other side of our room, and his presence takes me back to a time when we didn't have a care in the world. He is motionless in the chair and his face lacks emotion. I stand in silence, my body mirroring his. I want to tell him that everything will be okay. Drawing a shaky breath, I stand up straight and look him in the eye.

"I'm going to the hospital. I'm going to track down Susan."

These words conjure up a certain hope in me, and I straighten my back before heading down the stairs. I feel time slipping away as I walk. My heart pounds as time ticks away. My eyes are frozen on the parking pad out front. With my heart practically in my throat, I race forward, grab my keys, and go out the door. The engine powers up slowly, as is often the case. I look at the house and plead with God for the millionth time that my prayer will be answered.

My head slips into the palms of my hands, and I look up, feeling hot tears slide down my cheeks. And then I scream out. *Why? Why is this happening to me?* My head falls back against the headrest.

Why is this happening to me? I have sacrificed everything, everything. I have sacrificed everything to be on this earth.

As I lower my hands, I breathe deeply, feeling my voice echo against the windows of my car. I really shouldn't be driving with epilepsy. I shouldn't put myself at risk again. But this is a mission that I must carry out, not for me, but for the ones I love. Chris and Ben are the two most wonderful people I could ever ask for.

As I stare at the road before me, my cell phone rings, and Chris's voice pounds through. He sounds terrified. "I heard a scream outside. Are you okay?"

I hate to lie. I really do. But I can't tell Chris the truth about my emotions. Tomorrow is his birthday, and I can't burden him with the pain I feel right now. Maybe Susan is at the hospital. I can't be sure.

I exhale and keep my eyes on the road, speeding against the dense Seattle wind. Finally, as I reach the hospital's entrance, I smile.

Upon entering the oncology floor, a familiar face stands before me. From the sight of the tall stature to the dense brown hair and chocolate brown eyes, it is clear that I am standing before Susan. She pauses and looks at me, and her eyebrows flex with worry.

"Mrs. Rylan. I'm so sorry I haven't called you. Things have gotten really hectic, and we have a lot of people in the rooms right now," she says, glancing behind her. Her eyes seem to plead, as I look at her. Perhaps she knows something. I smile at her, my eyes lingering on her face, and I feel a sudden calm.

"What's wrong?" she asks, glancing briefly behind her.

"I need to talk to you."

Susan knows me. She knows me in a way that few women ever have. Though I am usually articulate, I can barely bring myself to speak. "I have epilepsy, and Chris thinks I'm going to die from it."

Her expression softens, and she appears more concerned than I have ever seen her before.

"You feel it," she says before looking away for a moment. Her eyes return to me after several seconds. "You felt the wind and saw the bright sun."

I nod.

She walks over and places a hand on my shoulder. "Mrs. Rylan, you don't know how many patients I've met who have nearly died. Many of them have told me about the sun and the colors, the rainbow."

I stare in amazement. In my mind's eye, I am suddenly transported back to that place. "But how do you? How do you know?"

"I see it, honey. I see it in your eyes. You wouldn't believe how many patients try to dismiss it and say it's a figment of the imagination or a hallucination of the brain."

"I know. It is wonderful, but what about the epilepsy? Can they do anything?"

She pauses. "You had the scans, right?"

"I did."

"And you're on meds?"

I nod. "Yes. I take Lamictal, Keppra and Valproic acid. I hate it, Susan, I really do."

"You're doing what you should to keep everything under control," she says, looking at me and shuffling some papers in her hands.

"I know you love Chris. He needs you, but I can't tell you what to do. Whether or not you take your meds is up to you."

I look at her softly and look away, hoping she doesn't question me further. "He wants me to tell him that everything will be okay."

She turns, her gaze frozen, as though it is cracking into ice.

"I'm not saying that you should stop taking the meds. Just think about your husband. Your heart will tell you what you need to do."

"But … but is there some type of cure?"

Her silence is telling. She looks around the lobby, steps forward, and touches my shoulder once again.

"Come to my office."

I follow her to the third floor and sit down in the chair across from her desk. The smell of the room is eerily familiar. As she sits down, I look behind me and see people scurrying through the hallway.

"Unfortunately, there is no cure, but you need to take your meds for him, for Chris."

I can feel my voice getting louder, but I can't help it. "It's just so hard, because he wants me to be with him forever. And I know … I know that that's not possible, no matter how hard I try."

I swallow and stare forward.

"It's okay, Mrs. Rylan."

"It's Lilly. You know me. Call me Lilly."

"Lilly, look at Chris. Look at your son. Look at all the wonderful things you have in this world," she says.

She stands up and walks around her desk. Now placing her hand on the side of her desk, where a pen lay, she looks at me.

"The scans didn't find anything?"

I shake my head, smooth a hand over my hair, and continue to fight my quivering lip. "There was nothing there."

She turns her head toward me. "You know what you have to do."

I nod, knowing that her advice goes against all of my desires right now. I want to be with Chris, but I long for that bright sun. However, I can't let Susan see that.

"I know. I have to live, and I will live for him."

She pauses and scans a paper on her desk.

"But Lilly, don't ever feel guilty for wanting otherwise. It's a gift you've been given. Someday Chris will understand."

"Okay."

She looks at me in a way that she never has before. Her eyes smile at me, and she slides a hand under her hair. Her smile is a reminder to me that there truly are other angels here on earth. Right here, as I gaze at Susan, I smile because I know that she is my angel on earth.

Her angular face turns toward me, and she pushes a lock of hair behind her left ear. "They didn't find any arteries, did they?"

"No. They just saw a cloudy spot that might be scar tissue."

I feel tears building, so I bite my lip. Silence suddenly envelops the hallway, and I know that I must drive home. A half hour later, I walk out of the hospital's door. As I stand next to my car and turn my eyes to avoid the sun's reflection on the building, I draw a dense breath, and I look back for a minute, breathing in the memories.

Now, as I speed down the highway, I realize that the once red leaves are now brown, and my eyes lift in response to a crack of thunder in the distance. Breathing in, I get a feeling that I have many times before. I feel joy, pure joy, now that I have been awakened.

Though the rainbow tunnel is delightful, I feel grateful that I know what I must do. I must keep Chris for the rest of our days together. And I know in my heart of hearts that that will be a long time.

The sky is getting darker now. The air is getting crisper, I realize, as I roll down the window for a moment and smile against the wind. Rain begins to fall, pounding a soft rhythm, as I continue forward. The rain pounds the roof of my car and grows in intensity, creating a song of nature. It is absolutely beautiful. My eyes lift, and comfort fills my being.

I find a charm about the rain. It is a reflection of all of my emotions as my eyes lift. I have experienced many wonderful things when the rain is falling. And now, as I pull into the driveway, I look at a bright window in the living room in our house. And now I smile, because I see Chris standing there. Right there in front of me stands my reason for living.

Chris disappears from the window as I turn off the car before closing the door. When I reach the front stoop, he opens the door and I lift my hands to his face. I smile because I know this is what he wants. This is what I want. My mouth drifts into his, and I feel sudden joy, as his tongue caresses mine.

He is so much more beautiful than I remembered him a few hours ago. As I look at his bright blue eyes, I am once again transported back to moments spent on the beach. I back away from him, and I feel my eyes lift to examine his face.

"What did she say?" Chris asks.

"She said that there is unfortunately no cure."

"Nothing?"

I shake my head and drift into his arms. "No. As long as I take my medicine, I should be fine."

He looks at me for several seconds, but doesn't say a word. If eyes could speak emotions, no words are necessary at this moment.

I lift my hand to his cheek and touch his lips, warm with the breath of life. As I look at him, my heart swells with love—pure, overpowering love.

An overwhelming mixture of remorse, expectation, and excitement rise within me, but I don't let these emotions take over me. Now is a time for living life to its fullest extent.

Three days later, the rain pours ferociously, pounding against the roof, creating a whirlwind of sound. I sit here wondering what the next moment has in store for me. It seems these days that my life changes in a split second. And this morning, it feels as though the rain echoes my emotions, steady and forceful like wind in a hailstorm.

Now, as I sip my coffee, I look up and hear something like a faint, tonal sound. It is persistent and creates a ringing in my ears. I pace toward the phone, which is buried under some papers, but I don't recognize the number. Exhaling a heavy sigh, I fumble through the papers and pick up the phone, despite the fact that I neither know this person nor want to talk right now.

However, I pick up the phone, slow and reluctantly, before bringing it to my ear.

"Hello?"

The voice on the other end of the line is soft and feeble, yet it is familiar. It is my grandmother.

"Lilly, sweetheart," she says, her voice sounding as weak as my body right now. "I know you're sick. Grandpa is coming over to see you."

My mouth drifts open, and words refuse to emerge as I stare in confusion. My grandfather died three years ago, or so I had thought. I had lost contact with my grandmother a year later. Until now, her whereabouts had been a mystery.

"Listen, Lil, you're going to pull through this one. I always told you that when you find the right one, you'll know it will be forever. That boy has been at the hospital all hours of the night trying to figure out what he can do to keep you—"

"What happened to you?" I manage, my voice barely audible. "I haven't heard from you or seen you in a long time."

She hesitates. "You know, it never hurts to call. A grandmother likes to hear from her grandchildren from time to time."

The statement rattles me, and I find it even hard to speak. I swallow, close my eyes, and worry that I will say the wrong thing. This could ruin our relationship, if we still have one.

"How did you know about Chris? How did you know about my epilepsy?"

"Your husband tracked me down at the local senior center and said the matter was urgent. Epilepsy is not something to be mess around with. You need to take your meds."

My eyes dart against the darkness, because of the rain, and I clear my throat. Our phone conversation continues, and I am fighting the urge to cry.

"What about grandpa? I thought he—"

"Died. I know. As it turned out, he was held in captivity by some drug lords in the United Kingdom, and they wanted his money. They declared him dead, but I went over there by emptying my entire savings account. It was worth every penny."

"So he's alive?"

She chuckles and her voice halts for a second. "He was grimy from head to toe. Hadn't bathed in a year, but we were able to get him home."

I hold a hand to my chest. "Oh my God. I can't believe he's—"

There is a sudden lift in her voice. "I know. He's still here."

I enjoy speaking with my grandma, and I am delighted to hear about my grandfather, but there is still a part of me that is suspicious. Chris will be home in five hours and we need to talk.

The hours tick by and feel like eternities, as I listen to the wind whipping against the front door, anticipating the arrival of my grandfather, a man I believed had gone to the other side.

"Anyway," my grandma says, her voice halting briefly, "you're grandfather should be there in a few minutes."

We exchange pleasantries before I muster a feeble "I love you." It feels different now, disconnected because of the years gone by. Her whereabouts are still uncertain in my mind, but I have bigger things to worry about right now.

As I stand here, rolling the phone within my hands, the doorbell rings, and I look up, feeling my eyes freeze with a sense of urgency. I tug open the door, and right there before me, I find a man I barely recognize. His hair is white and oddly long. His dense locks rest just below his ears and are frizzy. His hair looks as though it hasn't been touched for months. Yet it still holds a crisp white color that is shocking, yet familiar.

He now has a white mustache, and the once subtle wrinkles that used to rest below his eyes look like sandbags, sagging like uneven waves at the top of his perfectly rounded cheeks.

"Grandpa, you're … here."

He steps through the door as though he has done it a million times, and he reaches out to give me a hug. I had known him for a long time. And it is clear by the smile in his eyes that I have met him once again. Slowly, he comes toward me, and I inch my arms around his shoulders.

"You're still beautiful, Lilly, so grown up now."

"Thanks," I say, admiring a man I thought I had lost. I hear a clinking sound as he fumbles something in his left hand.

He is holding a bag in his hand, I notice as I release him. It is a tan-colored bag and appears to hold something significant, judging by the sudden lift of his eyes. Without a word, he takes a deep breath and holds my great grandmother's emerald necklace in the palm of his hand.

"You must take this with you," he says. "Wear it wherever you go. Consider it a gift from your great grandmother." I have no idea what to say, as he shuffles the gold necklace forward and into the palm of my hand. I have not seen my grandparents for a long time, and figuring out what to say is difficult.

"What's this?"

"You'll know when the time comes."

At this moment, I am at a total loss for words. As I look into my grandfather's eyes, I see many people I have loved. In his green eyes, I see my mother who once danced around me when I was a child. In his face, I see every loved one who has come and gone. And in my hand, I run my fingers over the deep green stone. I squint my eyes. Surely, it is an emerald.

"Now," he says. "Now you must be with Chris. Keep him. Stay with him, and take your seizure medication. I can't tell you what to do, but I will remind you that you made a promise to that boy."

I watch him leave through the window and silently rejoice that my grandparents are still here. It is a miracle, of course. But it is my miracle. And though I know my mom is no longer with us, a part of her is here with me, because of my grandparents.

It is now nearly December, and despite the fact that my eyelids are heavy, I cannot go to sleep. It is nearly midnight, and Chris walks in after writing a paper. His form catches my eyes, as he walks through the door. His head rises slowly and he reluctantly meets my gaze.

"We need to talk."

Chris and I talk into the night, and he explained that he needed to connect with someone who knew me other than him. He said he can't speak common sense into me when I'm so bullheaded.

In the process of trying to track down old relatives, he found a piece of paper with my grandmother's phone number on it. The paper was in the drawer to my desk, buried beneath old receipts and papers that I can't seem to let go.

It is now two days later and I find myself standing at the kitchen counter. My hands are cracked, and I am not wearing makeup. It is a typical occurrence given my condition and my frame of mind most mornings these days.

I must keep Chris forever. I must keep writing in the diary and give him a reason to live. I know that we have many experiences left. I know that we still have many passionate nights left to spend together.

As I sit here, I feel it. I feel his mouth upon mine. I feel his fingers upon my skin. These are the joys that keep us together as one. It is his laughter that keeps me smiling, and it is his arms that keep me warm.

These thoughts slip in and out of my mind as I begin tonight's diary entry.

Dear Chris,

I'm sure you know by now that I have given up on writing my book. I lack the inspiration to keep telling a story I know will never be read. The only meaningful story I've ever authored is Keeping Chris, the diary that someday will be yours and yours alone.

I love you with every ounce of my being, and I live to keep you breathing, to keep us smiling and making love in the darkness of night. Your touch is the light that keeps me shining, and your love is the air that keeps me breathing.

I have not always told you through words how much you mean to me, but know that I have loved you through everything. I have always loved you. I will continue to love you, as we walk side by side. Your hand is the treasure I hold, as I move forward through each day. Every night, I whisper your name into my pillow, as you lay sleeping.

Love is everything. Love is the air I breathe when I am beside you. Love is the force that draws my hand into yours. Love is the one thing I will always give you and the one thing that I will never take away, no matter how far we may travel on this road we call life.

I have so much love to give, and that love is yours forever.
Love you with all my heart,
Lilly

As I close the diary, I pause and exhale softly. My eyes glide over the diary's cover. Why am I lingering? Why do I keep looking at this diary when I know at some point that I will no longer be able to write in it?

I dismiss the thought and walk over to the bed. The room becomes darker as I sit down. It's hard to come to terms with the fact that I no longer see the world in the same way I did before. But I continue on, remembering every good memory that has ever traversed my mind.

Every exciting, exhilarating moment I have spent in Chris's arms has fueled my desire to live and be the fiery, passionate soul that I am. However, the thought of living without him is utterly terrifying—terrifying to the point that living at all would seem pointless.

Though I know that my days here on earth are filled with a headache that never goes away, my love for Chris keeps me looking forward to the next day. Except today. As I rose this morning, I felt a horrible heat in my legs and a tingling in my fingertips. My days are not meant to start like this.

My days are not meant to be painful. I simply don't understand why my family and Chris are doing this to me. Why do they torture me and beg me to stay in Chris's arms forever? He has a mission to fulfill, but his days are not meant to be ruled by pills and tainted with the fear of drifting into a convulsion.

As these thoughts race through my mind, my eyes remain steady on a thermometer on the table. I look at it silently for several moments before I bring my eyes the mirror in front of me. Right now, as I draw a dense breath, I run my hands through my hair and realize for the first time that not every strand curls perfectly.

My eyes trail away, slowly at first, and now, they fall to the door behind me. There is a knock at the door. I don't answer right away, but instead, I stare in silence before placing the thermometer in my mouth.

This is it. The moment of truth, I think, as I slide the thermometer out of my mouth and look at it. No fever. Just pain.

Now, the knocking comes again.

"Lilly, let me in. I need to talk to you about something."

"What is it?" I ask, fumbling a lock of my hair and spinning around.

"We have a date tonight, remember?" he says, moving forward and putting his arms around me. I detect a sudden yearning in his eyes as he pulls me closer. His lips are soft and reminiscent as he brings his mouth to mine. As I open my eyes slowly, he falls to the floor.

"Chris," I scream, struggling to pull him up. "Oh my God. Are you okay?"

"Lilly, help me," he says, his hands trembling and reaching for me like a child.

Chris fights nature too much. He forgives easily, perhaps too easily, given the fact that I have put him through more than a husband should ever have to deal with. It is catching up with him now. And despite his best efforts to stay strong, I see the redness in his eyes. The sight tugs me back to a time when I watched him in his hospital. I have been there before.

"You need to see a doctor. You know that," I say.

Chris stares, his eyes suddenly pleading. I know what's in his heart. He has made a choice—one that comes with a price. He tries to be strong, he really does. But the pain is mounting. It's strong, overpowering. And yet, he continues to fight it.

"Lilly," he says weakly. "You know how I feel about that."

"I know."

All I can do is stare. He keeps his eyes on me, and I continue watching him and cupping his face with my hands.

The night slowly fades into the soft hush of morning. Now, it is 5:44 a.m., and I am finished with a restful slumber. Slowly, I open my eyes. It's a wonderful feeling to wake up every morning and know that you lay next to someone who loves you. As I sit up and hear red leaves crackle on a soft wind outside the window, I realize that I am still basking in the afterglow of a life lived to the fullest. Perhaps I have been too hard on myself.

This is a dawning. A new awakening. This is how life is meant to feel—thrilling but also touched with sadness. This is life. Yet I can't help but wonder if I'm supposed to do more. He's been throwing up from time to time, yet he brushes it off as though it's no big deal. This is my reality.

"I am sore, Chris."

Chris shifts restlessly and breathes deeply against the covers. I scoot close to him and feel the warmth of his presence beside me. And now, he wakes. His eyes slide open, vibrant and full of life.

"Chris," I say with a sense of urgency as my eyes straighten against the dim light of morning. "I want you to hear more stories from my diary. You have no idea how many stories I have written and brought to life within its pages."

"Okay. How long are these stories?" he chuckles. "I must warn you. I like pictures."

I smile, flash him a playful grin, and give him a gentle slap. Now, I shuffle my arm under his back.

"We need to read my diary. There are some stories I want to tell you," I say, as he stares back at me with his mouth curling into a soft and tender smile.

He chuckles, his eyes softening as I look at him. "I must be special if you have written that much about me."

I grin, slowly removing my eyes from his face and chuckling into the palm of my hand.

"You're a bit of a narcissist. It's not all about you. I am in the diary, too. Within it, you will find not only my joys, but also my sorrows. My innermost thoughts are yours to find."

"Geesh," he says, shaking his head. "You're so smart with your words. I can barely string two sentences together."

"Ah, such is the brain of a scientist," I chuckle, throwing my arm over his left shoulder.

Out of all the dreams I have held, Chris is the dream that has given me the most inspiration. When I find my spirits sinking, I return to the moments that have brought me the most joy. In my mind, I return to the day Chris and I went canoeing on the lake, only to get lost several miles from the shore.

No one was nearby to find us, and as we looked out, the only solace we found was the sun's reflection on the waves. Chris knows that I have no sense of direction, and that day, he found amusement in telling me we were about to fall over the edge of the sea. I remember the fear that filled my stomach as I looked out upon the waves. His laughter was comforting, but our lack of direction was utterly terrifying. I miss those moments—moments when we didn't have a care in the world and the pressures of life had yet to become a concern for us.

We were free and careless, and I made a point to do as many spontaneous things with Chris that I possibly could.

Oh, how I miss those moments. If only we could reinvent them. If only we could take out the canoe and wander aimlessly. For the longest time, I had no interest in going out in the canoe again. But I realize now that I only felt that way, because I thought Chris was divorcing me.

The dock where the canoe sits currently is now a place of hope. Hope for the future. Hope for the rekindling of a dream. Hope for a life that is once again filled with adventure. Our most recent plans have for the most part been for doctor's visits and trips to the pharmacy.

My memories of our tender moments now come back to me at all hours of the day when I sit by my desk and stare at the wonders of the world outside the window.

Every day, I watch squirrels gather nuts in preparation for the long winter that lies ahead. As I look at my diary every night, I am reminded of the many joys that Chris and I have shared. And I ponder for the longest time how much time is left. Is there really time for dreaming?

Yes, we have many treasures to behold, not only right here, as I sit, but also as we venture out on new journeys. Perhaps it is the memory of him spinning me around town that gives me hope. Perhaps it is the way his lips feel against mine that keeps me motivated. But even so, I wonder if he knows what the future holds for him.

I know. I have seen his future before my eyes. Sometimes I feel guilty for seeing his future, for listening to the conversations of angels. I know his life is meant to be long, and he is the driving force for my existence on earth.

Yes, I believe in angels. I have seen them, and they have held my hand as I learned about what I am meant to do to keep Chris safe. Knowing Chris's fate is a burden on my heart, but in my mind's eye, I saw that we would be apart at some time. I saw a divide that would undoubtedly affect our future.

Why, I wonder, do I think about this so much?

Love. It is the driving force in my life. I remember a time in my childhood when I longed for companionship and found nothing but distance in the eyes of other children, who later became teenagers who rejected me completely.

Chris, on the other hand, has been the only constant in my life. I have watched his face grow older, and he has seen every line in my face deepen, turning me into an adult who still treasures her memories of childhood.

When so much is lost, you hold on to the one person who has given you the most inspiration and encouragement. I remind myself on a daily basis that I am fortunate to have so many wonderful people in my life.

The absence of my grandparents for so long taught me to be stronger and to become my own person without having my mother by my side. Now that they have returned so unexpectedly, I worry that they too will be taken from me.

These thoughts slip in and out of my mind as I sit here this evening and think about reading more stories from my diary to Chris. And as soon as I close my eyes, anticipating Chris's reaction to my stories, I hear footsteps. The footsteps are loud at first, but suddenly come to a halt.

"Sweetheart," he says, walking around my chair and looking at me with a soft and demure gaze. "I would love to hear some stories from your diary. Do you have the time?"

I look up, straighten the jacket draped over a black cashmere sweater, and bring my eyes to him.

"Sure."

My heart pounds for several moments, as I remember the many stories I poured into my diary's pages. Tears moisten the corners of my eyes, and emotion poured out of me earlier as I scratched my pen across its pages. This is a monumental turning point in our relationship, I realize, as I draw a deep breath and rise from my seat.

The lines in his face have deepened. As I look at him, I feel tears grow ever stronger. I have known this man for a long time, and though he knows me like no one else ever has, a part of me has yearned to show him the true and unending depth of my love for him.

I have to read him the stories now because there will be no turning back when my final days arrive. Much like the other mothers I have known, I am a nurturer. My love for others is fervent. As my eyes glide over the drawer that contains the diary, and Chris lingers nearby, I feel a sudden need to hold him. He sees the yearning in my eyes and takes my hand.

"You are beautiful, Chris. Truly."

By his smile, I can see he hears the sincerity in my words, and I am suddenly drawn toward him and toward the bed.

Slowly, we lower ourselves back onto the bed. The room is silent, and the only sound in the house is the subtle tick of the clock against the wall in our bedroom. Even that is becoming fainter, as my attention focuses on the moment, and I touch Chris's hand.

I shift restlessly against the bed and breathe softly against the covers. His breath is soft and rhythmic, and I feel a sudden lift in my stomach at the sight of his eyes.

"You've been thinking about this a lot," he says, turning to me.

I chuckle, and a soft smile curves my lips. "I've been thinking about this diary for the past 19 years, sweetheart."

His lips curl and a sudden chuckle comes out of his mouth. He smiles and pats my hand. For the longest time, I have kept these stories to myself. They have been my own secrets up until now. Now my eyes lift, and my stomach does tumble salts.

Pounding furiously in my chest is the heartbeat that has kept me writing. A writer's work is often one of solitude, so the mere fact that I am sharing these stories proves that I am no longer alone in my work. However, at the moment, my emotions are so strong that I simply stare. I am taken into silence, because I know that life will change as soon as I begin reading to him.

Chris is and always has been a gentle and humorous soul. He has made me smile through the years, and he will continue to be my best friend and companion. Now it is time that he hears the words that will invariably change his life and mine at the same time.

I pause, take a deep breath, and look at him quietly. "Do you know how many times I have wondered if you truly know how much you mean to me?"

His eyes meet mine, but he does not say a word. Instead, his eyes lift, as though he is reflecting on a long forgotten dream.

"I'm special, I know," he says, raising his eyebrows. Suddenly, I see his dry wit come out, as he brings his face close to mine. He is quiet for several moments.

From his silence I sense his emotion.

"Oh, sweetheart," I say.

He turns and touches my shoulder. "You mean the world to me, you know?"

I am touched, and I look at him, feeling myself let go of all my reservations. I smooth my fingers over the blond hairs on his arm.

"Is it crazy to think that you are meant to be with one person and one person only?"

His gaze meets mine, and his eyes dart as though he is deep in thought.

"That's a heavy question to ask someone," he chuckles, "but no, it is not crazy."

I smile, because I was terrified of asking this question. I cannot think of anything to say in response, so I stare for several seconds. "So I'm not crazy?"

He turns. "You feel that you are meant to be with one person only. You always have," he says, brushing a lock of hair from my face and slowly enfolding me in his arms.

I nod, knowing in my heart of hearts that I am reading my diary to him for a reason. "Yes."

"You have always been my reason for living, Lilly. You are my life, my heart, and soul."

"As you are mine."

The moment feels surreal, given the fact that his tone has suddenly grown serious.

"You're not dying again, are you?"

I pause for a few seconds and look for any hint of fear in his eyes. He has nothing to fear, but as he looks at me, his eyes grow red. His eyebrows flex as he stares back at me.

"Oh, sweetie," I say, placing my hand on top of his. "Don't be sad. This book isn't about death. It's a celebration of life—our life."

Though my statement about death isn't entirely true, I don't want Chris to be upset. I can't give him a premonition of what the future holds. His life on earth is meant to be lived without fear.

I fear nothing, because I know what is out there. I know what awaits me, and I know what Chris will do if he is at his wit's end.

"You're perfect," he says.

"As are you," I say. I smile lovingly, and his lips curve upward. His eyes are brilliant, crystal blue and pure.

I stretch my hand forward, and he reaches for my fingertips. I inhale as his hand reaches mine, and like a child, he holds it loosely.

As his hand grows tighter upon me, I once again see the boy who lifted me and threw me over his shoulder. As I look at him, taking in his warmth, I think about the rainbow tunnel and the sun. And I realize for now, that I must remain here in his arms. I realize how much he means to me and how lost he would be without me on earth.

I am not trying to keep the truth from him. I just know the nature of Chris's soul, and though he can be stubborn at times, he has a tender heart that needs to be shared with me. I realize, as I sit here pondering, that my mind is being taken somewhere else.

"Anyway, back to the diary," I say, once again feeling the softness of his fingers warm upon my face. I smile, lift my hands from his, and look at the sweet face I have loved for so long. "I love you."

"Love you, too. Come on," he smiles, rolling his hands forward. "Where is the diary?"

"Hang on. Hang on, Mr. Impatience."

"Oh, you're just jealous that you are not the star of a storybook."

"Anyway," I say, "I have kept this diary hidden away from you for years now. Do you know how difficult it is to find something positive to say about you all the time?"

He chuckles deeply. "Oh, come on. You know I'm perfect, and now I know you love talking about me."

"Okay. Enough of that," I chuckle, throwing my arm over his shoulder once again.

I know he is filled with emotion. He appears to be deep in thought, judging by the absence in his eyes.

Amid the silence, I ponder the possibilities. I indulge in the memories as I rub my hand over his.

"Can you do something for me, sweetheart?" I ask, rolling something over in the palm of my hand. "Can you put this on me?"

I hold up my hand with my fingers spread wide open to reveal the chunky gold and emerald necklace my grandfather gave me.

"Put this on me," I say, smiling deeply while watching his face full of concentration.

After clasping the necklace around my neck, Chris kisses me softly and once again brings his eyes level with mine. I know he is curious. I can see it in the softness of his gaze, as his face slowly turns away from the drawer in which I keep the diary. With a soft and gentle smile, he brings his forehead to mine, but he doesn't say anything. No words are needed at this moment.

He smiles at me for the longest time, but I don't need to tell him how I feel. It is written on my face. If I'd had the choice of a million other men, Chris is still the greatest match for me. He will always be my hidden gem. He is forever the only one who can keep me smiling.

Anticipation builds within me, as Chris continues looking at the drawer that contains my diary. He continues to look at the deep brown wood, and I feel a sudden excitement come over me. It's not sensual, but instead, it is explosive and rejoicing, because I know for the first time, I can celebrate all of our special moments alone with him.

"Well," he says, suddenly bringing me out of my thoughts. "When can I see more stories?"

As I walk over to the dresser, a feel a sudden mix of happiness and sadness wash over me.

He opens his hands and looks at me. I await his next joke, pausing briefly before I take two more steps to the dresser. This is an emotional move, one that will bring me one step closer to showing Chris everything he needs to know about me and our relationship. From its start, our relationship has been beautiful. Who knows where it will end? Or will it ever end?

The lamp in the room instantly illuminates the open drawer as I tug it open. I breathe in, and his breath rises too, as I turn to look at him for several seconds. I wish I could keep his spirits this high forever.

"You're taking a long time you know," he says.

Right now, as my eyes linger on the drawer, I comb my fingers through my hair and stand silently.

I amazingly have my composure at the moment, but I know that soon will change.

He motions me forward and holds out his hand, as I run a hand under my nose.

"Sweetheart, what's wrong?"

CHAPTER TWELVE

LOOKING BACK

Opening the diary without breaking into tears is much harder than I had originally anticipated. As I hold the diary, I turn and look at the box of tissues on my nightstand, feeling my throat crack with even stronger emotion.

I want to tell him more than life itself that everything is going to be okay. But I realize by the urgency in his eyes that now is not the time to bring up the tingling in my arms and legs or my headaches.

I am not well, I know. But instead of showing my pain, I stand silently before bringing my eyes to him. "So here goes," I say, looking at him briefly and biting my lip.

As I retrieve the diary from the top drawer, feeling its rough exterior against my fingers, my jaw trembles. However, I cannot let him see my sudden trembling. Exhaling a soft breath, I climb back onto the bed and regard Chris softly.

"Do you think we could read it in the light downstairs?" he asks.

"Sure."

Taking my hand and leading me down the stairs, Chris's eyes smile. He turns on the light next to the sofa and sits down beside me. As I look at him, his smile is soft, reminiscent. Though I am excited to share the diary with him, there is still a part of me that is a little nervous about reading it to him. Resting my head on his shoulder for a few moments, I feel the warmth of his shirt against my skin.

"Now, for the moment of truth," I say, breathing in and flipping over the diary's cover. "Wow, this is hard. This is really hard."

His eyes lift and linger on the page.

"You seem upset. Is everything okay?"

As I look at him, fear descends into the pit of my stomach. "No, I'm fine."

He pauses for several minutes and gives me a soft pat on the arm. "You can tell me anything. You know that."

As I look at him, I see a sudden denseness in his eyes. "There's a lot in this diary that I haven't shared with you," I say. "So I want to do it now."

Because Chris has been my lover and best friend for nineteen years, there is nothing I am afraid to tell him, until now. He has always been able to see straight through me. Realizing that, I pause before speaking.

"Lilly? What's wrong?"

Right now, I feel sadness overtake me. "Okay, here goes," I say, placing my left hand on the diary before clearing my throat. I begin reading Chris an entry about a day back in October 1999. It was the day we started talking about marriage. Though we were young and naïve about the responsibilities of marriage, we knew we were meant to be.

In my mind's eye, I can still see that day. I can still see Chris throwing up his arms in excitement and smiling beside me.

I look down at the diary and inhale deeply.

"We were sitting on my parents' deep blue couch, and you, as always, slipped your hand into mine. You were wearing your characteristic tennis shoes with jeans and a white t-shirt, and I was wearing a green dress and white flip flops. You wound up getting down on one knee, as I looked at you excitedly."

"Yeah," he says, his voice lifting. "You said it was too soon to propose, so we wound up fooling around in your room."

"No, Chris," I remind him. "We wound up making love in my room."

He throws his head back and cackles loudly.

"Correction," he said. "We had sex, and there was nothing soft about it. My God, you were rough."

I smile at the memory. Picturing that day, I bring into focus the image of Chris unbuttoning my blouse.

"You were a frisky little thing," he says with a fleeting look of amusement.

"What?"

"Yeah, sex. It's your favorite thing to do, remember?"

"Ha ha, very funny," I say, remembering his hands upon me, feeling his skin as soft as silk upon me. "Then, you asked me to marry you a year later. Besides, you said you wish you could do that to me forever."

"You mean fucking?" he says, flashing me a toothy grin. "It was so awesome."

Right now, I am silent, feeling my hands caress the silky fabric of my shirt. As I sit here, my eyes linger on the pages, and I bite my lip in reflection.

"A penny for your thoughts," he says, pausing and sliding his hands softly across my body. I move instinctively toward him and wrap my arms around him from behind. Now, as I once again breathe in the scent of his skin, I rock back and forth softly. Slowly, his hand drifts into mine.

"I'm not well, Lilly. You know that, right?"

My breath rises, and he stares, his eyes moving slowly while remaining upon me. His lips drift into mine and seconds later, he slowly drifts back against a dense pillow on the couch.

I feel the words come out of my mouth too quickly. "Promise me you'll be mine forever."

"Oh, Lilly, sweetheart, I will never leave you," he says, running a hand along my cheek. "You're my girl."

Whether or not our future together holds prosperity is not a concern at this moment. All that matters is the feeling of his hand within mine. He is perfect, I realize, as I look into his glittering blue eyes.

Some people think that you can love several people over the course of your life. I disagree. For me, there is only one love. And though time may separate us, at least for short periods of time, I know in my heart of hearts that Chris will never leave. His smile broadens, as he looks at me, and I lift a trembling hand to my chin. His movements are hesitant, and he moves slowly toward me, as though he thinks I will break. I am, however, fragile. I am fragile in my thoughts, fragile in my emotions, and fragile in my bones.

I can see from his sudden shifting in his seat that conflicting thoughts fill his mind right now. His eyes are intense on the diary, and I turn the page.

I look at him, trying to read his thoughts. This time, it isn't working. "What do you think of this … this diary entry?" I ask.

His eyes linger on me, and he brings his head level with mine. "I know I've asked this question before, but are you dying?" he asks, as a tear rolls slowly down his cheek.

"No," I say, rubbing my head. "I've just got this headache." I groan and close my eyes for a brief moment, cringing against the pain.

Chris enfolds me in his arms, as I lean back, allowing my head to drift back against him.

"Have you been taking your medicine?"

I stare in silence, because words elude me at this moment. I can't bring myself to tell him I didn't take my pills this morning.

CHAPTER THIRTEEN

THE AWAKENING

Why am I fighting this pain? Why do I hold on to this life when I know the pain is too great for me to bear? There are some things that can't be remedied. Some things just can't be fixed, no matter how hard you try.

I am fighting. I am fighting way too hard to be here, to be everything to everyone who loves me. My grandparents are still living, and they deserve each and every moment they have here on earth. They are still vibrant and full of life. Somehow, though, my grandfather seems to know something.

Could he have seen that I died several times? But that is not possible. He was not here when I died, nor has he been here when I had seizures. Chris, of course, took it upon himself to track down my grandparents. Now, he needs to see the truth. He needs to have an idea of what is coming.

This is the beginning of my awakening. Yet it is the ending to a beautiful fairytale that will never cease in my heart. If I could take Chris with me wherever I go, I would be eternally blessed. But Chris exists on his own free will, and wherever his journey concludes is entirely up to him. Right now, I am examining every page of my diary, smiling briefly at my scrawled handwriting.

I pause, rest my chin in the palm of my hand, and wipe the corner of my eye, anticipating tears that I know will inevitably fall from my eyes. As Chris looks at me, I bury my head in the diary's pages, avoiding his familiar blue-eyed gaze. Now, I bring my gaze back to him, feeling my lip beginning to tremble.

As I examine the silky hairs on his arms, I shudder at the thought of being without him. Here I sit, flipping through the pages of my diary, remembering our early days and reliving our every touch, our every kiss. I see the faces looking down. I feel the wind on my face. What's the point in leaving when I no longer have wings to fly?

As I hold the diary in my hands, seeing our memories within my mind, I pause in reflection. I can feel my eyebrows flex and my throat tighten, as I run my fingers across the lined paper. Now, as I raise my eyes to Chris, I lift my hand and motion him toward me. As I breathe deeper, he lifts a hand to my chin.

"You know, there's another reason I'm showing you this diary," I smile, looking up. "I want you to keep reading it on your own. And someday, I want you to pick up where I left off. There are so many more stories that need to be told. Once you do that, your journey will be complete."

"What are you saying?" he asks, his brows furrowing and his voice growing raspy. He looks at me with his body facing me, as if he's reliving a memory.

I look at him and smile. "It doesn't make sense to simply live life without looking back on the good moments and treasuring them for all that they were. Even the tough times in our lives have a way of shaping who we are."

His eyes are suddenly distant, fearful. All the moments I have captured in the diary are wonderful. They are beautiful in my mind.

I hope he reads the whole diary someday. But I know he will not be able to bring himself to do such a thing. I know this, because I see the pain on his face. And I know from past experience that dealing with intense emotions is difficult for him.

In many ways, he is weak, yet he is the rock that keeps me strong through every storm of my life. His hands lift reluctantly to my shoulders, and my heart aches for him, because I know he worries. He does not know what is on my mind.

And perhaps he shouldn't, because I know that I cannot be everything he wants me to be. I cannot promise a future that's filled with hope, but I can promise him my love, which is everlasting. I feel that love swell within my heart every time he looks at me.

"On to the next entry," I smile, pausing briefly to regard the soft silky hairs on his face. "We have a lot to read here, don't we?"

I look down at the next page and chuckle lowly. I remember writing this entry. And as I shuffle my fingers toward the top of the page, I smile.

"This entry is about the time we flew in a helicopter above the Grand Canyon. I was petrified and couldn't bring myself to look out the window. Then, you held my hand and got me to look out at the trees. When I looked at you, I felt completely safe."

He sniffs because he knows these entries are filled with our history. He can't remember all of our stories. His brain is overloaded from writing research papers. His heart, I know, is heavy with guilt, because he wishes he could do more to save me. Or is that even possible?

There's no cure. There's no way of repairing the damage. And I can see from his eyes that it weighs heavy on his soul. He will feel guilty again, I know. Then, he will feel sadness. He knows that I don't want to take the medicine. He knows I think doctors prolong the inevitable.

I wish I could offer him reassurance that I will never have another seizure, because I cannot promise I'll take my medicine every day.

I forget about my condition far too often. Forgetting my medicine has not hurt me, but it has the potential to wreak havoc on my treasured husband's heart. This is it, the awakening. This is the moment that he learns that we must soak up every moment.

"I remember the Grand Canyon," he says, looking at me with a glint of admiration. "I was so proud of you. We conquered one of your fears together. That has always been special."

Unable to hold back, I surrender to the lump in my throat. "I know."

"And that's what will always make our love special. You are everything, Lilly … everything."

He slips his hand into mine, and I place my hand on the diary. "Chris, you are everything to me, forever."

I turn the page and look at him, tracing the lines of his face with eyes that are growing deeper, more pronounced. I am 35, but I can feel in my body that so much is changing. Growing older shouldn't happen this quickly.

I know the nature of Chris's heart. Though he can be moody at times, he is kind and very loving.

Two days later, on the edge of dawn, the blaring sun shines down, and the bushes outside are like silhouettes against the lawn—a sign of the impending winter chill that will soon arrive.

Somehow our conversation continues, and it is now seven days later. I am sitting in the dining room, feeling the rising sun against my face. Much like my soul, it is warm with love. Thank God Chris is here.

Chris's voice quivers, as he squints against the sun, and his eyes rise slowly to meet mine. "You took your pills this morning, right?"

"Yes."

"Please keep taking them, Lilly. I have waited my whole life to have this much happiness. I treasure every moment, and I pray that we will find joy together until the sun sets on our lives."

I sniff deeply. He seems poetic, and I hold onto his words, as I lose myself in my thoughts. My eyes remain on his, as I fumble the sleeve on my shirt. My voice cracks as my eyes rise again, this time reluctantly, fearfully.

He knows how much I love him, yet he questions everything. Such is the brain of a scientist, I suppose.

"With everything I have in this world," he says, his voice quivering. "I would give it all away just to keep you here by my side. Lilly, will you stay with me forever?"

This is the beginning of the torture. This is the beginning of my pain, I realize, as I slowly blow out my breath. I look at his eyes, which I know will soon trail away with sadness, sadness that will soon give way to weeping.

How do I know these things? I know, because I have seen the future. I have seen his heart break time after time when I have seizures in his presence. But still, I'm avoiding his question. Smoothing a hand over my hair, I pause before looking at him and hold his gaze. Somehow I am finding it difficult to speak.

"I'm always going to stand by you, until the day I die, until eternity arrives."

His body freezes as he sits in his chair, and he stares at me. "Eternity?"

"Yes."

I tug softly at the collar of my sweater and run my fingers over the pages of my diary. As I begin to feel his worry, I lower my head and move my eyes toward the wall, attempting to avoid his silence.

This is hard. Wow, this is really hard.

I hate having heavy conversations with the man I love more than life itself, but death is a journey we must all take. It is something we must be ready for at any moment. This, I know, because I have lost so many people I love in split seconds. And I have been left to pick up the pieces of their lives, while struggling to hold on to their memories.

"You've been seeing the mountains again, haven't you?" he asks, his eyes freezing. He looks as though he is trying to digest reality. He swallows slowly and wipes his eye. I have seen this look before. And I know from the bottom of my soul that I will be forced to tell him the truth once again.

He needs to know how much I love him. He needs to know how much I want to keep him. The question is: Will he love me forever? Will he wait for me? Or will he continue on?

I stare at him in silent reflection, and my throat tightens and releases, seemingly at regular intervals. I shut my eyes tightly, holding back warm tears that continue to build.

He can't see me this way. Knowing this, I close my eyes, hold my head within my hands, and lift my head slowly. He can't see me like this. Not now, not as I tell him the hardest thing I have ever had to say.

I sniff deeply, take his right hand, and bring my eyes to meet his. I struggle in vain to keep my composure as I wipe the top of my hand across my forehead. My lips tremble and, like a waterfall, tears begin streaming down my cheeks. I lower my head to my hands and lift it once again, allowing my head to drift back upon my shoulders.

He is silent, and his eyes are more intense than I have ever seen them before.

"I came back here for a reason."

"What? You came back for what?"

"I came back to—"

He slides his hands down his cheeks. "Lilly, don't do this to me. Don't do this."

I lift my head, lick my lips, and bring my eyes level with his. "I came back for you. They wanted to take me and shelter me from the pain of my condition."

Now, tears are flowing down his cheeks, and he sniffs deeply. "Lilly, don't do this. You made me a promise. Your grandfather even told you—"

This conversation is agonizing, because I know what it will do to Chris.

"It was time for me to go, and it was so utterly beautiful."

He stares, sniffing, and placing his head in his hands, but he does not speak.

"But," I say, pausing, "there is time."

"You brought me back," he chokes. "You brought me back to keep me. You couldn't bear the thought of living without me."

Oh God, this is painful. This hurts.

Feeling my chest tighten, I try to look away, but the tears in his eyes only bring my eyes forward. The pain in my heart is nearly knocking the air from my chest and radiates throughout my bones. I get up and sit by myself for several minutes in the sunroom, taking it all in, taking in Chris's tears, taking in my decision to either go back or leave it all behind. *Oh God, the pain is killing me.*

These thoughts run through my mind as I look out at Chris's canoe. It is now dormant, sitting in the corner of the yard, awaiting the birth of next spring. My eyes linger on the dusty brown wood, and Chris's innocent childhood face comes to its full beauty in my mind.

I see the freckles on his cheeks that slowly faded during our late teenage years. I see his soft lips twisting into a warm smile. I see him bringing his mouth to mine, and I see him hugging me as we giggled, seemingly into oblivion. I see these memories fade like still photos into my mind.

I see him. I see him twirling me around in his arms. I hear his laughter. I feel every intense emotion we have shared through the years. In my mind, I see every glorious moment we have shared. Is there ever a time I could say that he was not the one for me?

No. I lick my lips and slowly, and my eyes descend to the carpet. I hear Chris walk into the sunroom. Slowly raising my head, I inhale and feel his soft hand upon mine.

This is harder than I ever expected it to be. It breaks my heart to bring up the subject of something happening to one of us. But I have to. I want to. Nothing should ever be left unsaid.

It is now the end of the day, and I am still staring through the door and watching the sun sink into the lawn. I look out at the canoe and blink, taking in the memories. *I can't do this. I simply can't do this.*

I have been blessed with many years of happiness. I reflect upon these thoughts, while running my fingers over the emerald necklace around my neck. My heart pounds within my chest and my eyes tremble, remembering my grandmother's silky smooth hands.

Now, as I exhale slowly, I suddenly realize that the emeralds do have meaning. I look down at the green stones, breathing in their wonder. And now the memories come, rolling in like a waterfall into my senses.

My great grandmother had given this necklace to my grandmother decades ago for taking care of her when she had emphysema.

Suddenly, there is a sound, and my eyes are instantly drawn to an acorn on the deck outside the door.

The air is getting colder now, I think to myself, as I bring the blanket in my lap closer to my shoulders. Chris is upstairs once again writing about science topics. I can feel my eyes growing dense, as I anticipate our next conversation.

Now I jolt my hand toward my head. The pain rises once again. It begins as a dull, aching sensation and slowly it intensifies like needles against my already fragile skull. It's a headache. That is all. Drifting back in my chair and sinking lower into its plush fabric, I feel my arms go rigid. The aura begins, turning slowly red, as it always does.

Like a child, I am helpless, surrendering to a convulsion that takes hold of my body and rocks my nerves to the core.

Pins and needles radiate up and down my arms, and my nerve endings jump at lightning speed. My eyes, now frozen wide open, can see everything, yet I am frozen like an iceberg, paralyzed by fear.

Despite my utter loss of control, I struggle to bring my thoughts back to the conversation I need to continue with Chris. I cannot speak as my muscles twitch, and for a moment, my mind goes blank. I can no longer muster a single thought. I am on the floor, my arms pounding like bongo drums against the plush carpet. At the moment, the fabric is anything but a comfort, as my nerve endings pulsate.

Right now, I am struggling to regain my composure, as I slowly and weakly rise from the floor. My vision, now coming back into focus, becomes crystal clear.

Now, as I rise to my feet, Chris's characteristic jeans are like a haze of blue in front of my eyes. His head jerks quickly, and his arms slide under me, enveloping me in a peace I have never felt before.

"Are you okay?"

I look up and suddenly realize that my honesty is about to get me in trouble again. As he walks over, fear overcomes my body, and my chest tightens as I lay here, helpless. I stare in silence, shakily combing my fingers through my hair. "I had another seizure."

I see the lines of his face crack with worry and sadness. His eyes begin to tremble, and his lips quiver. "Lilly, please. Don't do this to me."

I am too honest, and I am being heartless at the moment by telling Chris that time is running short. Time is running out. Or is it? Could there be a cure for epilepsy in the future? Perhaps an operation could take it away completely.

I hold my trembling arms against my sides and allow them to gently fall to my sides in surrender.

"We need to make the most of the time that is left."

He freezes and looks at me with a face that is crackling with pain. The look is so intensely terrified that emotion descends into the pit of my stomach. The feeling lingers, rising slowly to my heart, and Chris's eyes radiate with fear.

His lips quiver, and a lone tear trails down his left cheek. Now, as his eyes reluctantly come to mine, I sniff deeply.

"What? You promised to keep me forever."

I lick my lips and stare forward. Lifting my gaze slowly toward his topaz blue eyes, my mouth opens, and I draw a breath that is neither dense nor placid. Suddenly, I am like a deer caught in headlights, my body frozen like ice. I am unable to turn away.

"I am yours forever, and I know this is hard for you," I say, feeling my vocal cords tighten. "But not all promises can be kept on earth."

At the moment, he is like a statue, frozen in time and unable to move or speak.

He turns and wipes his eye.

"You can't. You can't do this to me."

"Something feels different," I say, holding a hand to my head.

He backs away. "Lilly, you can't go."

All I can do is stare. My eyes are like frozen green jewels against a sadness that begins to envelop me.

"It's not that easy."

He drops to his knees suddenly and lifts his arms. His voice becomes louder. I had known this was coming. I can't avoid it, so I just stand here.

"No, Lilly. Don't … go."

He screams for several moments with his head facing the floor and, slowly, he lifts his chest.

"Oh, sweetie. We have many happy moments left together, probably several years. I just … I just feel something changing. We just need to make the most of the time we have."

As I struggle to look away, the pain in my chest grows tighter, and I take a step toward him. Looking away is not an option at this point. My emerald eyes are overtaken with his love, and I look up, sheepishly accepting his outstretched hand.

I want him. I need him. But still, a force is drawing me away. As these thoughts race through my mind, I pause for several seconds. I stare forward. The pain will go away, I'm sure.

I feel the pain intensify hot under my skull, but I sit and try to push through it. Now, as I stand here shivering, I hear music, and I pause, feeling warmth rising within me.

I suddenly find my attention being drawn toward the ceiling, as a sun slowly brightens in the distance.

"Anyway," I say, trying to take my attention away from the pain radiating inside my head. I nod slowly.

"We should do something spontaneous."

His eyes are once again aglow with expectation, and he scoots up a chair, moving closer toward me. Fearfully bringing his hands toward mine, he speaks.

"Come and sit with me."

I can't believe how easily he comes to me, even during times like these. At this moment, as I am barely able to speak, he draws my hands into his. As he traces a heart on the palm of my hand, his eyes start trembling. I feel my eyes fill with moisture as he brings himself closer to me. His characteristic thick lipped smile dims, as his lips descend.

The soft look on his face causes my heart to pound.

"You are everything," he says, kissing my palm. "You are everything in this world to me."

I place my hands on his arms and lean forward. "And you are everything in the world to me."

"But—"

I place my hand on his, and I can feel my voice fall to a whisper. "But there is nothing to worry about. There is nothing to worry about— ever."

Ben is with Matilda after school today, as he has been for two weeks, and I attempt to smile at Chris.

Sensing my reluctance, he stretches his arm around me. "So about that something spontaneous. Let's be like the teenagers we once were."

"What do you mean?"

"Let's lie together in the grass behind the bushes in the backyard."

My eyebrows lift, and he grabs my hand, motioning me toward the back door. "I think we have something to do before we go out back," he says, grabbing my hand and bringing his mouth to mine. He kisses me slowly and sensually, and suddenly, he lifts his eyes.

Since I inherited my parents' house when my mother died, I have been blessed with a house filled with history, a history of love and memories. Dad got an apartment shortly after I graduated high school. He couldn't bear the pain of being in such a big house without Mom. Chris and I have known this house from the beginning of our relationship.

Despite the fact that Chris lived with his parents when we met, our history traces back to the house in which I grew up. It is now our home and our hearts, which right now seem to beat as one.

I reach for Chris's hand and bounce to my feet. And like the teenager I once was, I giggle as we run through the back door.

"I'll race you to the bushes," he squeals, throwing his arms around my waist and flinging me up into the air.

"Oh my God, Chris," I squeal. "I love you."

"I love you, too."

We kiss behind the bushes, which are now growing stiff with the crispness of the bright fall sun. Feeling a soft wind caress my face, I smile.

"You know, this is the place we first made love."

His eyes catch mine, and he lingers, his face softening in response. "I know. You were beautiful then, and you're beautiful now."

"Chris," I say, feeling my head beginning to hurt. "Hold me."

Slowly, he lifts me into his lap and wraps his arms around me. Now, as he rests his chin on my shoulder, his jeans are warm upon me.

His blue eyes as vivid as topaz gems draw me closer. "This is so familiar, so beautiful."

"It is."

"We should go somewhere beautiful. Remember the lake where we used to take out the canoe? Take me there."

His head turns, and he releases me from his arms. Now, he looks at me, folds his arms around me, and holds his hand against my heart. He touches my face.

"Yes, we will go there."

Running my hand along his face, I whisper. "Take me there, sweetheart."

It is now two weeks later on a Saturday morning, and the early winter air is made manifest by the foggy windows in our living room. They are cold to the touch, and I stand here, feeling the chill against my fingertips.

Despite the air's crispness, it is the perfect day to take the canoe out on the lake. "Take me out on the lake," I whisper in his ear, rubbing my right hand upon his shoulder. An hour later, we are slowly paddling out on the placid crystal water. I look out, realizing that we are totally alone.

The geese have flown south. The animals of the summer have gone into hibernation, and it is now only us alone in the peaceful silence of the lake.

I am drawing a deep breath and feel the crisp air in my nostrils. "This is beautiful, absolutely gorgeous."

As I say this, I realize that these few words sum up every day I spend with Chris. Though our relationship has had its fair share of storms, our love is the light that keeps us shining. Feeling a sudden shiver, I look up for a moment, breathe in the air, and feel the fall sun shine, warm against my skin. As Chris paddles us back away from the horizon, the sun reflects on the rippling waves. The evening's solitude is ours to share. The day has faded quickly, too quickly.

This night is one of inspiration, and as I now sit here at my desk, I hold a pen above paper. Opening the diary, I begin to write my latest entry.

To my dearest Chris,

There is nothing we can't do together. We can sail the seas and chase rainbows together. Yesterday we saw a rainbow. Those rainbows are one of my greatest treasures, because I share them with you. In one another's hearts, we find companionship, joy, and passion. But most of all, we find love. I find everything in you.

I find peace in your soft smile and comfort in your tender touch. Every dream I could ever dream comes true when I reach for you. Your heart is one of peace and happiness. Don't ever think that I will go anywhere without you. Wherever I go and in whatever I do, I carry a piece of you with me.

Our love is like a rainbow that grows brighter in the distance. It unites us on the tops of purple mountains, in the depths of the deepest seas. Every one of our kisses brings me a slice of Heaven and a reason to stay strong in every journey I take.

No matter where I go, my journey is not complete without you. I will follow you wherever you go. Even as the sun sets on the breath that is our lives, you will find me next to you. We could live a million lives together, and that would never be enough. Not until I hold you in my arms.

If I could keep us together through everything, I would do it. I would break down walls for you. I would take your hand and lead you through a light that shines. If I could assure you that everything will be perfect in life, I would do it. But inevitably, tears will fall, as they do in every person's life.

If I can, I will carry you home, as long as you are here beside me on earth. No matter what happens, there is a way for you to come with me, to be with me.

Love always,

Lilly

As I look up, my eyes are drawn to the window. The blind is still open, and darkness falls upon the world.

Some nights are easier than others. As I close my diary against the beautiful dark navy sky, I sit here reflecting on every precious moment that has gone by.

Why, I wonder, does it feel so beautiful now? Why do I no longer worry about Chris? Why am I sitting here, instead of dreaming by his side?

The answer hasn't come to me yet, so I lie down on my side of the bed and wait for Chris. He is shuffling something downstairs. As soon as his head hits the pillow, I will close my eyes.

The beautiful and peaceful darkness gives way to brilliant morning light, but I can barely bring myself to open my eyes.

I am barely awake, but I hear a voice. I must open my eyes, even though my eyelids are like sandbags, heavy and full.

"Lilly, did you feel that?"

"Huh?"

"Did you feel my hand on your cheek? I touched it ten minutes ago, and I think you were numb. You didn't move. Oh, God, you scared me. I thought you were sick, having a stroke or something."

I roll over groggily. "You're reading into things too much. I was just sleeping."

By now, I am wide awake, but I sink back into my pillow, and motion Chris to sit down.

"I didn't have a stroke, sweetheart," I say, rubbing his back and feeling a sudden tingling on the left side of my body. Now, as I groan deeply, pushing against the mattress, I look at him.

His face suddenly softens as he removes his hands from me. This is scary, Lilly. We're both sick." His voice cracks. "What's going to happen?"

"There's nothing to worry about. "I know, Chris. But we can't focus on that. We're going to make it together in this world. I promise."

I clutch his hand. His eyes linger on me for a long moment, and now he speaks. "Really?"

"I promised you that we'd be together forever, and I will keep that promise." His eyes lift, and he rests his hand on my arm.

"If anything were to happen to me, I'd want you to be happy. I'd want you to enjoy all the things that make you happy."

His eyes rise slowly with mine, and I look at him, noting the worry on his face.

"Why? Are you thinking about the broken heart?" I ask.

He nods, licks his lips, and looks away as though he wants to avoid my reaction. "I was just reading about the broken heart syndrome. It's called stress cardiomyopathy, and you're right. Dying of a broken heart does not mean that you kill yourself. It's the stress and pain that take you."

I feel my eyes freeze, as I attempt to figure out what he is talking about. "Are you thinking about it?"

He is silent for several moments. The whole thing about dying of a broken heart intrigues him.

"I was curious about what they called it," he said, seeming somewhat ashamed.

Feeling my eyes beginning to close again, I slump back down into the pillow, and I feel my face grow dim. "What brought this on? You got really mad at me for writing about dying of a broken heart in a diary entry. What are you worried about?"

He shrugs, shifts restlessly, and looks at me, with his eyes trailing downward. "Nothing, just the whole dying of a broken heart thing … it intrigues me. I wonder if—"

His voice suddenly trails away, as his gaze turns slowly toward me. His blue eyes are illuminated by the rising sun, blazing sadness into my heart.

"Oh, sweetie," I say, running my hand over his back. "You'll never die of a broken heart. You're strong, a lot stronger than me."

"What do you mean?"

I wave my hand and look away slowly. "I mean that you're a lot stronger than me physically."

His head turns away slowly, and I can tell by his silence that I did not give him the answer he wanted.

"I have cancer, Lilly—the kind that kills you."

I kiss his shoulder quickly and place my hands over his eyes playfully.

"Anyway, this talk is too heavy. We need something fun," I say, crunching my hands over his shoulders.

He is silent for several moments, his pose frozen like a silent statue. He doesn't say a word. The worry on his face draws me closer, and I smooth a hand over his chest. "It's okay, baby. It's okay."

In an attempt to diffuse his worry, I remove my hands and place them over his eyes. "What are you doing?" he chuckles, flipping his arms backward and grabbing my hands.

As I take my hands away from his eyes, he turns and smiles in amusement. "We do need to do something fun."

I fall back lazily onto the bed, feeling a sudden lift in the pit of my stomach. "So we'll go dancing."

As my heart pounds furiously in my chest, I feel my spirits lift. Now, as I move closer, bringing my lips to his, he looks at me in a way he never has before. Slowly and effortlessly, I allow myself to drift into his arms.

"We'll go dancing," he says. "You can hold me to that one."

His voice brings a sudden smile to my face, and I bury my head in his shirt. He smells wonderful, just like he did the first time we kissed.

The day passed quickly. And now, as my eyes slide open, it is Thursday morning, five days later. Everything seems to be a blur. Chris helps me put on my pink dress. He cuts off the tags quickly and raises an eyebrow, as he shuffles the dress over my head.

Now, as we walk out onto a dance hall in the city, he stretches his arm around me and allows it to descend lower.

"Gee whiz," I say, swatting his hands, "have a little decency. I am a lady."

He chuckles, as he always does, and looks at me with a fire in his eyes.

"Sure, a lady. Keep telling yourself that," he chuckles. "After all, I'm not the one with her hands on my hips," he says, as we walk over an ornate tiled floor. Slowly, I remove my hands.

The pink gems on my dress shimmer under the lights in the room. As I look up at the crowd of people and enjoy the slowly dimming lights, I close my eyes. "This is beautiful," I murmur to myself.

"You are gorgeous. You're truly a gift," he says, twirling me around. Now, as he holds his cheek beside mine, I feel a sudden longing within me.

"When we get out of here," I say, drawing down my voice to a whisper. "When we get out of here, let's make love on the street bench again."

He raises an eyebrow, pulls me closer, and begins dancing more quickly. "That would be wonderful. I would love it."

I raise my hand to my head and look forward, feeling the warmth of his arms around me. "I know, Chris, but something is changing. I don't feel well."

I try to ignore the jumping nerve endings that radiate in my arms, as we continue dancing. But the tingling begins, and I stare forward, feeling my heart pound.

With my arms clasped around him, I feel the urge to hold him tighter, but my legs go limp beneath me. The pink haze appears and I drift down to the floor. Chris tries to catch me, but as his hands open wider, I fall to the floor. "Chris, hold me. I'm about to have a seizure."

The seizure is short, and I soon find myself drifting out of it. My vision becomes astoundingly clear, but something is off. Something is changing, and Chris sees it as I stare back at him, trembling.

"Chris, something is different."

"Lilly, please. I love you."

"Chris, you can't keep something from happening. No one can."

He lifts me into his lap and holds my chin in his hand. "Lilly, please," he says, his voice quivering and wiping a tear from his eye. "Is this really goodbye?"

"No, it's not goodbye forever. Trust me. Feel it in your heart," I say, holding my hand against his heart.

I wake up in our house two days later.

CHAPTER FOURTEEN

LOVE NOTES FOR CHRIS

Is there truly a danger to living in a world where you clearly cannot remain? I am a romantic in my heart, but I am beginning to become a realist. I now see the world for what it is, a place to love and be loved.

But if love cannot keep me here on earth, is it truly worth staying? At the moment, the answer eludes me, and Chris is in the kitchen. He is quiet, very quiet.

Right now, I am standing above a table, looking at a tray that is filled with my epilepsy medications. They are beautiful in their own right, because they keep me well, or as well as I can possibly be.

I am being called once again, not by Chris, Ben, or Matilda. They are all busy. Chris is cooking. Ben is at school, and I am here, wondering—wondering why there is a field filled with poppy flowers in front of my eyes.

The sight calls out to me, and the smell is familiar. The smell of the poppies is strong and sweet against my senses, but I have to look away.

Today is a new day. And though these visions now come to me on nearly a daily basis, I must push on. I have things to do.

Running into a field of poppies would be a beautiful way to leave this world, but now is not my time. Chris now strolls over to the sofa, and I sit down next to him. As I move closer, I place a hand on his left arm and rest my head on his shoulder.

I wrote a diary entry last night that will hopefully bring Chris peace and help him find his way back to me. As I run my fingers over the page, I read it silently to myself. I must leave the room to avoid falling to pieces.

Sunlight shines on the floor, and I walk upstairs, feeling a rasp in my throat. Now I stare at my open diary, reading the entry I wrote last night.

To my dearest Chris,

If you are reading this entry right now, I know you are scared. I have gone to Heaven, and you are here on earth. Please know that there is a way to get to me. Come only if you want, and allow yourself to let go. Don't hold on to a place where you do not yearn to be.

If you want to hold my hand, just call out to me, and I will bring you back into my arms. I may not be physically able to carry you back to me, but I will come to you anytime you call my name. All you have to do is call me. I will hear you.

Love,

Lilly

As I close the diary, I smile, knowing in my heart of hearts that there is nothing that I would not do for Chris.

With love, anything is possible. As long as he remembers me and calls out to me, we shall never be apart.

Finding it difficult to be away from Chris, I walk to the kitchen and stand next to him. As I look at him, I feel love overcome me, and I smile.

"You're beautiful," I say. "I love you."

He looks up and appears confused. "Love you, too. Are you okay?"

"Yeah," I say.

My eyes suddenly fall, and I once again look out on a field filled with poppy flowers.

I have lived with the knowledge that I may not live out my days on earth like the many people who live into their eighties or nineties. My time will be shorter. I was told this many years ago, but it's hard to understand something that heavy when you are six years old. Not everyone is meant to live into their eighties or nineties.

In a vain attempt to dismiss the thought, I look at Chris and feel a sudden sadness come over me. "Chris, I need to be honest with you. I'm going to die. It's not going to happen right away, but it is going to happen."

His eyes become dense. He looks at me for several seconds and swallows. It is becoming clear to me that my transition is going to be much harder than I had anticipated.

"Lilly, please, don't do this to me. Give me five more decades."

I stand in silence, attempting to keep my emotions from bursting forth. I am not frustrated. I am simply here.

I swallow and look at him through watery eyes. "Chris, I can't be everything to everyone."

"Lilly, please."

I can feel my eyes move slowly toward him. I hold a finger over my lips, avoiding the terrified look on his face.

"Eight decades are the typical lifespan of the average American. I can't go on that long. It's not the path I am meant to take."

His voice cracks. "What do you mean?"

"I'm living," I say, licking my lips. "I'm living for you. I'm living for you and Ben, but I'm not living for me."

"Why? Why are you doing this to me?" he cries.

I stand up. "Why people die is a complicated thing," I say, "but it's like you have said to me before. At some point, one of us will have a broken heart. I don't want to break your heart this soon, but that's life."

His body freezes as he stands here, his blue eyes trailing away before returning briefly to my eyes.

"Lilly, that was just something I said after I found out I had cancer. It didn't mean that I wanted to leave and escape to some other place without you. This just doesn't make sense."

"It doesn't make sense to you," I say, pausing.

His voice grows dense. "What?"

By now, my emotions are bubbling at full speed at the sides of my vocal cords. This isn't good. He looks up, but he doesn't see my eyes trailing downward.

I can feel my left hand tingling, and I breathe in, feeling pins and needles once again. I bring my right hand to my face and look out the window.

I took my medicine, so I am safe. Nothing is going to happen to me.

"I need to go out for a bit," I say.

He turns, his hands remaining on the countertop. As his eyes linger upon me, he attempts a smile, but sniffs before looking away. I know that look, and my heart drops because I know his pain. I wonder what he is thinking. I don't ask what is on his mind, though. Instead, I do what I have done for the past nineteen years. I smile, push forward, and face the world with confidence. But before I leave, I pause and look over at him. My bottom lip trembles.

Instead of surrendering to the emotion in my throat, I smile sweetly because it calms him, and he feels safe for a while.

"I'm going for a walk," I say, touching a finger to my cheek and winking at Chris. And with that, I slide a hand over my hair, turning my eyes to the front door. "Give Ben a kiss for me," I say, looking back at his blond hair, his angular jaw, and the lips that I have kissed time and time again.

Now turning, I run back to Chris and look for any trace of sadness on his face. For now, his face lacks expression.

Love fills my chest as I look at him. My feelings keep me here, I realize, as my eyes linger on his face. I pause for several moments, looking at him. I turn and run to him, grabbing his shoulders and allowing my mouth to crush his. My tongue slides in and, for a moment, I relish the warmth of his mouth. Drawing back, I give him a soft smile. Love swells within me, as his hands lace with mine.

"Well, that was a surprise," he says, smiling and lingering on my gaze.

Now, I pause for a moment, tracing the lines of his face with my eyes. "I love you so very much."

I turn and sniff for several moments before bringing my eyes to look at him one more time. As I walk out the door,

I breathe in, taking in the crisp air and looking at brown leaves that continue to fall gently to the ground.

He awaits me, I think to myself, drawing a deep breath and blowing it out, as I push forward against the wind. I continue on, breathing deeply, and see my breath as I exhale. It is white against the wind.

Now, after walking swiftly down the stairs, I pause briefly to once again look at the trees and move swiftly forward down to the sidewalk. My steps are heavy against the pavement, and sudden warmth overcomes my body, rising slowly throughout my limbs, and now moving up onto my shoulders.

I have to get home quickly. Right now, as I look at the cloudless blue sky above, I run forward, allowing my legs to pound like a horse's hooves against a radiant landscape.

Aside from the rush of the wind and the leaves floating gently from trees, there is no one in sight.

I throw my right hand against my cheek, tossing my hair back while struggling to catch my breath. This is not the way it's supposed to happen. I have to get home.

My heart pounds furiously within my chest, as my legs give out. Slowly, I drift to the ground. My breath is now much heavier, and I scream out, allowing my hands to fall to my sides.

"Chris," I scream out. My eyes dart against the sky and slowly lift to the house in front of me. Now, there is joy and peace. I see Chris in the distance, his legs chugging furiously against the sidewalk.

"Lilly!"

His eyes, which were mellow just minutes ago, suddenly fill with a sadness I have never before.

He needs me here. I know this. But now, I know there's no escaping what I suspect might happen. Knowing his pain, I lift my head and feel my hands go numb. "Take me home," I say, trying to lift my hand to his face.

It is impossible, I realize, as weakness overtakes my body. "You are my best friend. You will forever be the love of my life."

"Lilly, I'm carrying you home. Don't say goodbye. We're almost home and safe together," he says, running steadily with me in his arms.

"Oh, Chris."

He holds me tight against him, quivering and gasping. "We are going to make it together. I'll do whatever I have to do to get you well."

Perhaps the artery inside my head is bursting. I breathe deeply, and then I gasp, struggling to hang onto Chris. While moving, he breathes air into my lungs by bringing his mouth to mine. He weeps and kisses my mouth, and I once again feel his warmth, kissing him deeply and putting my arms around his neck.

"I'm here, baby. I'm here," he says, as he pulls me closer against his chest.

The softness in his voice is familiar and comforting, and I feel his love as he carries me up the steps. As I feel him climb the steps on our porch, surrounded by crisp and golden mum flowers, I take in the sweet smell of his skin and close my eyes. Resting my head back into the warmth of his hands, I feel a sudden weakness in my limbs. Now, ever so softly and slowly, he places me on the couch. He lifts my hand and kisses it.

"Oh my God," I say, jolting my hand to the right side of my head. "These headaches are killing me. They hurt, and I am weak, very weak."

By now, I am barely able to speak, but I manage a few words. "Hold my hand. Let me feel the softness of your skin one more time. Grant me this one last wish."

Unable to deny me one final touch, Chris lifts up my shirt, wiggling his fingers under my delicate lace bra. His touch is warm and soft, as he melts into me, his body becoming one with mine. I am feeling better now. And with the soft and gentle rhythm of his hips upon mine, sensation rises within me. Perhaps this will keep me safe. Like a child, he looks at me, with a sweet innocence in his eyes.

"This is the thing I love most about life. Making love. Making pure, sweet, and passionate love to you."

I can't believe my eloquence, even in spite of my pain.

Chris lifts me up and shuffles me into a sitting position. As I try to keep looking at him, my vision becomes blurry. The emerald necklace around my neck breaks and falls onto Chris's knee, as his hands slide under me.

"Lilly?"

I look up and struggle to speak. Chris's eyes are dense with fear, and I now feel something hot underneath my skull. As I fight to remain conscious, an explosion of pain ricochets like bullets in my brain. The pain slices through me, radiating an unbearable slicing feeling deep under the surface of my skull. Weakly, ever so weakly, I bring my hand to my head.

"Oh my God," I say, struggling to bring Chris's face into focus.

"Stay with me, Lilly," Chris says, holding me tight against him and frantically grabbing the phone. "I'm calling 911. You have to stay with me. Keep breathing, like this," he says, placing his hand upon my chest.

"Chris."

He softly pats a hand on my heart. "Like this, baby. Steady and strong."

I look at him through my blurry eyes, and for a moment, sadness soaks through my being. I feel his teenage hand within my mine.

"Come here," I say, lifting my trembling hands toward him. "Kiss me again."

Tears now fill his eyes, but he obliges and brings his mouth to mine. Softly, I take in his warmth. I feel the soft touch of his hands, and I once again see the pristine purity and innocence that has always lived in his eyes.

The ambulance arrives minutes later. Four men rush through the door. They are all very tall, I realize, looking at their bodies, which race forward at lightning speed. Everything feels surreal, like I am lingering in a dream.

I hear one man speaking, as he lifts me onto a stretcher and places me on its plush fabric. One paramedic's hands are upon me, searching for vital signs, but they simply do not compare to the comfort I find in Chris's arms. My chest tightens, and a sensation of pins and needles flows through my left side.

This can't be it. I can't leave yet. I haven't said goodbye. My thoughts suddenly halt as a veil of blackness hovers in front of my eyes. For several seconds, my eyelids open, and I can see everything.

"She's showing symptoms of a brain aneurysm. We touched her left hand and tried to get it to move, but she's weak. Might be a seizure, partial paralysis. We don't know," the paramedic says.

Another paramedic wearing green scrubs lifts up my head and examines my eyes. "It's okay, ma'am, we've got you. We're not going anywhere."

With that, he places a breathing mask over my mouth and puts tubes up my nose. The tubes propel air up into my nose, and I suddenly cringe at the rushing air against my nostrils.

Despite my pain and weakness, I look at the medicinal supplies in the ambulance. My eyes glide over tubes, and I breathe in the cold and medicinal air.

As the pain continues to pound within my head, I squint and open my eyes. Oh my God. I can no longer think, but I continue looking at Chris. He is truly beautiful. The love we share is beautiful.

We manage to make it to the hospital and out of the ambulance, but the pain on the right side of my head radiates so strongly that my eyes close tightly against the pain. For a few seconds, I open my eyes and am able to see. But still, it hurts. Struggling to hold on, I watch the waiting room disappear, as I am rushed into the neurology wing. The silver rails are cold against my hands, as my arms fall away from them. Finally, we are in a white hospital room.

"I love you, Chris," I say, feeling his hand squeeze upon the bottom of my right leg. "I will always love you."

I can barely breathe, let alone speak, but I manage the strength to say one thing. "Please hold me."

"This is terrifying," I think, surrendering to the pain and wheezing. Every moment passes like an eternity, bringing sadness into my stomach.

Every moment becomes a blur, as I struggle against the pain.

"I'm tired," I say, feeling the weakness grow stronger upon me. "I need to close my eyes for a moment."

I am utterly confused, and I find my eyes being drawn toward some tubes above my head. As I look up, I see Dr. Smyth standing over me, her eyes dense with concern. Her face is fuzzy, but it becomes clearer, as I open my eyes again. This is what happens every time my head pounds.

She places a warm hand on mine and tells me to squeeze her fingers. "We've got you right here, Mrs. Rylan. You've had a brain aneurysm. We're going to get you in for some scans, okay? We're right here."

Fear descends into the pit of my stomach.

"I need to be with Chris," I say weakly.

He comes closer to me and places his hands on my arms. His crystalline eyes are darting, and he looks away for a second, as though he is looking for someone who can save him. I see his jaw quiver as he moves closer to me.

"Lilly," he says, his voice quivering. "You are my sweetie."

"Chris, I need you to keep writing in the diary," I say to him, attempting to raise a trembling finger to his cheek. It's so hard, so painful.

"Promise me that you'll write the rest of my story. Let it be our story now."

He clutches my hand and tightens his grip around me.

"It's our story, baby. It's always our story," he cries. "When will I see you again?"

"I don't know, baby. Don't look away when you see the light."

His arms are warm and comforting, just as they have always been. As I look at him, I smile and once again feel the connection of our hearts.

"Finish writing the diary for me, sweetheart. But before you finish it, read all the stories in it. You'll find some new ones to help you on your way."

Chris places his hand over my arm and kisses my forehead.

"I love you, Lilly. Always know that."

"You have always known how to make me smile. I will always be with you," I say, looking up. "Now keep smiling until we meet again. Promise me you'll go on."

He shakes his head, and tears fill his eyes. "Will we meet again?"

I smile at him weakly and struggle to draw breath. Quietly, I whisper. "I love you, sweetheart."

I look at Chris's face and breathe out slowly.

Now, I find myself standing in a warm and wonderful place.

As I look up, the soft wind is comforting as I walk into a field of poppy flowers. I walk through an endless line of pink, yellow, and red poppies, feeling their softness against my skin.

This field has no end, I realize, as I look up and see a rainbow brightening in the distance. Slowly, it grows brighter and comes toward me like a tidal wave, giving way to a calm that is warm and inviting.

I look up and smile, but I do not hesitate. This time, I step in, watching the colors brighten and feeling myself being lifted into a large and brilliant tunnel.

I see Chris's face in the colors. I see the face of every person I have loved on earth. I am standing in the wind. The sun brightens slowly, and joy swells within me. And now, I walk up to the mountain, my purple mountain. Softly and cautiously, I lift my hands and stand here, looking out.

I can see the world beneath me, but this time, I smile and turn away.

Chris raises his head in the hospital lobby and wipes tears from his eyes. The emerald necklace that fell from my neck is in his hands, and he holds it against his heart, breathing in. His eyes are still frozen, as he gazes back at the room in which I took my last breath. As he looks up, his head falls back upon his shoulders, and tears stream down his face.

"Never in my life did I think this would happen. We were supposed to be together," he cries out loud, moving forward toward the doors, which are foggy and seemingly thicker than usual. Staring out at people passing outside, Chris draws a deep breath and lifts his eyes to the sky.

"Lilly. Oh my God, Lilly," he cries, unaware of the people passing. His eyes freeze for a brief moment and tremble against the cloudy sky outside. Now, after turning back to look at the hospital's lobby, he crashes into a chair inside the hospital, allowing himself to sink into its plush fabric. He stares out the window for several moments, but knows that as soon as he leaves, life as he knows it will change.

Exhaling a dense sob, Chris scans the lobby and runs a hand over his now lush blond hair, which is as full and as beautiful as it was the day we met.

Struggling to hide his emotion, Chris swallows, and his eyes linger on a few paintings on the wall. Now, he pauses briefly to look back at the door to the neurology wing. Closing his eyes and drawing another dense breath, he lifts up his left hand, pausing briefly to run a hand under his nose. He walks through the door and holds up his palms, feeling soft raindrops soak through his skin.

He has my diary in the car, and as he reaches for it, emotion tugs at his throat. As he lifts his eyes above the steering wheel, warm tears trail back toward his neck. Suddenly, he sees my emerald green eyes and my curly brown hair. He sees me smiling at him in the backyard when we were teenagers. He sees everything that made us what we were. He sees me running circles around him. Now, as he closes his eyes, he feels my soft hand slipping into his.

As he pulls into the driveway, the words he had fought to hide inside the hospital come out of his mouth in a tidal wave of emotion.

"Oh, Lilly, why did you have to leave me?" he cries, placing the diary in his lap and running his hands over its blue exterior. "I have your diary, and I am going to finish it in your honor."

He holds up the diary in his large and trembling hands.

Finishing the diary is a mission for Chris—one that he knows he has to carry out as a tribute to me. His expression of his grief is made manifest as he squints his eyes against the diary.

Opening the diary's cover and reading my first entry, Chris circles a finger around a heart I had drawn on the side of the first page. His eyes lock on the heart, and he begins to read.

Keeping Chris, A Diary

Chris, my dear Chris:

If there was ever a time for me to celebrate, it would be this moment. Chris and I met on this beautiful spring day when beauty filled the world. The birds were singing. Flowers were bursting into bloom. And as Chris lifted me over his shoulders, I couldn't help but smile. I swear that I'm going to spend the rest of my life with this boy. He's so wonderful to me, and he's so sweet.

Oh my God, his kiss. His kiss is incredible. I never thought I'd feel this way about anyone. He cupped my face with his hands when we kissed. As I looked into his eyes, I wanted more. I wanted more of his touch and more of his embrace. I may be just a teenager, but I know he likes me. And I know in my heart of hearts that I am meant to be with this boy. Maybe he will love me someday.

Chris, if you're reading this right now, I want to make you a promise. If you fall in love with me, I promise that I will keep you forever. I will never leave your side. I will keep you forever.

Until next time,
Lilly

My grandmother used to say that it is at our lowest times that we truly find ourselves. And I think this is the case with Chris.

As he looks at me at the funeral, he places a hand over his heart and kneels down next to me. He lowers his head and places a kiss on my hand. As he kneels, I place a hand on his shoulder.

As he cries with his head in his hands, I touch him once again and smile. Now, I am floating back to the rainbow tunnel. As I turn, I blow him a kiss, knowing in my heart that I will come to him every time he calls my name. He may not hear me speak, and he may not see my face. But no matter what, my hand is always outstretched for him.

Chris drives himself all the way home that afternoon. As he does, the sun rises through the trees, and the remaining leaves on the trees around him crackle against the late autumn wind.

Feeling as though the wind has been knocked from his chest, Chris tightens his hands on the steering wheel and rushes forward. As the world disappears behind him, he looks up, rolling down the window and sniffing against the wind. As he does, he takes in the wonders of the world, but somehow they don't feel the same as they did before. A bright red leaf falls softly from the sky and lands on his windshield. As he continues forward, smelling rain in the air, he pictures my face. Now, as he gazes at his hands, he whispers.

I love you.

When Chris gets home, he has a talk with Ben and explains that Mommy went to a better place, a beautiful place. Once Ben is in bed, emotion takes hold and Chris falls into the sofa. He sobs deeply and smoothes a hand over Molly's head.

"Hey there, girl," he says, looking at Molly's wide brown eyes, as she stares back at him. Her stout tail wiggles back and forth, and she barks.

Two weeks later, as the sun cracks the horizon, Chris's eyes flutter open. And the phone rings. Shifting restlessly, he clutches the receiver, and his eyes tremble.

"Hello?"

It is Susan from the hospital. Her voice is soft as it cracks through the phone. "Mr. Rylan, I am so sorry to hear about your wife. I just heard about her death. I am so sorry. She loved you, you know. She loved you more than anything."

Chris talks to Susan for a little while, explaining how much he loved me, but he knows he has to move on. His heart, on the other hand, is telling him something entirely different. He hangs up the phone, picks up his pen, and shifts toward the diary. After reading over my last entry, which is scratched with blue ink, he sniffs and nods.

Oh, sweetheart, he writes, scratching his pen across the paper. *You were too young to go. But I promise I will see you soon. It may be years from now or possibly just moments. Either way, I pray that I will see you again. I hope with all my heart that you will come back to me somehow. If bringing me to you is possible, please take me to where you are.*
  Love,
  Chris

Chris's curiosity grows, and he soon finds himself reading all the pages of my diary. Now that I am gone, it is his diary. It is a compilation of my memories that will live on with him, wherever he may go.

A few days later, he comes across my entry in which I told him I would come and get him if he no longer feels like he needs to be on earth. The entry was not meant to be morbid by any means. I wanted him to know that he doesn't have to live in pain, that there is always hope for a happier future. Wherever that may be is up to him.

I wrote the entry to show him that my departure from the earth is not the end of our life together, but it is a stepping-stone to something bigger, something greater than a life together on earth.

Whether or not Chris chooses to live out a few more decades on earth is up to him. At this point, he is the master of his own destiny. I am no longer with him to keep him, but I am constantly there with him. His eyes linger on the last paragraph of the entry, and his head lifts. Right now, he doesn't know that I'm here. I stretch my arms around him, but he doesn't feel me, as I watch from over his shoulder.

Silently, his eyes glide over my words, and I look at my scrawled handwriting right there in front of his eyes. He is beautiful.

As I rest my hand on his shoulder, I lift my head and allow it to drift to his chest. I can feel his heart beating. I can see his face, and I can feel his soft breath rising and falling against my hand.

As he reads the entry, tears fall from his eyes, and his gaze freezes on my every word. As I look at him, I feel his pain, and I touch his shoulders. I look into his eyes, once again seeing those vivid blue eyes and those beautiful wisps of blond hair. I can't help but sit here for a few more moments, taking in his presence and sitting on the bed where I once slept.

Perhaps I'm hoping for a miracle. All I know, while I look at him, is that I need to drift back to the place where I now live.

But before I go back to my purple mountain, my eyes linger on the diary. A few minutes later, he picks it up and holds it against his heart. Opening to a random page, his eyes remain intense upon the diary's pages, and he reads another entry.

Now, I turn and drift back into Heaven. Still, as he sits there quietly, his eyes are bright and shining against the pages.

Perhaps this is where his journey ends. Can he truly live without me? These thoughts drift in and out of my mind, as I sit here watching my only love.

His eyes are intense, watery. In spite of his tears, I sit here, watching him with love filling my being. He sniffs deeply, as though he is being called back into a memory.

Dear Chris,

No matter where you go, I will enfold you in my arms. Just call me. Right now, even as we are worlds apart, I think of you. I come to you. I hold you in my arms. And I reach out to you when tears begin to fall. You were everything to me on earth, and some things never change. You are still in my arms and forever in my heart.

If you want to be with me again, go back to earlier entries in my diary. Read the entry about a broken heart. Read it all. Take it in, and know that you can come to me. I am always with you. I know that as you read this, it may be painful, but

I want you to know that I have always known what would happen.

I have always known that we would be apart at some point, but there is a way. There is always a way to reach me. So here I sit, two nights before my departure from my time on earth, telling you everything you need to know. Call my name. Cry out to me. Talk to me. Do anything you can to get my attention. I will hear you.

You can come with me, but only if you are ready to come to a new place.

Love you forever,
Lilly

Anticipation builds in Chris's heart, and his hands tremble with the sudden realization that I thought to write him before I died. He pauses, draws a deep breath, and slides his hand over the page that slipped out of my diary in his hospital room. I taped it into the diary after he found it at the restaurant.

An hour later, Chris brings an apple into the room. Now, as he looks at my entry, he feels hungry.

"How to die of a broken heart," he whispers. "Lilly, come to me."

His eyes lift to the crown molding at the ceiling, and he sees my face in his mind. I am not in the room with him, though. I am watching from afar, seeing the softness of his face, seeing that he wants to hold my hand. He runs his fingers along my side of the bed, smiles, and breathes into the soft fabric of the comforter.

He takes a bite out of an apple and sits it down on the table. Now, he picks up his pen and scratches a heart onto the next page.

To my dearest Lilly,
I love you so much. We lived a beautiful life together on this earth, and I loved you from the start. From your shining green eyes to the way you touched me, I had everything. I just never thought you would go so soon.
I have read all your stories, and I now know where I want to be. I want to be with you forever. I don't care where I have to go or what I have to give up. All I know is that I would give away everything I own to be by your side.
You deserve happiness and peace. Now, I long for your happiness and joy. I want to hold your hand. I don't know where you are, but I need you. I just need to see you.
Love,
Chris

Three paragraphs are all he needs, he realizes, as he places his pen down on the mattress. Now, he opens my laptop and goes to Google, his favorite search engine.

His heart pounds furiously within his chest, and he breathes in deeply, typing the keywords, "how to die of a broken heart."

Quickly, in front of his eyes, a series of links appear. As his eyes glide quickly across the screen, he chuckles, feeling a sudden lift within his stomach. His eyes glide over the pages, and he holds a hand to his chest, suddenly panting. After flipping through the pages, his fingers linger on another page of my diary. As his eyes glide over the paper, he stares forward and is suddenly transported back to our earlier days.

Dear Chris,

It is two weeks before our wedding, and here I sit, picturing my life with you. With you, I can imagine only a life that's filled with hope and love. I know that we will someday have children and see ourselves in a little child's eyes. I know that we will sit silently together, feeling total peace in one another's presence. In two weeks, you will lift my veil, and we will make a promise to each other—a promise to love one another against all odds.

I honestly never thought I'd find someone as quickly as I found you. Then again, I never thought I would marry the first boy who touched me. I just have this feeling that we were destined to be together. A lot of people get cold feet before their wedding, and they question everything. As for me, I question nothing. I know that you are my true love. I have loved you from the start, and I will love you forever.

Love,
Lilly

Chris pauses for a few seconds, smiles, and opens my diary to read about how to die of a broken heart.

Right now, as he looks at the computer screen, his topaz blue eyes are intense with a sense of purpose. As he presses the enter key, his eyes are met with a series of search results that talk about stress cardiomyopathy.

It's not suicide by any means. Dying of a broken heart is something that happens when you lose a partner you have loved for a long time. There is no shame in it, Chris realizes, as he turns off my laptop and closes his eyes for a moment.

His eyes lift, and the stillness of the room allows him to finally relax. Now, as he breathes excitedly, he opens his eyes and looks out the window.

He smiles sweetly as he pictures my face and once again remembers my hands upon him. His jaw quivers, as he lowers himself to my side of the bed.

Breathing deeply, Chris smoothes a hand over his chest and his gaze freezes. With his head tilted, he pictures himself lacing his hands with mine. And as he lay there, he smiles, once again feeling my soft skin and my delicate fingers. Feeling his heart pound within his chest, Chris lifts himself from the bed and struggles to catch his breath.

The stunning realization that his body can change causes his lips to curve upward. Slowly, he relaxes. As he closes his eyes, he sees me tugging him through the front yard. Instantaneously, he sees me grabbing a tire swing and swinging across the lake. He sees me sitting in his hospital room, reading my diary to him, and he pictures me walking down the aisle at our wedding.

After an hour, he manages to bring his eyes to my laptop. His gaze lingers on the screen, and he squints to bring the small print into focus. As his vision becomes blurry, he turns, feeling something beside him.

I sit down for a second, but stand up as soon as I see him scan the room. As he turns, I feel as though he can see me. But I realize I must leave, at least for a little while.

As Chris's eyes scan through the text on my computer screen, he wipes the corners of his eyes and sniffs deeply. The words seem to blur in front of him, and the corners of his eyes moisten with joy. Tears begin to trail his cheeks, and he stares silently, feeling empowered.

"Lilly, I miss you so much," he wails, feeling a sudden tightening in his chest. "You're my sweetheart, Lilly," he says, looking around the room. "I want to be with you. Please come to me."

His head falls into his hands, and his eyes close against the silence as he breathes in, attempting to bring me into the room. He must wait a little while. I slide my hair behind my ears and silently walk back into the room. He cannot see me, and he does not feel me. As I stand here, watching him, his head turns.

I stand beside him as he rolls the apple within his hands. "Chris, no!"

Chris reaches for his apple and attempts to take a bite, but suddenly falls back against the covers. His chest aches, and he wheezes against the bed. "Oh my God," he cries, his hands trembling helplessly against the sheets.

This day is milder, the strong wind disappearing and giving way to a sudden heat wave. After 40 minutes of lying on the bed, he looks up at the ceiling. His vision is growing fuzzy, as he stares up, feeling something elongate in his chest.

"Chris, no," I squeal, feeling powerless.

"Lilly, I'm coming to see you." His lips curve slowly, and he looks away. I know he can't hear me, but he can't do this. "Chris, don't!"

"Oh my God," he says, holding a hand to his chest and laughing in a sudden release of joyful emotion. After a few minutes, he coughs deeply and once again struggles to draw breath. He closes his eyes for a long moment, feeling his chest tighten with more intensity than it had minutes earlier. Slowly, he looks over at the diary.

He can't die of a broken heart. He just can't. Knowing this, I touch a hand to his chest, and his breath returns, stronger than ever before. As he gets up from the bed, he breathes deeply and wipes his eye. Some things just aren't meant to be.

So much happens in a lifetime, and to Chris, the past seven months have been filled with many accomplishments. He watched Ben graduate from preschool. He finished the diary. And now, as he sits on the ground at the edge of the lake in our back yard, he takes a bite out of an apple and tosses it out on the water. The canoe is wobbling on the dock, and he breathes in, taking in the soft summer air. Chris is holding my diary in his hands and looks out on the water. Drawing a deep breath, he kisses the diary, and places it in the canoe. Standing up, he pushes the canoe out onto the water. Slowly, it drifts away, sailing into a blue and glistening sea.

As Chris sits down on the ground, watching the boat cast ripples on the water, a lone tear falls from his eye.

"Lilly, are you there?"

He begins to stand up and feels a sharp and sudden pain in his stomach. I see him clutch his stomach where the tumor in his body resides. He is succumbing to his cancer, closing his eyes and opening them at regular intervals. He is in pain, I know. I can tell by the way he is breathing. His breath is growing shallower now, and he looks up, his eyes still sparkling in the stillness of the brilliant blue sky up above. He takes a few steps and feels tightening in his chest. Slowly, he falls into the lush green grass beneath his feet.

"Lilly?"

A sudden hush comes over the yard as Chris lifts his eyes, relaxes, and feels a gentle wind against his face. A red leaf falls from a tree above, and drifts ever so slowly over his body, before falling upon his hand. As he begins to drift away, he feels a sudden calm come over him, like rolling waves on a soft and sandy shore. Warmth comes upon him, and he sees a rainbow above.

Even though Chris and I saw so many rainbows together, not one of them was as beautiful as the one before his eyes. We have to let those rainbows go.

Right now, my bright white wings rise up on my back. This is the most beautiful moment I have ever experienced as I gaze at Chris and look at the beauty of the world surrounding him. Now, I stretch out my arms and carry a man with blond hair and blue eyes into the great beyond. Together, we disappear into a bright white light.

Printed in the United States
By Bookmasters